The End of Promise

by

Rita A. Popp

A Bethany Jarviss Mystery, Book 2

Cover Art by *Tina Lynn Stout*

The Wild Rose Press, Inc.
PO Box 708
Adams Basin, NY 14410-0708
Visit us at www.thewildrosepress.com

Publishing History
First Edition, 2024
Trade Paperback ISBN 978-1-5092-5543-6
Digital ISBN 978-1-5092-5544-3

A Bethany Jarviss Mystery, Book 2
Published in the United States of America

Dedication

For Toni and Boz, and in memory of Mc

Praise for Rita A. Popp

"If you like to decipher clues as you read light cozy mystery stories, curl up with a cup of tea and check out *The First Fiancée*." (*The First Fiancée: A Bethany Jarviss Mystery*)

~ *Nicki Pascarella, author of the Miranda Albright, Ph.D. Mysteries*

"Rita A. Popp's debut delivers a brilliant whodunit set in the winter-chilled New Mexico mountains." (*The First Fiancée: A Bethany Jarviss Mystery*)

~ *Margaret Mizushima, author of the award-winning Timber Creek K-9 Mysteries*

"A poignant slice of life tale about letting go of some things and opening the door to others. A heart-warming read!" (*Passing on the Farm,* a novelette)

~ *Amy Rivers, author of the A Legacy of Silence series and 2021 Indie Author of the Year*

"Popp's characters are dynamic and realistic as they find new love, discover new truths, and heal from the past." (*Passing on the Farm,* a novelette)

~ *Kathleen Donnelly, author of the award-winning National Forest K-9 series*

Acknowledgements

I wasn't taking notes for this mystery novel in my years as a college student, university writer and editor, community college adjunct instructor, and literacy tutor. But this novel provides the opportunity to thank the many friends I made along the way at the institutions that educated and employed me. A special thank you, as always, goes to my husband, Professor Emeritus Tony Popp, for the unwavering support of my fiction writing habit. I am indebted, as well, to Melanie Billings for the sharp-eyed edits, and to Rhonda, RJ, and the entire team at The Wild Rose Press for encouraging my creative growth as a Rose in your flourishing garden!

Chapter 1

College custodian May Zeller, who considered herself a tough old bird, didn't scream at the sight of Professor Paul Kiefer's body in the leather recliner he had added at personal expense to his office décor. She dropped her feather duster and pressed a work-worn hand to her mouth, stifling any sound of weakness. No doubt the young fellow was dead. Someone had wrapped his head in clear packing tape, squashing his handsome nose and mouth like a child's features pressed against a window for a joke. And if that wasn't indignity enough, coffee from his steel travel mug, overturned in his lap, stained the crotch and thighs of his neatly pressed khakis.

Who on earth would do this to an education professor? May backed up, pulled the door shut, and ran as if chased by bloodhounds to tell Department Head Eleanor Jarviss.

As usual on a Tuesday evening, Eleanor had gone back to her office after teaching her night class. She stopped packing her briefcase at the sight of May's pale face.

"Ma'am, you got to come. It's Dr. Kiefer. His head's wrapped up in plastic like a ham." The custodian's eyes conveyed having witnessed something more than a student prank. "He's dead, Dr. Jarviss. It's horrible!"

"Show me."

Eleanor regretted her four-inch sling-backs, worn to

increase her height, as she clicked along the slick hallway. May skidded to a stop before Paul Kiefer's door and opened it with a passkey. Seeing Paul's head, Eleanor understood what May meant by a wrapped ham. She swallowed bile and reached for Kiefer's desk phone. "Stay outside, May. Close the door."

Eleanor called 911, the campus emergency line, and the dean's home number. She sent a shaken but capable May down two floors to wait for the first responders. Soon came the campus and city police—the black and the blue, her mind quipped—and the EMTs in white.

Eventually, a pair of city officers, both young men, escorted her back to her office to give a statement. Obediently, she pressed her fingertips to the screen of a cell-phone-like device. Paul, the curriculum and instruction department's teaching-with-technology expert, would have loved that modern gizmo for taking one's prints.

****

After midnight, Eleanor slumped on a stone bench near the splashing Mexican fountain in the dimly lit Old Quad. Few others shared the space bordered by New Mexico University's administration and College of Education buildings, Alumni Hall, and the student union. Most of the gawking crowd had dispersed with the departure of the emergency vehicles, including the silent ambulance that had taken away Paul's body in a zipped bag.

She had not admitted to the police that Paul had been her least favorite colleague, prone to giving her static, rather than respect, as his new department head. Always pushing for more computers and specialized software the college could ill afford, always itching to travel to one more conference, teach one less class than a full load, all justified by some research project. To be honest, she didn't much mind his demise. Any number of faculty members would share that loathsome thought. But who in the world would have matched action to it? Paul hadn't taped his own nose and mouth shut. Light-headed, Eleanor leaned forward on the hard, cool bench. The murderer might be lurking behind the education building in the faculty parking lot. Too scared to walk to her car, she would have phoned Wayne had he not been out of town. That left Bethany, who would be fast asleep at her house. Eleanor speed-dialed and reached her sleepy daughter on the third ring. "Bethany, something terrible has happened. Paul Kiefer has been murdered in his office."

Eleanor heard a gasp, then, "Mom, what did you say? Paul? Murdered?"

"That's right. I've been with the police for hours. I'm still on campus. I hate to ask, but since your father is out of town, can you come and get me? I'll wait on Main Street."

Eleanor appreciated that Bethany didn't ask more questions but said, "Good goddess, Mom! Give me fifteen minutes."

In more like ten, Bethany drew up to the curb in her SUV. Eleanor hopped in and fastened her seatbelt, but the car didn't move. Streetlights illuminated her daughter's beautiful, strong-featured face.

"Mom, are you okay? Can you tell me what happened?"

Eleanor felt her lips quiver. "You've met our custodian, May Zeller. She found Paul Kiefer dead and came to get me. What a terrible sight! Someone had wrapped his head in clear tape—packing tape, I suppose. He'd spilled coffee from his travel mug all over his lap."

"Did you see any blood?"

"No, just a big coffee stain."

"Someone must have put something in his coffee to knock him out, then smothered him," Bethany said.

"A deliberate murder. I can't believe it. It will be the talk of the campus by now."

Eleanor described the crowd she'd been part of: the police, the university president, the college dean, bystanders recording with their cell phones, and student journalists and the city media in hot pursuit of a breaking story. As she spoke, she accepted a tissue Bethany offered. It seemed she was crying. She dabbed at her eyes and tried to get control of her emotions.

"Who could have killed him, Mom?"

"I can't imagine anyone doing it." Eleanor blew her nose, grateful that the dean and the president hadn't seen her in this state.

"Someone in the college? One of you guys, a professor. Or maybe a student," Bethany said.

"Surely not! All hell's going to break loose, isn't it? Bethany, I have an idea."

"I know what you're going to say." Bethany drove away from the curb. "The answer is no."

"When Joni needed help, you found that killer. Your sister will always be grateful."

"A fluke. Besides, that was a cold case."

Eleanor glanced at her daughter, but Bethany didn't take her eyes off the sparsely trafficked street. "And you found out the death of that college girl in Albuquerque was a murder, not an accident."

"Manslaughter. It wasn't planned."

"You'll be on campus in a couple of days," Eleanor said as they sailed through a yellow light. "To award the Foundation scholarship. Slow down, dear."

Bethany eased up on the gas. "Assuming the luncheon isn't canceled."

"There's that. But I expect it will be held as usual. You could talk to people. Of course, the police will investigate, but they didn't know Paul. You did."

Well beyond the heart of town, they approached Las Cuevas's hilly outskirts.

"We had dinner together. I didn't really know him."

"But surely, you want his killer caught. As soon as possible."

The SUV left the pavement and tackled Eleanor's subdivision's gravel road. She could barely see her daughter's profile in the dark.

"Even if the killer is somebody you know, Mom?"

The car hit a rough spot. Eleanor grasped her seat belt and didn't reply.

****

An hour later, her mother insisted she would be fine by herself. Bethany headed back to the historic center of Las Cuevas to her small, silent house near the university. She climbed the stairs, peeled off her jeans, and got into bed in the T-shirt she had donned when she responded to her mother's call for help. By her side, Nathan Fuller slept, his face turned away from her. She wrapped an arm around his waist and curled her five-six frame into his five-ten one, savoring the memory of making unhurried love. But the easiness of his visit would surely end now. The murder of a professor in the department her mother led wouldn't go away with the morning light. Eleanor and her colleagues were bound to be on any suspects list.

Bethany knew she might also come under suspicion despite her encounters with Paul having been brief and superficial.

Bethany closed her eyes but couldn't sleep. Might as well consider what she knew of Associate Professor Paul Kiefer. Good looking in an entirely different way from the man asleep beside her. While Nathan had a compact, muscular body and the easy-going personality of a New Mexico cowboy, Paul had been a tall and slim former Chicagoan, driven by the need to excel in his work. A few years older than Nathan, mid-thirties to Nathan's twenty-nine. More suitable for her thirty-two, people adhering to lingering social norms might have said.

But she and Paul never made it to the lovers stage. Unlike the rumored scores of women lusting after the man, she found him too sure of being a great catch. He was too secure in a smug braininess, too prone to dominate a dinner conversation. The curriculum and instruction department's star, he conveyed a superiority over other faculty members. He even hinted that a promotion to full professor, at a younger age than anyone else in the department, was in the bag.

The thought came unfiltered: Paul Kiefer had been a flagrant egotist. Nothing like the sweet man beside her in bed. But on the surface, more of a logical choice for a lover than Nathan. People might ask why she, Bethany Jarviss, the Jarviss Foundation's charitable grants administrator, a woman pursuing an MBA, dated a ranch hand. Nathan's highest academic achievement was a dusty high school diploma, and his glory days of bull riding had faded in the dust too. But he was a decent, modest, kind-hearted, loving, and yes, smart man. While

Paul Kiefer had taken her to dinner to curry favor that might lead to a Foundation grant for his research, Nathan never seemed to want anything but to be with her. She pressed her face into his back and soaked in his distinctive smell, like sagebrush stirred by a breeze.

Chapter 2

Bethany awoke to another scent—bacon frying—accompanied by Nathan singing one of the songs about women he'd learned at his mother's knee. Now, he belted out, "Lady of Spain, I adore you!"

Bethany didn't have a Spanish bone in her body, but the song didn't mean she had a real-life rival. Nathan also sang at times about Michelle, Peggy Sue, and Barbara Ann, complete with air guitar. "My mom raised me alone after my dad died," he said soon after they met. "She collected songs about women. It helped keep her strong. As far as I know, there's no song about a Bethany, and seeing as I'm no songwriter, what can I do?" The story touched Bethany's heart, and she came to appreciate the female repertoire and his pleasing tenor.

In the kitchen, he stopped transferring the fried bacon to a plate with his left hand, the uninjured one, long enough to kiss her on the lips. "Eggs?"

"One, please."

He broke eggs for them both into the skillet. "Over easy?"

"Sounds good." She helped herself to coffee and took a breath to tell him about the murder, but he beat her to the punch. "What's up with your mom?"

"You heard the call? Knew it was her?"

"You did say 'Mom.' I heard you go out. Her car break down?" He flipped the eggs with a plastic spatula and pressed gently on the whites. The eggs would be perfect.

She said to his back, "A professor in Mom's department has been killed."

He turned off the heat under the frying pan. Their eyes met. "Car crash?"

"No. It's horrible. A murder, apparently. At the university."

"Shot? Did they get the guy?"

"It wasn't a campus shooting, thank goddess. It appears someone taped a professor's eyes, nose, and mouth shut. His coffee—drugged probably—had spilled in his lap. The custodian who found the body took Mom to see. Mom phoned the police and the dean. He got there pretty fast, and so did the university president. It could have been a movie scene, Mom said. The police in crisis mode, the building cleared, the media buzzing around. Mom had to give a statement. Afterward, she was too shaky to drive, and with Dad away, she phoned me."

"Holy hell." He took her hands in his rough ones. The scars from the injury to his right hand and the surgery to partially repair it crisscrossed like roads on a map.

"I want to see how Mom's doing and give her a ride to campus. Her car's still there."

"First, you need to eat something."

She dropped slices of whole-wheat bread into the toaster, and he dished up the bacon and eggs.

"Who's the professor that got killed?" He said it between mouthfuls. His mother must have taught him his good manners. He didn't chew and talk at the same time.

"Paul Kiefer."

"Did you know him?"

"A little. He specialized in training future teachers to use technology. The latest thing in computers, teleconferencing, robots even." She didn't mention she'd had a couple of meals with him.

Nathan took a turn making toast. When she declined a second slice, he ate both slices slathered with her only margarine—diet—and her low-sugar strawberry jam. He started to clear the table, but she stopped him. "Don't you have to get on the road?"

"Back to the ranch," he said with a touch of cynicism. He'd come to Las Cuevas to pick up kitchen and bathroom tile he and the ranchers' teenage son were expected to cut and lay. The order hadn't arrived, so he'd stayed overnight.

"That tile might not get here today either. I may still be cooling my heels in Las Cuevas."

The night before, he had admitted to tiring of being a jack-of-all-trades and said the job had him "trapped like a hog-tied calf. Five years of my life gone. After that big bull got me good, I was grateful for the work. But I haven't laid eyes on the Carters' herd for weeks."

When Bethany asked why not, he said the cattle were grazing the forest lease, and the boss didn't need help checking on them with his ATV. "Pretty soon, the wife will have me hemming curtains."

She had laughed at an image of Nathan pushing fabric under a sewing machine's bobbing needle. Mid-laugh, he kissed her, and they had made cheerful love. This morning, she had expected they would talk about his quest to find other work. But now, the house phone rang. Eleanor signaled her readiness to go to campus.

"That was Mom," Bethany said. "I'd better get moving. I'll drop her off on the way to the Foundation.

If your ranchers' tile doesn't get here, I'll be glad of your company tonight." She deliberately infused the words with a sexy innuendo.

"Likewise, ma'am," Nathan said in the same playful tone. "You go fetch your mama. I'll clean up." He kissed her and popped a piece of bacon into his mouth.

****

Gazing at her parents' dream house, Bethany saw a jumbled pile of boxes, all angles and glass, with squared-off balconies stuck on here and there. They'd had it built by a famous architect after she and her adopted siblings left home. It was their taste, their money. Set on a hill, the house was spaced a good distance from the other showplaces dotting the suburb. It stood out as odd, but visitors given directions couldn't miss it. "Look for the house with no curves, the one that doesn't blend with the landscape. That's the Jarviss place." Bethany had to admit that against a blue morning sky, the house had a certain modern-art appeal. Inside, her mother had chosen pleasing, warm colors to contrast with the stark exterior. But today, Bethany did not want to go in. She tapped her horn, and phone in hand, waited for Eleanor to appear. Almost immediately, she received a text. —*Give me five!*—

It was seven-thirty. Eleanor had better get a move on to make it to the office at a quarter to eight, her usual arrival time. As department head, she aimed to start the day before her secretary or anyone else showed up. Eleanor took her job seriously; she'd held the position less than a year. She didn't want anyone to think she was a slough-off like the now-retired department head, a man who'd rarely been around when his faculty members needed him. Now, Eleanor was gaining the reputation of first one in, last one out five days a week, and often in her office on weekends. No surprise she had been on hand to witness the university's first murder victim—if no one counted the young man in 1910 who had been shot in a bar fight off campus, hours after graduating in a class of twelve.

Bethany beeped her horn. "Hurry, Mom!"

Moments later, Eleanor slid into the passenger seat with profuse apologies. "The dean called right after I texted you. A press conference is scheduled for 11:00 a.m. in the quad. The news media have been pestering him and the president all night. I got calls too, but they both instructed me to ignore them. Apparently, reporters know May Zeller found the body, I called the police, and it's Paul Kiefer who died. I never imagined I'd have to face anything like this. Do I look as much of a mess as I feel?"

Bethany gave her a quick glance of approval. "Let's see. Serious suit. Smooth hair. Very formal."

"Like for a funeral one dreads."

As she drove, Bethany considered if she should bring up something bothering her. Why not? She had a good relationship with her mother and could talk to her about almost anything. "Mom, remember me saying I went out to dinner with Paul?"

"That seemed natural. You're single, he was divorced, and you were about the same age."

"The thing is, I didn't tell Nathan. He stayed over last night. I mean, I told him a professor was killed, but not that I dated him."

"Didn't you go out with him only once? Nathan would have understood."

"I made the mistake of dating the guy twice. I should

have known right off the bat he only wanted one thing, and I don't mean the usual thing. He wanted a grant for his research. I didn't like him at all."

"Me either, dear. Between us, and I've never said this to anyone else except your father, I couldn't stand the young man. And now I feel awful about that."

They had left Las Cuevas's quiet outskirts. On Main Street, as traffic picked up, Bethany slowed down through her neighborhood of old houses and mature trees. Where the university spanned both sides of Main, she offered to stop at Campus Coffee Roasters.

Eleanor said she didn't want coffee. "I keep thinking of that stain on Paul's pants. By mid-morning, I'll probably be raging for a cup, though. Can you drop me near the president's office? I've been summoned, along with the dean. The campus police chief and the University Communications director will be there. It's necessary to get our ducks in a row for the press conference. Remind me sometime why I agreed to be department head."

Bethany knew Eleanor had been pushed into it when the last head retired. Eleanor's best friend, Charlotte, had urged her to become the department's first woman administrator. Dean Gerald Darwood had loved not having to lead an external search costing thousands of dollars. Eleanor only had to switch offices and order new business cards. An old family friend of the Jarvisses and a man fond of clichéd similes, Dean Darwood proclaimed himself "as pleased as a three-handed politician working a crowd" when Eleanor agreed to accept the position.

****

At the administration building, Bethany didn't park;

her student permit was no good here. Eleanor started to get out of the SUV but hesitated. "Perhaps I should suggest canceling the scholarship luncheon tomorrow."

Bethany gave it only a second of thought. "No, Mom. Go ahead with it if Dean Darwood agrees. The student deserves her five minutes of fame. I'll be there with the Foundation check."

Behind them, a car horn sounded. Bethany stuck her arm out of the window to wave the driver on.

"And then there's Spring Visitors Day," Eleanor said. "I wonder if the president will cancel it."

"I bet not. It's not like a deranged killer ran through campus, randomly taking lives. Paul Kiefer must have been targeted specifically."

"But why? That's what I keep asking myself. Did I tell you that last night, the police took my fingerprints and swabbed my mouth for a sample of my DNA? Routine, I suppose, but so upsetting!"

"Did you call Dad?"

"Oh, yes. He said, 'Don't worry. You have nothing to hide.' He offered to fly home immediately, but I said not to. He can't miss Don's golf tournament. Wayne's presence is important to both of them. It strengthens the father-son bond." Eleanor gripped her briefcase and stepped onto the sidewalk. "Here I go."

Bethany watched her petite mother, in her trim suit, stride into the administration building, an imposing stucco structure with a red-tile roof. The oldest building on campus, it sat near the education building where Eleanor spent her workdays.

Eleanor had not repeated the request to look into the murder. *Typical of Mom.* She tended to make a suggestion, then allow it to hang in the air, linger in the mind. Would refusing to get involved let her mother down, Bethany wondered as she drove to the Foundation office. With her father out of town, she was in charge. She hoped to slip in some prep for her master's degree class at 6:00 p.m. If Nathan hadn't left town, she would remind him she wouldn't be home until past eight.

****

Out of energy after class, Bethany felt her daypack weighing her down. But her heart lifted as Nathan met her at her front door, kissed her lightly, and announced a pizza had been delivered minutes before.

She started for the stairs to change out of her office clothes. "You didn't have to wait for me."

"I made a salad," Nathan said. "Bought a few things to put in it. You didn't have much besides lettuce, and that was kind of brown." He flashed her a smile. "Don't dawdle, darlin'."

As they finished dinner, Nathan asked if she'd heard anything more about the murder.

"Everybody in my MBA class knew about it. But in the business college, Paul Kiefer was only a name. Our professor and the other grad students expressed appropriate shock, but they're not affected like Mom."

"Did you talk to her today?"

"Briefly. She's under a lot of stress. A detective with the city police showed up at her office and asked her a bunch of questions."

"What kind of questions?"

"About her job as department head. About the faculty and staff. Conflicts among them, that kind of thing. She wasn't surprised, but it upset her to talk about her colleagues. She can't imagine any of them killing Paul Kiefer."

15

There were two pieces of pizza left. "Have the rest," Nathan said. "I've eaten the lion's share."

"No, I'm done. Go ahead."

She appreciated how he didn't argue but simply took another slice. Nathan wasn't one for false politeness or falseness of any kind.

Later, they watched the evening news out of Albuquerque, which led with a segment on the Kiefer murder. Ralph Ramirez, the NMU president—somber in a black suit too heavy for spring—used the words tragedy and community in what sounded like a rehearsed comment. He expressed his confidence in the police "to determine who committed this unprecedented crime affecting our entire Las Cuevas community."

Bethany fell asleep in Nathan's arms when the sports report came on. Sometime later, she became vaguely aware of him rousing her to go to bed. Brushing her teeth, she thought of how his presence comforted her. She hoped that her mother, all alone, could sleep tonight.

Chapter 3

On Thursday, from behind her desk, Eleanor faced the Department of Curriculum and Instruction's other two senior colleagues: her best friend, Charlotte Kline, a kind-hearted, disorganized associate professor to whom students confided their dreams and worries, and Gene Waverly, who, at sixty, had pretty much retired in place. They discussed who would take Paul Kiefer's classes until the end of the term. Charlotte volunteered for his one face-to-face class, which met during a gap in her own teaching schedule. Eleanor knew that Charlotte would stress about the extra work but would manage to cope. And Charlotte would handle students' reactions to a professor's death with sensitivity. In her flowing outfits, she exuded a New-Age, earth-mother quality that calmed her charges. Today, she wore an ankle-length dress in a red, green, and gold print that resembled those thin cotton bedspreads from India.

"Well, I can't take his online classes," Gene said. "Wouldn't know the first thing about running them."

Charlotte spoke up. "It's not that hard. The software's the same as for submitting grades. The learning curve isn't that steep."

"Says you."

Eleanor studied Gene's body language. Usually one to slouch, he had pulled himself upright, pushing out his chest so the pack of cigarettes in his shirt pocket bulged.

He hadn't bothered to snap the pearl button to conceal the pack. He was the department's only overt smoker; the other faculty smoked furtively or not at all. Too bad he remained a deliberate ignoramus at online teaching; he would be better suited distanced from students. She acknowledged the inevitable. "Well then, I'll find an adjunct instructor. One of the part-timers will want the extra month's pay."

"Only four weeks left in the semester!" Charlotte said. "Where did it go?"

He supplied an answer to the obviously rhetorical question. "Down the drain like all the semesters before it. Into the great maw of time."

Charlotte raised her eyebrows beneath her frizzy bangs. "How poetic you are today!"

Eleanor discreetly pumped the lever under her seat. She rose incrementally above her colleagues until only her toes touched the floor. Being petite had been a boon in high school when boys from short to tall asked her out, but it didn't benefit a leader of people who didn't see any department head as a boss. The head did all the nuisance work: class schedules, budgets, running interference with the dean's office. But one task came in handy: doing the annual evaluations that determined pay raises. She didn't totally lack authority.

Now, she exercised it in a small way. "Gene, I'd like you to attend the scholarship luncheon with us." She eyed the clock over her colleagues' heads. "It's in twenty minutes."

He mumbled about having plans, but she cut him off. "It will be much better food than what you'd eat at your desk."

"PB&J. Damned good lunch."

"Save it for a snack. The thing is, Alma Gomez attended one of Paul's classes, so I asked him to the luncheon. I don't want an obviously empty chair. You've taught Alma, yes?"

"Last year, not this one. In a big lecture class."

"Good enough."

"But surely Charlotte—"

"Charlotte will attend as chair of the scholarship committee."

"And because Alma has helped with my school reading and writing project," Charlotte added.

"Right. You're wearing two hats," Eleanor said. "Then there's the dean and myself. And Bethany, of course, to hand out the check. The university photographer will slip in at the end. Gene, it won't take more than an hour and a half."

His torso sagged. "Okay, I'll do it. The condemned man ate a hearty meal."

"You're a trooper, Eleanor," Charlotte said.

If they had been alone, Eleanor knew she would have been on the receiving end of one of her friend's intense hugs.

Gene fingered his bulging shirt pocket. "But terrible for you, Eleanor, seeing as you've only been in charge of the department since the fall."

The summer, Eleanor stopped herself from saying. That's when the job had actually started, almost ten months ago. Gene, the only other inside candidate, had stayed away all summer when he learned she had been chosen over him. Gene never taught summer classes, but he had been in town; he could have stopped by her new office to wish her well. Her other colleagues had done that. She understood; not having been a shoo-in when the former head, his crony, retired after decades in the position must have hurt. But after years as colleagues—friends, she would have thought—Gene might at least have offered a handshake.

He leaned toward Eleanor's desk. "What have the police told you? I saw the crime scene tape on Paul's door when they let us back into the building this morning."

Charlotte saved Eleanor from having to reply. "They did work fast to only keep us out yesterday. No one lost more than a day of class time Wednesday."

"And the Tuesday night classes after May Zeller discovered Paul dead," Eleanor said. "Two were interrupted by the police."

"It doesn't hurt to cancel class once in a while," Gene said. "The students love it."

Charlotte jerked her head in his direction, setting her beaded earrings swinging. "Not in this instance. Paul's death has sent a shockwave through campus. It's affected everyone."

Gene gave her a wickedly humorous glance. "You're right. I get a free lunch."

Eleanor rose, ignoring his bad joke. "You both have offices near Paul's. You might be asked to let the police take your fingerprints and swab your mouth for a DNA sample. I let them do both."

"Because you were at the scene," Charlotte said.

"Yes, and when I asked if samples would be needed from everyone who uses the building, including the students, they said that's likely."

Charlotte gasped. "Not from our students!"

"Students," Gene said, "must top any list of who'd want to kill a professor." He patted his shirt pocket. "If

I'm going to this lunch, I'd better fortify myself." He drew the cigarette pack from the pocket and left.

Charlotte glared at the empty doorway. "That man! He's treating Paul's death as a joke."

Eleanor sank back into her chair, wishing Charlotte didn't let Gene get under her skin. "You have an earring caught in your hair. On your left side." She watched Charlotte disentangle it. "At least Gene isn't displaying false emotion."

"He hated Paul." Charlotte lowered her voice. "Paul didn't respect us older faculty or anybody not enamored with technology. I'm sorry he's dead, but I won't miss that smugly superior attitude of 'I know something you don't' about computer systems and social media. Why didn't he go into computer science instead of education? He would have been right at home with those geeks on the other side of campus. Who do you think killed him? I can't imagine anyone doing it, much as we all wanted to at one time or another."

Eleanor took her purse out of a desk drawer and found her lip gloss. "We have to go to the luncheon. Now." As she moved toward the door, she dabbed at her lips.

Charlotte ran her fingers through her hair, making it messier than usual. "I'm not looking forward to this. I'm happy for Alma Gomez, of course. But shouldn't the luncheon have been canceled?"

Eleanor stopped in the department's outer office. Her secretary had left, as she often did, a few minutes before noon, a practice Eleanor made a mental note to put a stop to. She turned to Charlotte. "The dean wouldn't hear of it. Business as usual, he said. Cancel this and what would we cancel next? Spring Visitors

21

Day? Graduation? He thinks cancellations would signal a fear of some madman or, not to be sexist, some madwoman who might kill again. It could cause a widespread panic on campus. He believes someone had it in for Paul and that no one else should fear for their lives."

"He's probably right," Charlotte said. "In class today, I tried to reassure my students. We formed a circle and talked about the murder. I expected a number of no-shows, but I had a full house. One student said that with the number of campus shootings in her lifetime, she wouldn't be surprised if a masked gunman killed people on campus randomly. But one professor murdered in his office came as more of a shock. Everybody in the class agreed. I stopped them speculating, out loud at least, if a student or a professor or an outsider did it."

****

Eleanor normally looked forward to the scholarship luncheon. Her husband's family created the scholarship after she reached full professor when no one could say the gift helped her achieve that rank. She had no active hand in awarding the prize. This year, a student in her department would receive it, but it was open to students in all of the education college's departments. Wayne used to attend on behalf of the Foundation, but three years ago, he happily passed the duty of presenting a plaque to Bethany. The monetary award would be paid into Alma Gomez's university account. The scholarship would cover her tuition and books for the remaining two years.

Alma, a young woman almost as petite as Eleanor, showed up a few minutes early, right after Eleanor and Charlotte. Bethany arrived at the same time as Dean

Darwood. With a sweep of an arm, he shepherded Bethany in before him. Gerald played the natural host, Eleanor observed. He beelined it for Alma, leaned down to minimize his height as he introduced himself, and spoke to Bethany and the faculty members with an easy bonhomie. He shook Eleanor's hand, as if he hadn't seen her in years, with a firm bear paw clasp. In less than five minutes, he waved people into their seats. Gene sidled into the room at the last moment.

Eleanor and the dean faced each other at opposite ends of a conference table like the lord and lady of a manor. Last-minute place cards had put Charlotte and Alma to her left, and Gene and Bethany to her right so that Alma and Bethany sat closest to the dean, facing each other. No one else besides Paul had been invited.

A simple salad lunch had been planned by the dean's secretary. The student would not be intimidated by too many forks. Right on cue, a dining service staffer pushed a cart filled with covered plates into the room. She stood silently in her white apron while the dean made his opening remarks.

He cast an avuncular smile at Alma, who tilted up her chin. The girl had a beautiful profile and an elegant neck, and the dean had a commanding presence, Eleanor noted. He stood up and swung his huge head from side to side. His glance lingered for a moment on Gene sitting in what should have been Paul's place. The young professor's death struck Eleanor anew. She had a clichéd-but-true thought: she could hardly believe it. A picture of Paul's face—self-confident, too often self-satisfied—superimposed itself over Gene's aging countenance. She blinked to make the image of Paul disappear and to listen to the dean's remarks.

"We're here today to celebrate the awarding of the Jarviss Foundation Scholarship, this year to our outstanding student, Ms. Alma Gomez. Sadly, we are mindful of the death of Dr. Paul Kiefer, a promising young education professor who would have attended this luncheon."

Eleanor saw a look that was hard to characterize cross Alma's face. *Anger mingled with disgust?* The student's head jerked back as if she were repulsed by a bad odor.

Meanwhile, the dean said, "Dr. Kiefer's death is a tragedy. It's the subject of a police investigation, as I'm sure you're aware. The university intends to cooperate fully."

He paused and stared at two drink glasses on the table before him, one filled with water, the other iced tea. He took two quick swallows of the water, his Adam's apple bobbing like a golf ball stuck in his throat. Eleanor strained to listen, not laugh hysterically or think about Don's performance at his tournament.

Alma had assumed an appropriately solemn expression with downcast eyes. "President Ramirez has directed us to carry on as normal, a decision I fully support," the dean continued. "Classes are meeting. Occasions such as this one and Spring Visitors Day are taking place as planned. Now, let us enjoy our lunch and the scholarship presentation to follow."

If anyone had entered the conference room after that speech, they would have heard light conversation that covered an underlying tension. Eleanor, finding herself gripping her utensils tightly, tried to relax her hands. She supposed the chicken salad tasted as good as most university fare, but it stuck in her mouth. She only managed a bite of the chocolate cake before pushing it away. Seated flanked by Charlotte and Gene, she didn't need to make polite conversation. Charlotte turned toward Alma, the dean, and Bethany. Gene stared past Charlotte to the windows behind her, his fingers repeatedly touching the shirt pocket that held his cigarettes.

Dean Darwood encouraged Alma to tell him about herself. Eleanor heard snatches of the student's dutiful answers: parents and younger siblings in Mexico, a desire to return there to teach and later enter a doctoral program—plans Eleanor already knew.

As the server cleared the table, a skinny man in his twenties—the university photographer—appeared in time to document the plaque presentation. Without notes and not blinking at the photographer's flash, Bethany summarized Alma's accomplishments: a 4.0 grade point average, vice-president this year of the university's future teachers' chapter and the newly elected president for the coming year, plus volunteer experience, supervised by Charlotte Kline, in the public schools.

Eleanor had seen Bethany on previous occasions ably represent the Foundation at this and other award presentations and ribbon cuttings. Her daughter shone as a sincere young professional, a beauty with a prominent nose and eyebrows—softened versions of her father's features. Today, she wore the turquoise necklace Eleanor and Wayne gave her for a birthday years ago. Her glossy brown hair, which usually swept her shoulders, was secured by a silver clip. She fit into her linen suit as naturally as her preferred jeans. Eleanor's heart swelled with pride. Bethany wrapped up her remarks with a "Congratulations, Alma. Best of luck as you continue your studies."

The skinny photographer efficiently posed everyone for a group shot, placing the dean in the back row between Charlotte and Gene. Eleanor shared the front row with Bethany and Alma, more because of her short stature than her department-head status, she suspected. Alma seemed the taller in extremely high-heeled sandals with her mass of dark hair coiled atop her head in a fat bun. At Eleanor's side, the girl beamed a smile at the photographer's command. Even without the perfect grade point average, she would stand out among her peers.

A fanciful notion struck Eleanor: In another time and place, Alma might have been the bride of a Spanish don instead of a student from Mexico. Had she told her parents in Chihuahua that one of her professors had been murdered at this supposedly safe, small university? Probably not. She wouldn't want to risk being taken out of school, especially now that she had won this scholarship. But maybe the aunt and uncle she lived with had told them. Surely, everyone in Las Cuevas knew with the news all over the media. Eleanor's mandatory smile faded as the photographer nodded his thanks.

As the group dispersed, Eleanor drew Bethany to the side. "Good job, dear. Why don't you talk to Alma in private? I saw her face at the mention of Paul's death. She had a strange reaction, a mixture of anger and something else—disgust or scorn. As a student, she may know things about Paul that we don't."

"Oh, Mom," Bethany protested. "She must want to get away from us and relax."

Eleanor gave Bethany a verbal nudge. "She's leaving. Go after her! She can hardly refuse to talk to you."

"What will I say?"

"You'll think of something. Scoot!"

Chapter 4

Bethany shook out her hair and stuck the clip into her leather daypack. She exited the building behind Alma. The student, ably hefting a bulging backpack, set off in the direction of the student center. Bethany followed and entered behind her. The 1990s structure, dubbed by students the aquarium for its massive windows, was packed and noisy.

"No class at the moment?" Bethany asked, moving to Alma's side.

The student sucked in her breath in surprise but recovered quickly. "My next one would have been with Dr. Kiefer. We have been told to wait for an email about when it will resume."

"I don't have anything on my agenda either. Hey, there's a free table. Shall we share it?"

Alma's lips tightened. Obviously, she hadn't expected them to have further contact after the luncheon. But she said, "Yes, of course," and followed Bethany to the vacant table. The Commons area, bordered by a food court, held undergraduates and a scattering of apparent graduate students, faculty, and staff. Conversation, shuffling feet, and scraping of chairs created a useful atmosphere for a private conversation.

Alma set her backpack on a chair. "Thank you again for the scholarship. I'm honored to receive it."

This close, she appeared younger and less

sophisticated than the image she had projected at the luncheon. Her lipstick had mostly worn off, and now, she took a tube of it out of her backpack and freshened her lips without the aid of a mirror. She wore false lashes, Bethany realized. *How weighty they must feel!*

"Well deserved," Bethany said. "Alma, you mentioned being in Dr. Kiefer's class. Could I talk to you about him?"

Alma's eyes widened. "But why?"

"My mother and other faculty who knew Dr. Kiefer will provide as much information as they can to the police, but they have a limited perspective. They can't know, for instance, what it was like to be a student of his. You could help fill in that picture."

Alma extracted a water bottle from a mesh holder at the side of her backpack but didn't drink. "Does Dr. Jarviss think a student killed Dr. Kiefer?"

"No. I didn't mean to imply that. But would it surprise you?"

Alma's cheeks turned a deeper hue than she had achieved with blusher. "In Mexico, we have many murders. The gangs start wars and kill each other. Too often, innocent people get caught in their crossfire. In this country, you have mass shootings in public places by crazy guys. But I did not expect anyone to kill a professor at this friendly university."

"Nobody expected it. Tell me, Alma. What did the students think of Dr. Kiefer?"

"Many admired him, the techies especially."

"Techies? Engineering and computer science students?"

"Yes, and we have techies—geeks they are also called—majoring in education. In Dr. Kiefer's Teaching with Technology class, those students thought highly of him."

"You're not one of them?"

"I am not—what is the word?—a fanatic—about technology. Virtual reality and artificial intelligence are amazing, of course. But we students grew up with laptops, phones, and social media accounts. Technology is a tool, not the solution to all the problems of education."

"You sound like my mother," Bethany said. "She uses technology in the course of her work but doesn't rate it over human relations. I get the impression Dr. Kiefer didn't have strong human relations skills."

The artificial lashes flapped like a blackbird's wings. "I can tell you one other thing, Ms. Jarviss: Besides the techies, he favored the pretty girls in class."

"You're one of those girls."

Alma took a ladylike sip from her water bottle. She rubbed a thumb over the place where her lips had left a smear. When she spoke, she gazed past Bethany at the crowded Commons. "Once, when I had an appointment, he gave me nearly an hour of his time. Girls who are not pretty got maybe ten minutes."

"Did he help you in that hour?"

"To be truthful, only a little. He mostly talked about himself and his home in Chicago. He missed the big city. He asked if I felt homesick for Mexico. I told him no; I am not a baby. That made him laugh. I explained that I stay with my *tia*—my mother's sister—who, like my mother, was born here. My mother married a handsome foreign student—my father—from Mexico City, and that's where I was born. Long before I came to NMU, I visited Las Cuevas many times. It's my second home.

Dr. Kiefer said he envied me, that sometimes he felt out of place here, having come not too many years ago."

"He tried to connect with you on a personal level? And you think that's because you're pretty?"

"Yes. To think of it now, I can tell you how he seemed: like a guy on a first date, making an effort to sound caring, to impress a girl." Her voice took on a bitter tone: "As if he cared." She looked Bethany straight in the eye. "But he did not."

Her pulse racing, Bethany said, "What do you mean he didn't care? It might be significant."

"I doubt it, but I will explain. This semester, he said I failed to turn in an essay. When I told him yes, I did submit it online, he would not believe me."

"Did you show him a printout?"

"He refused to take assignments on paper. It was one of his rules. All of our work had to be submitted through the online system. He said I must have failed to follow the instructions, but I did follow them. I'm sure of it. And since he did not accept late work, he was about to give me a zero. So I asked to meet with him in his office."

"And he only talked about Chicago and asked if you were homesick?"

"No, no. That meeting took place earlier. When I was working on the essay and had some questions. Then, when he posted the grades for the assignment, and it looked like I had not done it, I asked to see him again."

"Did you meet with him a second time?"

"How could I? He was murdered, no?"

Alma paused as if for applause after a performance. Moments passed in which Bethany guessed Alma knew she had a motive for murder: a 4.0 GPA to maintain.

"You should tell that story to the police," Bethany

said. "Before they hear it from someone else."

"Why? It would only cause me a headache. It has nothing to do with what happened to Dr. Kiefer." She shifted her gaze to a tall girl threading her way through the crowded tables. "Here comes my friend Roxanne. She was in Dr. Kiefer's class too."

The student had a long neck and long, light-brown hair tucked behind her ears. She moved like a child unused to a body experiencing a growth spurt. A short cotton dress and thin, white sweater enhanced the childlike look, as did a face devoid of makeup. The overall effect signaled someone plagued by stress or illness. But as she approached Alma, she seemed set on being cheerful. "How did the dreaded lunch go? Bet you're glad it's over."

Alma dipped her head in embarrassment. "Roxanne, this is Ms. Jarviss from the Foundation."

"Bethany."

Roxanne flinched. "Sorry, miss, I didn't realize...I'm sure the lunch was nice."

"Join us?" Bethany pulled out a chair. The young woman dropped into it and clutched a messenger bag to her chest.

"We're talking about Dr. Kiefer," Alma said. "The dean, at the luncheon, did not avoid the subject as I thought he might do. He called the death a tragedy."

"It is," Roxanne said. "It's horrendous. Did you know Dr. Kiefer, Ms. Jarviss?"

"Yes, I know the C&I faculty. My mother is Eleanor Jarviss."

Before Bethany could add, "the department head," Roxanne said, "Dr. Jarviss is your mom? She's big on student success. She helped me so much when I was in her intro class last year. She cares about us future teachers. Not that Alma will be an ordinary teacher. She's such a smartie she'll get a Ph.D. and become a professor."

"You flatter me." Alma's words rang with insincere modesty.

"You'll be the famous Dr. Gomez," Roxanne said. "You'll write thick books about bilingual education and have a zillion followers." Roxanne appealed to Bethany for agreement. "It's true. Look who won the scholarship."

Alma waved a delicate hand. "Ms. Jarviss doesn't want to talk about that. She wants to be sure her mother did not murder Dr. Kiefer."

Roxanne's mouth dropped open. Bethany clenched her jaw and realized her face ached. Alma's directness startled her, a reaction Roxanne clearly shared.

A strained silence grew among the three of them, in contrast to the hum in the busy Commons. Keeping her voice calm, Bethany said, "I suppose my mother might be a suspect, along with everyone else who knew Dr. Kiefer. I hope the police find the guilty person as soon as possible."

"Dr. Jarviss would never hurt anybody," Roxanne said on the tail of Bethany's comment. "I'd tell that to the police."

Alma leaned toward her friend. "Don't be unwise. Don't speak to them unless they make you. Otherwise, stay out of their way. We are taught that in Mexico." Of the two friends, Alma was clearly the dominant one.

Bethany said to Roxanne, "I hope you don't mind talking to me, though, like Alma has been doing, about Dr. Kiefer. Did you like him?"

The student squirmed in her seat and toyed with the strap of her messenger bag. "He was my favorite professor."

"You liked his class? Teaching with Technology, Alma said it's called."

"It was okay, but I'm more of a book person." Roxanne pushed back a sleeve of her thin sweater to uncover a watch that looked huge on her wrist. "I have a bunch of homework. I better go."

"Of course," Bethany said, wondering why the student suddenly seemed flustered.

"Nice to meet you, Ms. Jarviss. See you later, Alma." She fled, the messenger bag bumping her side.

Alma sipped water and said deadpan, "Dr. Kiefer gave Roxanne very little of his time, but she adored him."

"Do you know how she was doing in the course?"

"Passing, I believe. But that was not her big issue. She had feelings for the professor. She would gaze at him with innocent calf's eyes and sigh. I don't think she heard a word of his lectures. She often asked to see my notes."

"Why do you think he affected her that way?"

"He affected, as you say, a lot of female students because of his good looks. But in Roxanne's case, it was because of what happened one day. She crashed into him with her bicycle. They ended up on the ground, but he picked her up and said soothing things with no concern for himself, only her welfare. She told me all this. I could see she fell in love with him at once, like a little girl who skins her knee and gets a crush on an older boy who gives her a bandage. At first, she said the accident was all her fault. Later, she mentioned Dr. Kiefer cut across the bike path in front of her. But he was her hero for taking her hand and helping her to her feet." She rolled her eyes under the false lashes. The eyes glimmered a remarkable green. *Colored contacts?* Maybe, but the color looked natural.

Alma palmed her phone. Studying the screen, she said, "Is there anything else, Ms. Jarviss? I should go too."

Bethany pulled out her own phone. "Can we exchange numbers? In case you think of even the smallest detail about Dr. Kiefer that you would like to share with me."

"If you wish."

As they parted, Alma said, "Thank you once more for the scholarship."

"You're welcome, Alma." Bethany watched her weave through the crowd. Quite a few others watched too, the females on the sly and the males with open admiration. Roxanne, in contrast, hadn't created the slightest stir. The two students, who had walked off in opposite directions, seemed unlikely friends.

Bethany bought a coffee at the food court and saw that the table she'd shared with the students had been claimed by others. She chose a booth by one of the Commons' glass-and-chrome walls, where she watched a stream of people flow by outside. She sipped coffee, grateful for the boost it delivered. At the luncheon, she had drunk only water and a mouthful or two of weak iced tea. Now, she pictured how her mother had described the murder scene. Paul, with coffee spilled on his lap and his face distorted in a wrapping of clear tape. Actions meant not only to take his life but also to rob him of his dignity? If that were true, whoever killed Paul must have hated him. If so, why?

Bethany recalled telling her mother she hadn't liked Paul. Once she realized he had made the dinner dates only to seek a Foundation grant, not because he had a personal interest in her, she told him flatly that the Jarviss Foundation didn't fund individuals' research projects. It provided the College of Education scholarship and supported literacy efforts, senior centers, daycare centers, community kitchens, and the like throughout New Mexico.

Paul had pressed a napkin to his lips and said, "Okay, fair enough." Their second date ended before he suggested ordering dessert. At her front door, he didn't mention calling her another time.

Grimacing at the memory, Bethany saw a text from Nathan. He needed to stay with her another night and would see her later. The message ended with four heart symbols. She texted him back, happy to be dating a guy attracted to her, not for what he might get from the Foundation. She headed back to the education building to report to Eleanor on the conversation with the students.

Chapter 5

In the reception area of the C&I office, Eleanor's gossipy secretary told Bethany that the campus police chief, Elisa Marcos, was in *the inner sanctum.* The door opened, and Eleanor ushered out a hefty woman in street clothes and black-framed eyeglasses.

"Chief Marcos, this is my daughter Bethany Jarviss," Eleanor said.

The police chief nodded. She didn't seem inclined to make idle conversation. "Were you on campus Tuesday, Ms. Jarviss?"

"No, I wasn't."

"Do you work at the university?"

"Bethany is an MBA student and the Foundation's grants administrator," Eleanor said. "She presented the Jarviss Scholarship at today's luncheon."

"I see," the chief said in an absolutely neutral voice.

Bethany endured being sized up. She couldn't tell what the chief made of her. Chief Marcos had excellent posture despite carrying extra pounds around her hips and middle. She would look impressive in uniform, and indeed, her navy blue slacks and white blouse mimicked one.

The chief turned to Eleanor. "I may need to speak to you again, Dr. Jarviss." She about-faced smartly and left without another word.

Eleanor gave a sigh of relief. "Come on in,

Bethany." To her secretary, she said, "Jereen, I'll shut the door so we're not disturbed. I won't take calls for a while."

The unsmiling Jereen, whom Bethany knew had served the previous department head for decades, said without enthusiasm, "All right, Dr. Jarviss."

Bethany assumed the police chief's visit would be known all over campus before long. Jereen expertly cultivated the staff grapevine, Eleanor had mentioned.

"So that was the police chief," Bethany said. "I'd never laid eyes on her before." She took a visitor's seat as Eleanor settled herself behind her desk.

"Few people have a reason to meet her," Eleanor said. "Her department is on the outskirts of campus and mostly deals with routine safety and security issues. I've only met her a few times at university events. She was among the police who responded to my call about Paul's death. She wasn't on duty that late in the day, I suppose, but she arrived soon after two of her campus officers. She stopped by today to say the city police are leading the inquiry into Paul's murder, although her department will be involved too."

"That's probably to be expected. The campus police must not have the resources to handle a murder investigation."

"She said as much," Eleanor agreed. "And that I should expect to be questioned again by either force. That I should prepare faculty, staff, and students to come under scrutiny too. She said she told May Zeller's supervisor the same thing. We'll be under a microscope, she said. She didn't mince words. I suppose she considers me a suspect."

Eleanor squared her slight shoulders, a gesture

Bethany had seen before when her mother faced adversity. Her admirable posture matched Chief Marcos's.

"I can't say she's warm and friendly, but I appreciate that she not only spoke to the president and dean but came to see me," Eleanor said. "A campus media person is coming to the office later today. I'd better get used to our college being in the news. I've already been getting calls from concerned and even hysterical parents. I can't say I blame them for being worried about their children's safety. I'm worried too. How can I reassure them our students are safe when I have no idea who killed Paul or why, or if the killer might harm someone else?"

Usually, her mother could calm upset people, Bethany had often observed. Eleanor spoke in a kind, clear way that soothed the highly strung. Her office didn't intimidate anyone. When she moved in as department head in July, she covered the walls with candid photos of herself with students, colleagues, and the family. She didn't trot out framed degrees and awards to impress others. She lined her windowsill with geraniums and African violets. Today, she had cracked open a window, so a spring breeze drifted in.

But although the office was restful, Eleanor was not. She fiddled with the lever on her chair, moving herself up several inches. Then she dropped to a less extreme height. It seemed she had forgotten about sending Bethany on a mission.

"I did speak to Alma," Bethany said. "In the Commons."

"Alma! Of course. I asked you to go after her. Did you find out why she reacted so strongly when the dean

39

brought up the subject of Paul's death?"

"I didn't ask her directly, but I persuaded her to talk about Paul."

"What did she say?"

"That he favored pretty girls. Young women, I mean."

"Really. In what way?"

"He gave them more of his time. Alma expected preferential treatment from him recently, but when push came to shove, that didn't happen." Bethany told Eleanor about the essay Paul said Alma had not turned in online.

Eleanor listened intently, with her small hands folded on her desk. Clear polish gleamed on her neatly trimmed nails. "Alma Gomez has a perfect GPA to protect," Eleanor said. "Oh my."

"And a motive for murdering the professor who could have ruined it," Bethany said.

"Yes, but surely, she wouldn't have taken such an extreme measure. If she couldn't have been given the benefit of the doubt by Paul, she could have come to me to mediate the issue. That's university policy. Well, you know that. I would have gotten Alma's side of the story, then Paul's, and then perhaps met with them together. If no solution was found, I could have taken the issue to the dean."

"I didn't think about that, Mom. I've been thinking about how a student could've committed the murder," Bethany said. "How could Alma have tampered with Paul's coffee to drug him? Because that must be how someone was able to tape up his nose and mouth."

"And his eyes." Eleanor squeezed her hands together so tightly that the knuckles went white. "I suppose she could have slipped something into his travel mug in a meeting in his office, then waited for the drug to take effect. No one has told me the coffee was tampered with, by the way. But you're right; it must have been."

Bethany thought of a possibly significant detail. "Mom, was the lid on or off the mug when you saw the body?"

"On. The lid was on. But you'd expect it to be. To keep the coffee warm."

"Yes, but that would make it hard for someone to casually slip a drug into the mug. I don't see how Alma could have done that. Where do you think that coffee came from? From Paul's house? A coffee maker in his office? Or this office?"

"Paul didn't have his own coffee maker," Eleanor said. "He contributed to a shared coffee fund. Most of us get coffee from the workroom near Jereen's desk. We put cash in a tin, and Jereen takes care of buying cans of coffee. All of us are honor-bound when we take the last cup from the pot to make another pot. That includes me as department head. Paul, I think, was known to take the last cup and sneak away without doing that."

Bethany could not help but grin. "Not making the next pot could prompt your fellow workers to have an urge to kill you."

Eleanor acknowledged that truth with a shake of her head. "I heard faculty actually say, 'I could kill him' as they brandished the empty pot in the workroom. Even Gene makes fresh coffee, although he never washes the pot first. It's mostly left to female faculty and Jereen to even rinse it out."

"Mom, about the packing tape? Do faculty keep rolls of that kind of tape in their offices? Did Paul?"

"I have no idea about Paul. The workroom contains supplies of pens, pencils, reams of paper, and a variety of tape, including packing tape, that we help ourselves to as needed."

"The killer could have brought tape or found it at hand in Paul's office. But in either case, since his coffee was drugged, the murder must have been premeditated."

"Well, I can't believe anyone at the university did it," Eleanor said with passion. "Not a faculty member, not Alma Gomez—a model student—nor any other student."

Her mother's comfortable world had taken a hard hit. Eleanor looked so small in the man-sized desk she'd inherited from the previous department head.

"I met another student who had a class from Paul," Bethany said. "A friend of Alma's stopped by to talk in the Commons. She gushed about you."

"Who was that?"

Bethany struggled to recall the student's name. "Roxanne somebody. Vale. Yes, Roxanne Vale."

A look of concern crossed Eleanor's face. "I know that student fairly well. Roxanne is a project. She needs frequent reassurance she will make a good teacher. Which she will. Of young children. Middle schoolers and teens would eat her alive."

"Sounds like she was in love with Paul," Bethany said. "At least, according to Alma."

Bethany recounted the bicycle incident. "Alma told me about it after Roxanne left us. I think it amused her to tell the story of how badly Roxanne had it for a professor."

Eleanor frowned. "Alma said the accident was Paul's fault, not Roxanne's?"

"I guess. He apparently crossed a bike path, and Roxanne ran into him."

"That would be Paul. He was a 'Look out world, here I come' type of person."

Eleanor went to her window and opened it wider. "Isn't it a beautiful day? The weather has been perfect this spring. I hope this summer isn't as sweltering as last year's. In August, Paul came to me complaining about the heat. It seemed the air conditioning wasn't working properly in his office. We don't have individual climate control. The central unit in the building brought the temperature down to seventy-eight degrees. Paul liked a climate of seventy-five and argued a cooler environment is better for computers. I suggested he buy a fan like mine." She gestured to an electric fan, not in use today, propped on a file cabinet.

"How did that go over with him?"

"Not well. When he said a fan wouldn't provide the climate control he needed, I advised him to fill out an online complaint form with the facilities folks. He'd done that, he said, the day before. As if that office should tend to his needs in a matter of hours. There are more than two thousand faculty at NMU, most of them happy to have air conditioning at all. I count myself lucky to work in this building with windows that open. Some of the buildings have sealed windows. I would hate not being able to open mine, not that I opened it for most of last August. I enjoyed the seventy-eight degrees the air conditioning system managed to achieve."

She turned to Bethany. "I'm rambling. Sorry about that. Thanks for talking to Alma, to both of the students."

Bethany rose to leave. "It was interesting to say the least. Alma seems to take her beauty and brains for granted. Roxanne is plain and awkward. She makes no effort to try to look otherwise, or at least she didn't today. I bet she's Alma's sidekick."

"Not an enviable position, a sidekick. Do you think Roxanne would do favors for Alma?"

"Yes, but kill for her? I hate to even think about it."

Chapter 6

Bethany opted not to spend the rest of the day at the Foundation's headquarters but to work in her home office, a minuscule, converted upstairs bedroom. At five o'clock, she checked for phone messages. None from Nathan but—surprise—a text from Alma Gomez. —*Plz come to Los Mariachis. 7 p.m. Someone U should meet.*—

Bethany called Alma's number, heard a recording, but didn't leave a message. Why hadn't the student sent a more detailed text? Who merited meeting at the popular restaurant? Sighing, she texted back, —*OK. CU at 7*—.

A knock sounded on her front door. She went downstairs to admit Nathan, who never used his key when he expected her to be home. He shed his ball cap and smacked it against his thigh.

"No tile yet," he announced. "I waited at the store for ages while they tracked it down. It's on a truck coming from the West Coast. Be here tomorrow. That's what they said yesterday, but did it get here today? No siree." He kissed her, a brief peck on the lips, and assumed his puppy-dog expression. "I'm here for another night if you can stand more company."

"If you're willing to have dinner with me at Los Mariachis." She told him about Alma and her cryptic message.

Nathan drew her close, burying his nose in her hair. "The best enchiladas in town. Good old boys blasting us with music. Hell yes, let's go!"

****

Los Mariachis restaurant and bar had been a local favorite since her parents were kids, Bethany knew. At the entrance, patrons could turn left into the tavern or turn right into the dining room, where antique sombreros lined the walls. As Nathan had mentioned, the enchiladas—red, green, or Christmas—were a local favorite.

At close to seven o'clock, customers packed the restaurant, and a four-man mariachi band held forth with gusto. The players were young ones tonight. They were hatless and wore white shirts with floppy red bows at their throats.

Alma hadn't arrived, but Bethany and Nathan placed their orders. As Bethany was getting tired of waiting, the band finished a Spanish ballad, and one of the members stepped forward to greet Alma. He took his guitar strap from around his substantial torso and passed the guitar to a fellow player. Three of the players headed to the back of the restaurant. Alma brought the player she had greeted—who looked to be in his late twenties—to Bethany, introducing him as Lenny Ortiz.

"Lenny is my second cousin," Alma said. "Dr. Kiefer was his thesis adviser in the grad program."

"That's why you wanted me to meet him?" Bethany asked. "Why don't you two join us for dinner?"

Alma and Lenny exchanged glances, then she said, "No, thank you, Ms. Jarviss. I'm meeting friends here soon."

"I'm good," Lenny said. "The band gets a meal

before we play, but thanks."

"Well, sit with us during your break," Bethany said. "This is my boyfriend, Nathan Fuller."

After they took seats around the table, Alma said, "Lenny is a full-time teacher at the high school. He's been teaching since he received his bachelor's five years ago."

Lenny had a broad, clean-shaven face. Above his collar, a spider's web tattoo covered the right side and back of his neck. Bethany wondered if his long-sleeved shirt hid other body art.

"It's cool you play in a band," Nathan said, his voice conveying sincere admiration.

"It's my passion, mariachi music," Lenny said.

A likeable guy, Bethany judged.

"Tell them about your thesis," Alma urged. "And what Dr. Kiefer said."

A waitress came to the table with water for Bethany and a cola for Nathan. Bethany encouraged Alma and Lenny to order soft drinks, but both said water would be fine.

"Your thesis?" Bethany asked. "What's your topic?"

"That's the problem," Alma said. "Tell her, Lenny."

"I want to write about mariachi music," he said, shifting his weight nervously. "We have mariachi classes at the high school and a mariachi club. Being in a school-sponsored band can keep kids showing up for their classes, and I know it keeps them away from gangs." He rubbed his neck, his hand partly covering the spider's web. "I should know. I was a gangbanger for a while as a teen."

"What's the problem with your topic? It sounds like

a good one," Bethany said.

Lenny spread his meaty hands. "Nothing that I can see. I want to survey high schools across the state that have mariachi programs and those that don't. The idea is to compare the school dropout rates. Dr. Kiefer wanted me to do something related to technology in the schools instead. He pushed me to survey schools to compare those with computer labs to those without. To prove that computers keep students in school. He was all for technology and didn't give a flip for music, definitely not my kind."

"What a jerk," Nathan said.

Lenny nodded. "You said it, man."

The waitress brought two more glasses of water. Lenny took a long, thirsty drink.

Bethany asked, "Where does your thesis project stand now? Did you agree to go with the topic Dr. Kiefer suggested?"

"No, ma'am. I didn't know what to do, to tell you the truth."

Alma rotated her glass between her hands. Seeing Bethany watching, she stopped and said, "Ms. Jarviss, I can tell what you are thinking. Was Lenny angry enough at Dr. Kiefer to kill him?"

Lenny gave a strangled cough. "What are you talking about, girl? I didn't off the guy!"

With a sweet smile, she said, "Take a breath, Lenny. You didn't kill the professor. Calm down and tell Ms. Jarviss what you told me about Dr. Kiefer's girlfriend. Well, now his former girlfriend."

"Who would that be?" Bethany asked. She guessed he meant Kim Lamont, an assistant professor in Eleanor's department. A good-looking woman several years younger than Paul. On Valentine's Day, Bethany had lunched with Eleanor and her friend Charlotte. Love had been Charlotte's topic du jour. Knowing Bethany had gone to dinner with Paul, Charlotte mentioned he was a free agent, no longer in a relationship with Kim. Bethany remembered laughing uncomfortably and saying, "No thanks. Two dates with Paul Kiefer were enough."

Lenny confirmed Bethany's supposition. "I mean Dr. Lamont," he said. "I'm in a class of hers this semester."

"Lenny told Dr. Lamont about the thesis issue," Alma said.

"Let me tell it, okay?"

Alma had let her hair down tonight. When she turned her head, the gleaming mass swayed around her face. "Sorry. I'll be as quiet as a little mouse."

"Right, cousin." He turned to Bethany. "I had an appointment to see Dr. Kiefer again about the thesis, to tell him I didn't love his topic, that in my heart, I knew mine was the right one. Dr. Lamont had said to write up a real professional proposal and send it to Dr. Kiefer online, which I did. He agreed to meet with me but didn't give me any idea what he would say. When I got to his door, I saw Dr. Lamont, of all people, there. I hadn't told her when I was meeting with Dr. Kiefer. She stood in the doorway, yelling at him like they'd had a big fight. The woman turned around and slammed into my chest. *Wham!* She didn't bother to apologize."

Alma tugged on Lenny's sleeve. "Tell her what she shouted at Dr. Kiefer."

"I'm getting to it, okay?" He shook his head at Alma's pushiness. "Chill, Alma."

Bethany held her breath and waited for what was to come.

Uneasily, he shifted in his chair. "Dr. Lamont yelled, and I swear these were her exact words: 'That's despicable! You evil bastard!'" He emptied his water glass with audible gulps. "That's what she said before she rammed me. Her face was all blotchy, and she had a wild animal look in her eyes. I've seen a few women rattled like that before, and it's not a pretty sight."

Alma put her fingertips to her mouth, her green eyes dancing. As Nathan grinned, Bethany asked, "Did you find out what Dr. Lamont meant by that?"

"No, ma'am. It could have been a lovers' quarrel. I found out later Dr. Kiefer had been dating her. Dr. Lamont never let on about that when she told me to see him again. She acted like any nice professor giving me advice about sticking to my guns."

"And the thing is," Alma added dramatically, "not long after that, I heard they broke up right before Valentine's Day. The students were talking about it."

"I wasn't," Lenny said. "I didn't know a thing about it until you told me."

"All the female students knew," Alma said. "The undergrads. You're a full-time teacher and not at the university as much, so you don't hear all the gossip. But maybe you heard Dr. Lamont break up with Dr. Kiefer. Ms. Jarviss, don't you wish we knew why she gave him a tongue-lashing?"

With three sets of eyes on her, Bethany felt like a target stuck with darts. "Yes, I do."

"Do you think Lenny should tell the police?" Alma asked.

"No way," Lenny protested. "Alma, you said I just

had to talk to Ms. Jarviss and that she'd look into it without getting me involved." His dark eyes conveyed alarm.

Bethany shook her head at Alma. "You promised him that without talking to me first? Alma, you shouldn't have. You had no right."

Annoyed, Alma said, "You asked me to get in touch if I thought of even the littlest detail about Dr. Kiefer."

At that, Lenny looked even more troubled. "Ms. Jarviss, Alma told me you came to her asking questions because Dr. Jarviss is your mother. She's a good professor. I had her for a class. I considered talking to her about what Dr. Kiefer said about my topic. That day, after Dr. Lamont left, I met with him, and he still dissed it. Now, I don't want to bother her. She must be crazy with worry about Dr. Kiefer's murder."

"You should ask to meet with her anyway," Bethany said. "Obviously, you need another thesis adviser, one who's on your wavelength."

"What if Dr. Jarviss thinks I killed Dr. Kiefer? Offing somebody to solve a problem is what you expect from gangbangers. I used to be one of those guys, but I never saw anybody get killed. And I'd never hurt a soul."

"My mom will appreciate that," Bethany said. "Go see her."

"Okay, but I don't want to talk to any cops."

Alma spoke up. "Somebody should find out what Dr. Lamont meant when she called Dr. Kiefer evil."

"Yeah. That's a heavy word," Lenny said.

They fell silent as the waitress brought two green-chile enchilada dinners and made the usual comments about the plates being hot. Nathan dug into his meal. Bethany ate a bite and set down her fork as Lenny said,

"Alma told me about you, Ms. Jarviss. That you're some sort of amateur detective."

Bethany swallowed hard. "I didn't tell you that, Alma."

"No, but you acted like one when you talked to Roxanne and me. I looked you up on the internet. You found out who was to blame for a girl's death in Albuquerque. And you helped solve—what do they call it? A cold case. Yes, a cold case that involved your sister."

Again, three sets of eyes focused on Bethany. She was the first to blink. "I've been lucky to piece together information that helped bring two killers to justice."

Nathan nudged her. "Lucky? Maybe. Smart for sure."

Lenny gazed to the back of the restaurant at his fellow mariachis. "My break's over. Ms. Jarviss, please don't go to the cops about what I said. You look into it yourself, okay? I don't want to get Dr. Lamont in trouble if she didn't do anything bad."

He pushed away from the table. Bethany watched him join the three other players. Soon, the band commenced singing a song in Spanish. Bethany caught the words *corazon*—heart—and *triste*—sad. A familiar song about a love affair gone wrong. She wished she knew what had gone wrong between Kim Lamont and Paul Kiefer.

"You will solve this mystery," Alma said with the confidence of a young person. "I see my friends waiting. I should go."

Bethany said, "Of course. You were right to have me meet Lenny. I'm sorry I didn't seem grateful at first. I am, truly."

With Alma out of hearing distance, Nathan said, "That's one sharp señorita. Now eat your meal, darlin'." He lifted the lid from a container, and Bethany took a warm, soft corn tortilla. The mariachi music washed over her but didn't soothe her mind. *Amateur detective*. A title as corny as the tortilla she chewed, but somehow it fit, as did the Mexican music bouncing off the restaurant's sombrero-covered walls.

****

In Bethany's bed, after they'd made love, Nathan said, "There's something I've been meaning to say, something important."

It was ten o'clock, and she was drifting off to sleep. Expecting a particularly heartfelt declaration of love, Bethany snuggled her naked body closer to his.

"I've got a chance for a new job," he said.

"Great! Tell me about it."

"It's on a ranch near Laramie."

Wide awake, she snapped on the bedside light. "Wyoming?" The word felt hard and alien in her mouth. "That's two states above New Mexico." She pulled the bedcovers over her breasts.

"Yeah, that's the hell of it. But it's a decent job that doesn't involve laying tile. It's working with horses and cattle."

He explained that the ranchers also ran their place as a guest ranch in the summer and a hunting camp for deer and elk in the fall. "I heard about it from a friend who got taken on, and he likes it a lot. They need one more hand before the summer season starts. My buddy says I should act fast if I want a shot at the job. He thinks the clientele would like a real rodeo cowboy—okay, a former one—around the place. He knows I got injured

53

but could still lead trail rides in the summer. Tend to the horses on the hunts, help out with the cattle. The pay would be better than I'm getting now."

Bethany listened without interrupting. When Nathan wound down, she rolled to her side, her back to the light, to face him. "Sounds like a dream job."

"Except maybe dealing with a bunch of rich greenhorns."

"I haven't heard that word in a while."

He laughed. "Tenderfeet then."

"Like that's a better word? You'd probably love the ranch's guests, and they'd love you. You're good with people." As she said it, she imagined other single women falling for her charming cowboy. Would he have casual affairs that ended when the ladies went home? Or worse, meet one of them he preferred over her?

"Guess I could manage the people part of the job," he said. "And sure, Wyoming's a ways from here. But I'd be back every few weeks, and you could come visit. There are cabins to rent and a trout stream. I saw the setup on the website."

He drew her to him, wrapped his feet around hers, and kissed the top of her head. "I can't stand much more of my current gig."

"When did you hear about this job?"

"A few days ago."

"But you waited to tell me until now?" Bethany's muscles tensed, and she pulled away from him, disentangling their feet.

"Yeah, I should've said earlier. I meant to, and then this murder happened. The timing wasn't right."

"But it is now?"

"If the tile gets here tomorrow, I'll go back to the

ranch to lay it, then take a few days off and drive up to Laramie to meet the folks that might hire me."

"Will you tell the Carters what's up?"

"Not yet; I have plenty of time off coming. They won't mind me taking a break with only scraps of work to do around their place. Heck, they probably expect to lose me sooner or later."

He stopped talking. After a while, Bethany slid from between the covers and donned her T-shirt and yoga pants. She went downstairs to the only bathroom in the house, closed the door, and fretted about the long stretch of Colorado between northern New Mexico and southern Wyoming. When Nathan didn't come to find her, she returned to the bedroom where, as usual after sex, he had fallen into a sound sleep. She switched off the bedside light, lay down beside him, and closed her eyes. Sometime after midnight, her mind stopped churning, and she slept fitfully.

****

In the morning, as they ate the salsa-drenched scrambled eggs Nathan had whipped up, his phone rang. The tile had finally arrived. He packed his duffle and kissed Bethany goodbye with a fierceness that stung her lips. "It's not a sure thing, this job," he said.

Yes, it is! Nathan would be an ideal hire for a guest ranch. He'd be popular with the guests and—an experienced hunter—knowledgeable stalking deer and elk. Was being sick of his current job the only reason he wanted a change? Or did he want to cool their romance? *No, of course he didn't.* Bethany phoned the Foundation to say she would work from home, but as she turned on her laptop, she couldn't keep her mind off her man.

At noon, Eleanor texted a request for additional

scholarship brochures for Spring Visitors Day. Good, Bethany thought; the depleted supply must mean the murder hadn't kept away the usual busloads of potential freshmen. She made it out the door in minutes.

Chapter 7

The Old Quad buzzed with teenagers taking advantage of free food, carnival-style games, and meetups for campus tours. Previously, besides the brochures, Bethany had supplied Foundation swag—pens, mini flashlights, and USB sticks—to the education college. She was glad the university hadn't canceled this event.

Eleanor, at the scholarship table, greeted Bethany and introduced her to a new college staffer, a young woman who looked about twelve.

"Julie, you've been out here quite a while," Eleanor said. "Why don't you take a break? I'll watch the table."

"Yes, ma'am. I could use a potty break."

As Bethany added a thick stack of brochures to others promoting various scholarships, Eleanor said, "You would think it's a normal visitors day. Like every other year."

"I know," Bethany said. "Look at Gene Waverly in the dunk tank. The guy's all wet." Eleanor grinned at the double meaning.

Two other faculty members caught Bethany's attention. "There's Kim Lamont and Vince Morrison. They're headed away from us."

"Vince was Paul Kiefer's best friend, and Kim was Paul's girlfriend for a time," Eleanor said.

"When Paul took me to dinner, I didn't realize he

was dating her. I did see Vince and Paul playing tennis on campus occasionally," Bethany said. "When I rode my bike near the courts."

"They played regularly," Eleanor said. "I heard Vince was the more accomplished player. That must have been good for his ego because other than that—"

"Paul was more successful," Bethany said. "How old is Vince, do you know?"

"Thirty-six or -seven. He's an associate professor."

"With prospects of promotion to full prof any time soon?"

"That would be talking out of school," Eleanor said. "I can say that in my department, Paul alone turned in paperwork for a promotion this year."

"Ah, Vince wasn't ready to go for it. I know him a little, Mom. We served on the Western Heritage Festival committee last year. He told me he grew up in Iowa. He's not a native Southwesterner, but he's interested in anything to do with the Old West. He seemed ashamed of the stereotypical views of the West back when he played cowboys and Indians as a kid."

"He cares very much about how Western history is taught," Eleanor said. "But he has a fondness for classic Western TV shows. His father has a DVD collection of those shows Vince hopes to inherit someday." She watched the crowd that had absorbed Vince and Kim into their midst.

"Mom, if I learn things about your faculty that might have a bearing on what happened to Paul, what should I do?"

She didn't answer as about fifty teenagers, led by an NMU guide carrying a pennant overhead, trooped into the quad. The guide stopped, and the line broke up.

Bethany got out of the way of a trio of boys who grabbed brochures and other items. When the boys moved on, Eleanor asked, "Did you hear something that ties Kim or Vince to the murder?"

"Nothing for certain."

"You have good instincts. Do what you think is best. If you want to talk, I'll be ready to listen."

"Okay, Mom."

"Kim and Vince volunteered for the college's burrito booth. I saw the sign-up sheet. Why don't you go get some lunch?"

"Did they sign up as a team?"

"Kim first, then Vince, for the current shift. I think he signed up because she did."

"Right. Good to know. See you later, Mom."

****

As Bethany passed Gene in the dunk tank, students from the tour group lined up to pitch foam rubber balls at a target over his head. Gene's hair and clothes were soaking wet, as were his bare feet. He waved at Bethany, then, as a ball hit the mark, dropped with a comical look of surprise into a kiddie pool, splashing water and sputtering. The students snickered and cheered.

Gene relished his role of dunk-tank victim every spring, Bethany recalled. His college students enjoyed his plight too. Some of them infiltrated the high schoolers' ranks, offering cash in exchange for the younger students' free tickets.

Farther down the line, the food booths did a brisk trade in mini donuts, hot dogs, pizza slices, and other fare. Bethany breathed in fast-food scents. At the burrito booth, a woman in an NMU Dining Services apron and hairnet fried a mixture of ground hamburger, diced potatoes, and chopped green chile. Vince, silly-looking in a similar hairnet and apron, filled a tortilla and inexpertly folded it into a plump package. Kim handed it to a student.

Kim was taller than Bethany and slighter in bone structure. She wore neither an apron nor a hairnet. She had twisted her hair into one of those deliberately messy knots Bethany could never quite master. A few feet from the portable cooker, Kim managed to appear cool in a pale pink blouse. Bethany knew her only enough to exchange nods when their paths crossed on campus.

Stepping up to the counter, Bethany said, "Hi, Kim. One burrito, please."

"Hello, Bethany." She accepted Bethany's five-dollar bill, made change, and with a cursory thanks, passed her a warm, foil-wrapped packet.

Seeing no one behind her, Bethany lingered. "Good showing of students."

"The normal world keeps turning." Kim sounded resigned to that reality.

Vince stepped forward and, as if the hairnet embarrassed him, whipped it off and let it dangle from his fingers. The guy had a noticeable receding hairline.

"Bethany Jarviss, the sleuth," he said. "I hear you've been asking people questions about Paul." It sounded half joke, half reproach.

Kim gave him a startled glance as Bethany said, "People?"

"One person. Lenny Ortiz. Why did you talk to him about Paul?"

"Because Alma Gomez asked me to. Lenny said Paul wasn't inclined to approve his thesis topic, mariachi music in the schools. In fact, he scorned that topic."

Two girls behind Bethany must have sensed tension in the air. "Let's get hot dogs," one said. They scampered off.

"If you think Lenny killed Paul, you're crazy," Vince retorted. "Paul probably would have approved Lenny's topic if he'd written a strong enough proposal. I told Lenny that. And I'll tell you this: We should respect who Paul was. A good man, a brilliant one." He gave Kim a sidelong glance. "And we shouldn't pretend he never existed."

The Dining Services woman cleared her throat. "This meat is done, Dr. Morrison. Almost overdone."

"Yes, ma'am." Vince dragged the hairnet back on and resumed assembling burritos.

Kim stared, aghast, at his back. "Vince, I didn't mean to ignore Paul's death. I just didn't know what to say."

When he didn't respond, she leaned over the counter toward Bethany. "You must have heard Paul and I were a couple for a while. I know you dated him. You must have seen how charming he could be."

In a low tone for Kim's ears only, Bethany asked, "Despite being an evil bastard?"

"Where did you hear that? Oh, of course. From Lenny Ortiz." She aimed another glance at Vince as four laughing teenagers strode toward the booth, brandishing tickets.

"I should encourage him to tell it to the police," Bethany said. "Or you and I could talk in private."

"All right," Kim said. "I have office hours until four. Come then. I'm down the hall from the C&I office."

Bethany moved away, the burrito she had no appetite for cooling in her hand.

****

At four o'clock sharp, Bethany passed a startling display of yellow tape proclaiming *CRIME SCENE. DO NOT ENTER* on Paul's former office door. Kim's door stood open. As Bethany peered in, a student scraped back a chair and scrambled to her feet. "Thanks, Dr. Lamont, for all the help."

"Come back if you still have questions." Kim smiled dismissively.

In leaving, the student trailed the faint baby powder scent of a common antiperspirant.

"A shy future teacher?" Bethany asked.

"She's nervous about a class presentation and worried about ever being able to face a room full of children," Kim said. "By the time she's a senior and student teaches, I tell her she'll gain confidence. At least, that's my hope."

The office might have been styled for a promotional photo. Its bookshelves were filled, but not jammed, with education texts. An uncluttered desk held an office phone, a laptop, a stack of papers, and a silver pen in a holder. On the floor, a sleek maroon briefcase rested against the desk.

"Would you close the door so we won't be disturbed?" Kim asked. "And have a seat."

She gave the instructions with the confidence of someone used to being obeyed. Paul had spoken in the same way. "Do order the steak," he had said. Bethany complied even though she had been in the mood for grilled chicken. Later, she wondered why she had done his bidding. Normally, she wasn't a pushover.

"You asked to see me," Kim said. No smile now.

"I hope you'll explain the words 'evil bastard.'

Lenny heard you call Paul that. He also heard you say, 'That's despicable!' You were leaving Paul's office as Lenny arrived for an appointment."

Kim fingered a pearl button on her blouse. "I guessed that he heard me. I'm sorry he did."

"Sorry?"

"Yes, because it related to him. Paul told me Lenny had asked to see him about an unfortunate choice of thesis subject, mariachi music. Paul told me he had no interest in what he called 'a lame, boring topic.' He was going to steer Lenny toward something related to technology."

Just as Lenny said.

"'I don't care if students wear sombreros and howl at the moon on their own time, but I won't waste mine reading papers about their hobbies,'" Kim said, mimicking a man's voice. "That's what Paul said. His attitude was despicable, and I told him so."

"But according to Lenny, you weren't willing to speak to Paul on his behalf."

"No. Paul brought up the issue. But his arrogant attitude upset me."

She doesn't look upset now. "To the extent that you called him evil? That seems an extreme reaction."

"I don't actually think I said *evil*. Or if I did, it came out in the heat of the moment. Did Lenny know we'd been talking about him?"

Bethany recalled the conversation at Los Mariachis. "No, I don't think so."

"Why did he tell you what he overheard? Because if I was angry enough to shout, I might have been angry enough to kill Paul? That's quite a leap of imagination. But, as I said, I doubt if I called Paul *evil*. I might have called him selfish. You must know selfish fit him."

"What do you mean?"

"He only cared about himself. He told me he only asked you out because of your Foundation."

"My family's Foundation."

"Whatever. He was trolling for a grant, wasn't he? He probably didn't notice you're an attractive woman. You were too old for him."

Bethany said indignantly, "I'm thirty-two. He was in his early thirties, I assumed."

"Thirty-five. I'm twenty-eight, too old for Paul, I found out. He liked his girlfriends young."

Two hot spots, like rouge, popped out on Kim's face. Bethany's face felt warm. Betting she also looked flushed, she asked, "Is that why he stopped seeing you? Because of a younger woman, an undergrad, maybe?"

Kim took the silver pen from its holder and opened the folder on her desk. "I'd better grade these papers." When Bethany didn't budge, Kim said, "He didn't stop seeing me. I broke it off. And I don't think he would have risked having an affair with a college girl. But what would I know? He basked in students' hero worship. He wasn't a mature man."

"That's why you ended your relationship? Because he lacked maturity?"

"Not that it's any of your business, but because he didn't see himself fathering children any time soon. He said if we married, maybe we could start a family in the distant future. I didn't want years to go by and eventually have a baby with a forty-year-old father."

"You sound upset."

"Dating Paul wasted my energy. I'm almost thirty. I couldn't afford to devote time to a man who wasn't interested in fatherhood. But I can assure you I didn't kill Paul. I had no reason to. And I have no idea who did. If you'll excuse me, I really have grading to do." She picked up a student's essay.

On her way out, Bethany said, "I see you accept work on paper."

"I prefer to read printouts, not stare at a screen. I enjoy using this pen. My parents gave it to me when I earned my doctorate."

The door swung closed behind Bethany with an audible click. Her head aching, she walked to the end of the hallway and out the exit to a staircase open to a clear sky. She descended one floor and plopped down on a concrete step to think.

What did she make of Kim's comments? Unlike Vince, the woman didn't mourn for Paul, that was for sure. Was it true she had broken up with him? He wasn't around to give his account of the breakup. Poor Kim, though. Longing for marriage and children, hyperaware of her biological clock. Bethany's ticked with a fainter, less insistent sound than Kim's, apparently. She and Nathan hadn't discussed their views on parenthood. She didn't know if she would ever want that responsibility, and she didn't want to scare off her cowboy. He might shy away from the topic like a spooked animal.

She brushed off her slacks and descended the remaining stairs, turning her thoughts back to Paul and Kim. Who might know more about their relationship? Someone with an ear for gossip—Charlotte Kline. Bethany phoned her and got lucky. Charlotte had charge of the C&I table on the quad.

"Things are winding down. Sure, I have time for a chat."

****

Charlotte sat with the department's website on her laptop's screen and a scattered display of brochures and swag on the table. She sipped a cold drink and wiggled her naked toes in the grass.

"You look comfy," Bethany said.

Charlotte yawned. "Not much activity late in the day. Eleanor sat out here earlier when the crowds were fearsome." She slipped her feet into her sandals and stood up.

"Yes, I spoke to Mom here," Bethany said. "And to a couple profs who seem upset about Paul Kiefer's death."

"About the murder? Eleanor thinks you're a young Miss Marple, but you'd better be careful, Bethany. We don't want you to be the next victim."

"Don't worry, Charlotte. I'll be fine."

"Who have you talked to?"

"Kim Lamont, for one. I just came from her office."

"Ah, the jilted lover."

"Jilted? She said she broke it off with Paul."

"Did she? Rumor had it he called it quits, but he could've given people that impression out of wounded pride."

"Kim claimed she ended the relationship because he didn't want kids, at least not soon."

Charlotte nodded. "It was common knowledge she's baby crazy, and he certainly wasn't. The gal worries about approaching the big three-oh-no. That's ages ago for me. I can't remember how it felt to be that young." She shook her head in amusement, setting her beaded earrings swinging.

"It's silly of Classy Kim—that's what I call her but

not to her face—to panic. Women have always given birth in their thirties and even forties. I told Kim I turned thirty-nine shortly after I had Toby and Theresa. I didn't admit that, at fifty-one, it's quite a task to keep up with twelve-year-old twins. It would be chaos at home without a good husband like Jerry. He keeps me grounded. What Kim needs is the right partner. Paul never could have been that man for her. Too self-involved."

Near them, faculty and staff packed up their displays. Charlotte scrutinized the items on the C&I table. "How did these get so scrambled? By the way, how goes it with that guy of yours?"

"We're good. Charlotte, if Paul dropped Kim, she had a motive for murder. Maybe she killed him because he stopped her from realizing her dream of marriage and motherhood. She hinted he had an eye for the female students. Ever hear anything about that?"

"An eye yes, but I don't think he slept with students. He did bask in the light of their adoration, our Dr. Charming."

"Is that what he was called?"

"By me, nobody else that I know of. Well, I should pack up. This event is as good as over. I need to take this stuff back to the office and then scoot to my yoga class." She powered down the laptop and closed the lid with a snap.

Bethany helped sort the remaining brochures and bind them with rubber bands. Charlotte stuffed the brochures and laptop into a tote bag stamped with images of Hindu goddesses.

"Let's walk and talk," Charlotte said. She picked up her drink. "This raspberry chamomile tastes okay, but it doesn't have a drop of caffeine. My fault for getting it at the Future Nurses' booth." She dropped it into the first trash can they passed.

"Do you think Kim would have been capable of planning a murder?" Bethany asked. "Drugging Paul's coffee and smothering him with tape?"

"Kim is capable of anything she sets her mind to," Charlotte said. "That's probably what Paul liked about her, a cerebral nature in that exquisite face and body. He probably didn't expect she'd fixate on becoming a mom." She stopped to get a better grip on the tote bag. "You said you talked to another faculty member about Paul?"

"Vince Morrison. Earlier, with Kim at the burrito booth."

"Vince tried his luck with Kim before she dated Paul."

"Charlotte, are you sure?"

"He saw her socially when she came to the university. It didn't last. But now, with Paul out of the picture, maybe Vince thinks he has another chance."

"Mom did tell me Kim signed up for the burrito booth first, then Vince. She hinted he volunteered because Kim did. He seemed awfully upset about Paul's death. And he got angry when I said a grad student I saw last night claimed Paul hadn't respected his thesis topic."

They resumed walking, Charlotte slower than Bethany's usual pace. "Can I take that bag, Charlotte?"

"No, I've got it. We're almost there. Who was the grad student?"

"Lenny Ortiz. Do you know him?"

They stopped at the front of the education building as a group of teenagers—high school visitors, no doubt—ran past them, probably to catch their bus home.

"Lenny teaches at the high school, and as you know, my specialty is the elementary grades."

"You won't take over as his thesis adviser, I suppose."

"Was Paul his adviser? That must've been a bad match. Lenny Ortiz is a local young man who grew up the hard way. Paul preferred to work with out-of-state master's students. He flattered himself that some of them came to NMU to study with him and maybe get their name as a research assistant on one of his papers."

"Lenny said Paul didn't appreciate his thesis topic, mariachi music in the schools."

"I didn't hear about it. Paul must have hated that topic."

"As Lenny said."

"For his own good, he'd better not mention it to the police. They've been around asking a lot of questions. I was interviewed by a pair of city officers."

"What did you say?"

"That I've agreed to take over one of Paul's classes, and before they think that's a motive for murder, it's for no extra pay and only until the end of the semester. And no, I don't keep clear packing tape in my desk. But they looked for it. As if whoever killed Paul wouldn't have disposed of the roll of tape! I've got to run. *Namaste!*"

Chapter 8

On the way to her car, Bethany spotted Gene Waverly, dry now in faded, baggy jeans, toting a duffle bag in one hand and a shabby canvas briefcase in the other. She had known him most of her life and found him sweet and harmless.

As she came up behind him, she called, "Gene!" loudly, to not startle him.

He broke into a broad smile. "What you doing on campus? Handing out more free money?"

"Nope, just brochures. Hey, I saw you get dunked."

He raised the duffle bag. "My wet duds are in here."

"Wise of you to bring a change of clothes."

"Yeah, from years of experience. But the gig's not the fun it once was. Used to be, students I knew by name would send me into the drink. These days, I lecture to a hall full of kids I wouldn't know if I met 'em on the street. At least I don't have a mass of 'em online." He resumed walking, at a relaxed pace.

"Some faculty prefer online teaching," she said.

"You mean Paul Kiefer. He was famous for it."

"I heard he had fans in his in-person classes too."

"True. The techie crowd. They called him 'Dr. Paul.' And some of the females buzzed around him like adoring honeybees." Gene picked up the pace.

"I've met students who didn't like him," Bethany said. "Alma Gomez wasn't a fan."

"Had her in one of my lecture classes, which is why your mom tapped me to fill Paul's seat at your scholarship do. Bet a smart girl like that wouldn't have fallen at his feet."

Silently, Bethany agreed. Roxanne, Alma's friend—a less confident student—seemed more prone to idol worship.

"You didn't like Paul," Bethany said bluntly.

"Arrogant SOB. Took himself and his job way too seriously. We're training young people to teach kids, not curing cancer."

"I've heard he did important research," she said to provoke a response.

"He wrote about all the new bells and whistles. Saw himself as superior to the senior faculty. And I don't mean only me. He didn't respect Eleanor before or after she took the department head job.

"You know, Bethany, I wanted that job. Felt I deserved it as the longest-serving full prof in the department. But I would've made a hash of it. I detest paperwork and meetings and setting so-called goals and objectives. All the stuff a head has to do. I'd hate to rate my colleagues and send a report to the dean with a thumbs up or down for raises and promotions."

"Or deal with a young professor angling for early promotion to full prof," Bethany said.

Gene halted at the edge of a faculty/staff parking lot, breathing fast. He dropped the duffle and briefcase and took a cigarette pack from a breast pocket. With a silver lighter, he lit up, took a puff, exhaled, and coughed. "Yep, there was a big to-do over that. Now, where did I park my buggy?" He scanned the lot.

"Did you think Paul had earned an early promotion?

Was he that accomplished?"

"At first, I thought no siree. But he had a strong case. I had to support it, much as I disliked the guy. He had a truckload of publications to his credit. A whole sheet full of 'em. He made some noise about how we should read his application packet online. In the end, Jereen had to make copies. She was put out about that."

"Did you read his publications?"

Gene shook his head. "Nobody reads each other's journal articles unless they're in your own area of interest. We saw a list of Kiefer's attached to his application, that's all."

"You're on the promotion and tenure committee?"

"All full profs are. Can't get out of it."

"And despite not liking Paul, you supported his bid."

He puffed hard on the foul-smelling cigarette. "Yep. Can you see my ride out there? Where the heck did I leave it?"

"I suppose you don't have a key fob to beep it?"

Gene yanked a set of keys from a pants pocket. "'Course not. The old rattletrap doesn't have fancy features. Ah, I remember. The lot was so full today, I parked way back, not in my usual spot." He picked up the duffle and the battered briefcase. "Good luck investigating Kiefer's murder. Expected you would be, with Eleanor the obvious suspect."

"Mom? Obvious? Why do you say that?"

The cigarette bounced in the corner of his mouth. "Anybody who was Kiefer's boss would want to kill him. You watch your back. I don't think Eleanor bumped him off, but whoever did won't want a clever gal like you nosing around."

Bethany watched him find his car, then sought hers in a more distant, student lot. As a longtime senior faculty member, Gene knew a great deal about his co-workers. It would be worth it to talk to him again. He lived near her house, across from a city park, where he walked his dogs. She might bump into him there *accidentally on purpose* as an old-timer like him might say.

****

Bethany's house was a welcome sight, her backyard a refuge with hummingbirds whirring around the feeder, jockeying for spots on the tiny perches. Trying to relax in her favorite garden recliner, she considered the day's conversations, foremost the one in Kim Lamont's office. Had Kim called Paul "evil" or not? Did her account of severing the relationship with Paul ring true? Would knowing even matter?

Restlessly, she tinkered with her phone. No message from Nathan, but her father had texted that he'd be back in Las Cuevas soon. She sent a quick reply, then tapped the like symbol on a social-media post from Joni about spring rates at the Sorrel Lodge. Bethany felt a lingering sense of satisfaction at solving, for Joni's sake, a cold-case murder near the lodge a few months ago. For Eleanor's sake, she would keep asking questions about Paul Kiefer's murder.

The hummers' feeder, low on nectar, needed tending. Time to go inside and make a new batch, about the only kitchen activity Bethany enjoyed. Rarely one to cook, she appreciated how Nathan, like her father, grilled a mean burger. Come to think of it, she might have a leftover one in the freezer. As she was about to go see, Eleanor called with an invitation. "Come and have a decent meal, Bethany. Bring Nathan."

"He hit the road this morning, Mom."

"Then it'll be the two of us. We don't do that often enough."

"Have a decent meal?"

"Get together without the men. You can tell me about your day. I know you talked to Charlotte. She phoned."

Bethany should have expected that. "Naturally. Right after her yoga class?"

"Before it. The instructor was late. Charlotte squeezed in a call before her first Downward Dog."

****

They had dinner on the deck with a lovely view of the valley. With satisfaction, Eleanor watched Bethany take second helpings of grilled chicken and asparagus. This daughter could be counted on to eat heartily rather than play with her food like Joni, who had suffered with anorexia since middle school. Bethany resembled her father, not only in looks but in temperament: sensible, reliable, easy to love. Joni, equally loved, had been a handful ever since her adoption as a five-year-old. But adoption hadn't made the difference. She and Wayne previously had adopted Don—no blood relation to Joni—and he was as easy as pie. At the thought, Eleanor said, "You might save room for dessert. I bought apple empanadas."

"This is a nice meal, Mom."

"I'm glad you like it. You haven't been over much in the last few months. But that's fine. Nathan's certainly one of the good guys."

"Do I hear a fishing line being cast? Angling for information?"

74

"Naturally."

Her daughter's dark eyebrows drew together, a troubling sign.

Eleanor set down her fork. "What is it, dear?"

"Okay, I might as well tell you. Nathan's considering taking a job in Wyoming."

Eleanor didn't interrupt as Bethany described the opportunity, obviously trying to see things Nathan's way. He would be happy working with horses and cattle, guiding the hunters, befriending the guests. Too often, his job at the Carters' place bored him stiff.

"You realize it's time he makes a change," Eleanor said. "But you worry about how it will affect you."

Bethany frowned again. Soon, there would be a permanent line between those dark brows. She'd developed a frown line at about Bethany's age. "How about ice cream with our empanadas?" Her daughter never could refuse a scoop.

"I can make room for that."

"Sit tight."

When Eleanor brought the desserts, Bethany had recovered her natural good spirits. "Mom, you're showing admirable restraint, but you must want to hear what people said about Paul Kiefer." She gave an abbreviated account of meeting with Alma Gomez and Lenny Ortiz at Los Mariachis.

"I'm impressed how readily people confide in you," Eleanor said. "No one would have told me half of that."

Bethany scraped her spoon in a nearly empty bowl. When she was a girl, she would use her forefinger, then lick it free of the last smear of melted ice cream. These days, she resisted the temptation, but her finger twitched.

"Do you think Alma trotted out Lenny to take

suspicion off of herself?" Eleanor asked.

"Could be. But even more, to throw suspicion on Kim Lamont."

Eleanor wished she had given herself a more generous serving of ice cream. Two scoops would have gone down well, but you didn't stay slim in your fifties without self-control. "What about Kim and Vince? Did you speak to them at the burrito booth?"

Bethany recapped what the two of them had said. "But then I saw Kim in her office. She doesn't remember calling Paul 'despicable' or 'evil' although she admits shouting at him. She says they argued over his attitude about Lenny's thesis topic. I'm not sure I believe that. Lenny may have heard a lovers' quarrel. Oh, and Kim said she broke up with Paul, not him with her."

"Did she say why she ended things?"

"Yes, because he didn't want children soon or maybe ever."

Eleanor's thoughts raced. "But did the end of their affair lead to murder? I can't see Kim Lamont committing such an awful act." She didn't say that Kim could be a passionate, angry person. She'd seen Kim come off the rails in departmental meetings. As could other faculty. "Bethany, you breezed over Vince. Does he have a motive?"

"Jealousy of Paul as the more promising academician. The chance for a relationship with Kim with Paul out of the way. But he didn't seem all that into her at the burrito booth. He basically accused her of not being upset enough about Paul's murder."

They shared a troubled silence for a while.

"You know I spoke to Charlotte. I saw Gene too." Bethany summarized the conversations. "Paul wasn't popular with either of them, as I'm sure you realize. The strange thing is, Gene supported Paul's bid for full prof."

"That puzzled me," Eleanor said. "But men tend to stick together. The dean adored Paul. I think if the C&I department hadn't supported Paul, Gerald would have overridden our decision. As it is, we'll never know. We hadn't taken it to a vote yet. And there was something else in the wind involving Paul."

"What, Mom?"

"Paul thought that as a man, he was the victim of reverse discrimination by me. He viewed Charlotte's service work—books for third graders in the schools—as outdated. You know she's supplied books for years and arranged for our education students, Alma Gomez for one, to help children gain reading skills. I wholly support what she does. Paul put it around that I approved the ongoing funding because Charlotte is a woman and my friend."

Eleanor's throat tightened in anger. "Paul wanted the project shut down and the funds used for that tech lab he envisioned. So I have a motive for murdering him. Charlotte does too."

"Thin motives," Bethany argued. "Academia is rife with controversy over who should get funding for their projects, but it doesn't lead to bloodshed."

"Paul's blood wasn't shed. Someone effectively silenced him, though, with that tape." Eleanor was hit with a vision of Paul's wrapped head. "I couldn't have killed anyone like that."

"Of course not, Mom. But could Charlotte? She didn't mention that he threatened her project."

"I can't imagine her harming anyone. Charlotte is a peace-loving person. She does nothing but good in this

77

world. Hundreds of children in our community read proficiently because they get extra help as third graders. Children who can't read by then are at a high risk of not graduating from high school. And Charlotte's project gives education students practical experience in the schools. Stopping it was one of Paul's more stupid ideas."

Together, they cleared away their meal and went inside to tidy the kitchen. Eleanor started the dishwasher. "Stay for an after-dinner drink? We could call your dad and brother."

"I'd better get home and do some Foundation stuff. I don't want to chat with Dad until it's done. I texted him before I came over."

Eleanor empathized with her daughter. "You have a lot to deal with without concerning yourself with Paul's murder. You can stop if you wish."

"No, I want to continue, but I have no idea what to do next. Any suggestions?"

Eleanor thought of another woman friend. "Just one idea at the moment. Why don't you go see Meryl Darwood at the tutor center? It's open on Saturdays, and she's usually there. She and Gerald know you solved that murder when Joni needed you most. Meryl won't be surprised that you're involved in this case on my behalf. She's one of the most astute people on campus. Her take on Paul might be valuable. And do congratulate her. Another of her novels for literacy learners has been published."

****

At 11:00 p.m., Bethany sat in bed, intent on her laptop, when Nathan phoned. He sounded cheerful and sexy. "Did I disturb you, lady? In bed reading a trashy

78

romance and thinking of me?"

She played along. "In bed reading a grant report. The awardees are a bunch of slackers, late with their communications."

"Like me. Ouch. I should've called sooner. My bad."

"Out with the boys?"

"Nope. Believe it or not, laying kitchen tile until now with a real slacker. Mickey, the Carters' son and heir. He showed up and pitched in for once. We started late but got it done. I'm in bed with a beer and feeling no pain. Not drunk, mind you. Tomorrow, I'm hitting the road to Wyo."

Bethany shunted the laptop to the side. "What about the bathroom?"

"Say what?"

"Don't you have to tile that too?"

"Some other time. Like I told you, I've earned a few days off. The rest of the tile job can wait."

"When will you leave?"

"As early as possible. I aim to make it in one straight shot, only stop for gas. I'm excited about this chance, Bethany. More than I thought I'd be. I'll find out the exact duties when I meet the owners."

A cool breeze drifted into the bedroom. Pulling the covers up to her chin, Bethany felt like a teenager talking to a boyfriend who might be slipping away from her. "I'll miss you, Nathan." She was unable to say more. She had never been one for romantic talk.

"I'll miss you too, but I'll be back ASAP. Say you're happy for me."

"Sure, I am, but you'll be pretty far away."

She could hear him sigh. "Only a day's drive. Not

much over the Wyoming state line. I'm crazy about you, Bethany," he said in a burst of passion. "You know that, don't you? No matter how many miles we're apart, you're always in my heart."

The rhyme made Bethany giggle, but hearing the sincere sentiment, she didn't make a joke. "I'm quite fond of you too, Nathan. Be careful on the road. Don't drive too fast."

"I won't."

Liar. Cowboys, heck almost everybody, put the pedal to the metal on long stretches of Western roads. When the only creatures in sight were cows, deer, and antelope, people ignored speed limits. It was plain bad luck to get caught by a sheriff's deputy lying in wait along a lonely road to give his or her quota of tickets.

"Watch out for the speed traps and cattle guards." She put a touch of humor in the warning.

"Yes, ma'am," Nathan replied with an exaggerated drawl.

Belatedly, he seemed to remember the Kiefer murder and asked if the killer had been caught.

"Not yet," she said without elaborating.

"How's your mama doing?"

"She's upset but carrying on with her job."

"You ladies take care," he said. "The police will find the bad guy." He didn't tell her to keep out of the investigation. She wouldn't have listened anyway.

Chapter 9

The next morning, Bethany biked to campus to see Meryl Darwood. The well-traveled route took her past the tennis courts, where she had seen Paul and Vince in heated competition once in a while. Was that Roxanne Vale up ahead? Yes, riding like an awkward child. Bethany imagined Paul crossing the bike path on foot and Roxanne slamming into him. The accident was likely his fault, but the student hadn't blamed him. Instead, it had caused her to fall head over heels for the man. It was easy to imagine that happening. Paul had been handsome and charismatic. If he had been a woman, men might have called him a tease.

Roxanne dismounted in front of the education building. Bethany slid to a smooth stop behind her and said hello. The student gave a startled jump, her messenger bag bumping her hip. "Oh, hi, Ms. Jarviss." She produced a tiny padlock key and, all thumbs, secured her bike to a stand.

"Saturday class?" Bethany asked as she locked up her own bike.

Roxanne shook her head. "I'm going to the tutor center."

"I am too."

They approached the building's entrance, where Roxanne stopped abruptly. "This place gives me the creeps after what happened to Dr. Kiefer."

"That's understandable, Roxanne."

"I can hardly think of anything else. Alma says we have to get over it. She's stronger than me. Brainier, but you know that."

Roxanne wore a thin T-shirt and lightweight capri pants on this cool morning. She seemed like a child without a parent to dress her for the elements. Bethany had the urge to take off her denim jacket and offer it to Roxanne but doubted the gesture would be welcomed. Instead, she tried to add warmth with words. "Alma won a scholarship, but that doesn't mean she's smarter than you."

They ascended the front steps, Roxanne with her head dipped. Inside, they took the stairway to the tutor center in the basement. On this weekend morning, it hummed with activity. Because the college tutors also were students, it wasn't apparent, from a casual glance, to tell who was tutoring whom.

Roxanne looked around the room, and another student smiled at her. "That's my tutor. Without her, I'd be doomed. Excuse me, miss."

Students like Roxanne—hardworking but struggling academically—had prompted Meryl Darwood to create this center a decade back, Bethany knew. On one side of the room, community volunteers tutored adult literacy learners. Somehow, Charlotte Kline found time to oversee that program, which the Jarviss Foundation supported.

At the back, the door to Meryl's office stood wide open. Bethany saw her in profile, fingers flying across her keyboard at a utilitarian, built-in desk. At Bethany's rap on the doorjamb, Meryl swiveled toward her.

"Am I interrupting?" Bethany asked.

"Never! Come in."

A comfortable fifty-something, Meryl was short and sturdy. She might have been a 1950s housewife in one of her flowered shirtwaist dresses and smooth, helmet-like hair. Her eyelids perpetually drooped sleepily, causing people to underestimate her. But Bethany never made that mistake. Eleanor said Dean Darwood owed his successful university career to his wife nudging him up the ladder in her encouraging way. Bethany's parents had valued Meryl and Gerald as friends since the Darwoods adopted their son, Louis, from China the same year Joni came to the Jarviss family and didn't fit in as easily as Don had. The two couples bonded in a support group for adoptive parents of troubled children.

"You look pretty busy," Bethany said.

"End-of-semester report. I'd rather talk to you. Close the door if you'd like."

With the steady hum of voices dimmed, Bethany took a seat. "I ran into a student who came to meet with her tutor. Roxanne Vale."

Meryl gave her a shrewd look. "She comes regularly for various subjects. How do you know her?"

Bethany explained about speaking with Alma and Roxanne after the scholarship luncheon and hearing about the bike mishap. "She's having a hard time with Paul Kiefer's death. I think she was in love with him."

Meryl didn't look surprised. "I didn't know about that accident, but it's true Paul had a definite effect on female students. I don't think he purposely caused hearts to break."

"He didn't have a thing for undergraduates?"

Meryl smoothed the shirt-waist's skirt as she considered the idea. Her nails, as usual, were unpolished.

"Gerald or I would have caught wind of it. I worry about Roxanne. Her tutor wonders if she's dyslexic."

"A peer tutor, right?"

"A junior. Our tutors aren't trained diagnosticians, but they're observant. I gently suggested to Roxanne that she take a battery of tests. But the tests are costly, and Roxanne says she can't afford them. But I'll figure something out." Her expression softened. "By the way, Louis asked about you in his last email. He fell in love with you for a while, you know."

"I seemed like a glamorous teenager to a middle-schooler. He recovered from that crush in a matter of weeks."

Meryl threw back her head and laughed, but her well-sprayed hair didn't budge.

Giving Meryl a chance to brag, Bethany said, "Mom says Louis is doing well."

"He loves the graduate program in Austin. He's immersed in his dissertation."

"Good for him. What's his topic?"

"Chinese opera from the Cultural Revolution to the present. He'll need to narrow the time frame. He wants to go to China this summer to see some performances."

"Sounds wonderful."

"I'm glad my boy is learning to balance work and play. At least he says he is."

"Mom told me you have a new book out."

"I do." Meryl took a paperback from a box on her credenza. "Have a copy with my compliments."

Bethany read the title aloud. "*Season of Dreams*." The cover showed a woman with two little girls in a Christmas tree lot.

"A single mom, recently divorced, is my

protagonist," Meryl said. "She has never worked outside of the home, never graduated from high school. But she has to feed her children, so she musters the courage to apply for jobs."

"She's hired to sell Christmas trees?"

"Yes, but she struggles to master a credit-card machine and to tell a spruce from a fir. Fortunately, she has a sympathetic and patient boss."

"A handsome guy?"

"No, a friendly lesbian. The book isn't a romance like some of my others. It's more about sisterhood."

"Would you sign it for me?"

"How sweet of you to ask." She signed with a flourish.

The book had a large, easy-on-the-eyes font. Bethany knew the books were purchased by literacy programs to give to adult learners. Book sales enabled Meryl to travel to conferences. She was an in-demand speaker on literacy topics despite holding a master's degree, not a doctorate.

Eleanor once commented that Meryl's roles as mother and wife came first. "She's Gerald's cheerleader. She's never had the kind of support your father gave me, Bethany. When I was pursuing my doctorate, he stepped up by parenting you three kids. Gerald is an old-style patriarch. But Meryl doesn't seem to mind."

Slipping *Season of Dreams* into her daypack, Bethany said, "I'll enjoy reading this." Meryl could tell a heartfelt story in simple words.

"I assume you didn't stop by for reading material," Meryl said. "By the way, I heard that you dated Paul Kiefer. How are you doing since his death?"

"Shocked as everyone else, but we only had a couple

dinner dates. Did Mom tell you that?"

"No, we haven't spoken. It must have been horrible for her to see Paul's body. And poor May Zeller, finding him first. Gerald made sure she was okay. You know she helps at our house parties. Will you be coming to our annual Spring Fling?"

"Wouldn't miss it."

"We must go ahead with it, I told Gerald. He acted appropriately by not canceling the scholarship luncheon." She spoke decisively.

"Did you have a hand in that decision?"

"I suggested the college should not deprive a worthy student of her moment in the sun."

"Did you weigh in on going ahead with Spring Visitors Day too?"

"The president made that call. With input from other administrators, himself included, Gerald said."

"Can I ask what you made of Paul Kiefer? Did you like him?"

Meryl didn't pause for thought. "No, but I admired his ambition, his self-confidence. Men like Paul are rare, don't you see? Many men are ambitious but lack self-esteem. They pretend to be confident. Paul wasn't acting when he talked about education's future and his place in it."

"Mom told me Paul wanted Charlotte's project for third graders to be defunded. That he wanted the money for his own purpose."

Meryl smoothed her skirt again. "I knew about that. He also wanted to revamp this center, set it up as a high-tech research and teaching lab, boot out the literacy program. He joked about our literacy tutors still teaching cursive writing. Said it was a waste of time, that

86

handwriting is a dying art. He was right that it's no longer taught in many schools across the country where students only learn to print. They can't even sign their names in cursive. Not here, though. Charlotte's project provides handwriting workbooks."

"Were you worried that Paul would get his way?"

"Not terribly."

"Because of who you are?"

Meryl didn't take offense. "The dean's wife? I'm not without influence. But aside from that, I cannot imagine Gerald preventing those third graders from getting their books, nor would he interfere with the literacy or college tutoring programs. Paul held some extreme ideas. He overvalued modern technology and social media. Face-to-face effort remains as important as it ever was. Gerald appreciates that."

"But what about the president? Could he have overruled the dean?"

"Yes, and the Board of Regents could have overruled President Ramirez."

"How did the president feel about Paul?"

"I can't answer that. My guess is he appreciated Paul's futuristic orientation."

"Do you have any idea who killed Paul?"

"No, Bethany, I don't."

"Or why someone killed him? Because he got crosswise with a colleague?"

"It's easy to assume that. But to what extent did anyone at the university know Paul Kiefer? I expect if someone digs deeply enough, they'll find he was killed over an issue in his personal life, not a squabble over college funding or the use of campus facilities."

"Town not gown?"

"I'd like to think the murderer came from outside the university," Meryl said. "It's unimaginable that one of us is responsible for the man's death."

****

Bethany took the stairs to the third floor. The C&I office was locked, the hallway empty of faculty and students on a Saturday. She added phone numbers on faculty members' doors to her contacts, passing Paul's door with a mental shudder.

Glad to get out of the building, Bethany retrieved her bicycle and retraced her route. Where the bike trail skirted the playing fields and tennis courts, she dismounted and took a sip from her water bottle. Paul Kiefer would never play here again. But would Vince Morrison?

What did she know about Vince? Eleanor had said the associate professor had not yet applied for full prof. He was a better tennis player than Paul. But his tennis skills must have been a small consolation to the less-accomplished academician! And Vince was going bald, an unfortunate genetic tic for a man in his thirties, especially with a handsome colleague who'd had no sign of the affliction.

Vince could have considered Paul his best friend while being jealous of him, especially about his relationship with Kim Lamont. Paul's sidekick, that's what Vince had been, like Roxanne to Alma. He probably had known Paul as well as anyone. *If he didn't kill him, he must want the killer caught.* Bethany had put Vince's number in her phone. Why not call and see if he was free for a chat?

Vince answered from Campus Coffee Roasters. "Why do you want to meet?"

"To talk more about Paul." She held her breath.

"Okay, if you must." He said it grudgingly. "I can give you a few minutes."

"Thanks. I'm on my bike. I'll be there as soon as I can." But he had already disconnected.

Chapter 10

Vince didn't notice Bethany arrive as he jotted notes on a legal pad. Coffee in hand, she squeezed through the crowd to his table.

He looked up as if he had forgotten to expect her. "Bethany. Right." He flipped the pad closed. "I was hard at it. Heritage festival stuff."

"You're working on it already? That's dedication."

"September will be here before we know it." For a good ten minutes, he bent her ear about the festival. The event would be bigger and better than last year, the parade more spectacular, with more horses, more buggies, and a larger contingent of NMU and high school band members.

Sipping her coffee, Bethany waited to change the subject to Paul, but she didn't want to get Vince's back up. Finally, seeing that they had drained their cups, she offered to get refills. "What are you drinking?"

"The house blend."

He waved cash at her, but she said to keep it.

When she returned, he said, "You didn't call to hear about the festival. Look, I admit I didn't treat you well last time. I gave you grief about being some sort of amateur detective. Sorry about that."

He took a drink, belched lightly, and excused himself. "Too much caffeine." He pushed his cup away. "I heard Paul's coffee was drugged."

"That's a reasonable assumption."

"I have a friend with the campus police who says it's true."

"Elisa Marcos?"

"No, Chief Marcos doesn't know me from Adam. I've played tennis with one of the cops. He said word is the coffee contained a big dose of an anti-anxiety med. He wouldn't say which one, only that it starts with an X, so I can guess. You know how many people take something for anxiety? Probably half the profs and a quarter of the students. The murderer must have dissolved a handful of pills in Paul's coffee. Then, with Paul out of it, they wound tape around his head. I keep imagining it." He rubbed his eyelids with the heels of his hands. "I'm not getting a hell of a lot of sleep."

Who is? "I don't know if Mom has heard what you've told me."

"If she doesn't, she will. It'll be public knowledge. My cop friend said Chief Marcos and the city police chief are releasing a joint statement this afternoon."

"Vince, do you suspect anyone in particular of killing Paul?"

"Not really. But I've been thinking about what he said about people. About conflicts he had with various colleagues. He was my closest friend. He told me things I doubt anybody else knew."

"Such as?"

Vince blinked rapidly. He had thick, black lashes almost as heavy as Alma Gomez's fake ones. "You're not going to get me to gossip, Bethany."

"Not gossip. Anything that might help catch Paul's killer. For instance, why Paul and Kim Lamont broke up. And who broke up with whom."

"No idea. Paul didn't talk to me about her. And if he'd wanted to, I wouldn't have let him."

"Because you care for Kim."

"I do. We're friends, but that's all." He looked past her, obviously uneasy about the statement.

"Friends. Because that's how you want it or how she wants it?"

"It's mutual, okay?"

"But you dated her before she started seeing Paul."

"Briefly. When she was new here."

"Did Paul steal her from you?"

He glared at her. "What did you hear?"

"Nothing. But if you dated her first…"

"Look, it was no big deal."

Bethany didn't believe him. "You didn't talk to Paul about their relationship? About the breakup?"

"No, I didn't!" At his raised voice, a group Bethany assumed were college students openly stared.

Bethany put out a hand to calm him.

In a quieter voice, he said, "Don't for a minute think Paul did anything bad to Kim. He wasn't ready to get serious about her or anybody. You probably know he was divorced. Well, he hadn't gotten over it. I think he wished he could've reconciled with his ex, but that was never going to happen. He did say something on that topic, though…"

"His divorce?"

"About divorce but not his. About Gene Waverly's. And recently, Gene and some woman. How if I knew the details, I'd be surprised. I scoffed at that. You only have to look at Gene to see he's not appealing to women. Can you imagine being attracted to the old fart?"

Coffee shot out of Bethany's nostrils. She blotted

her face with a napkin while he watched, grinning. "Can you tell me what Paul said about any other colleagues? Without gossiping of course."

"He liked Eleanor. He knew she wasn't keen on his ideas for sweeping the cobwebs out of the C&I department and didn't support his bid for full prof yet, but he expected she would. And he said he could count on Gene. He wouldn't say more than that. I suppose Paul and Gene consoled each other about their divorces, and that's why Gene decided to support Paul."

"Gene says Paul's long list of publications impressed him. Not that Gene actually read them…"

"Gene never reads anything. He wouldn't have thrown his support behind Paul because of his publication record."

"When did Paul say he could count on Gene's vote?"

"Um, let me think." He brushed a hand over his head, flattening his springy, sparse hair. "Oh, yeah, over coffee here after Paul returned from an ed conference a few weeks ago. We met to catch up. He'd presented a paper that people raved about and met the editor of the journal that was going to publish it."

"Who else in the C&I department attended the conference?" Bethany asked.

"Not too many of us. I didn't. Neither did Eleanor, as you must know. Kim went. She didn't have a paper to give, but she led a discussion session. I heard Meryl Darwood gave one of her talks, but she's not in our department and is only college staff. Gene attended."

"Gene? Did he present a paper?"

"Nah. For him, conferences are junkets. We can attend one a year whether we present or not. To keep up in our field, supposedly. But some senior faculty mostly hang out in the bar and whine about their low salaries and serving on pointless committees. That's what Gene probably did."

"But you think that after the conference, he threw his support behind Paul's bid for full prof?"

"Maybe. I remember being surprised. As a full prof, Paul would've pushed for the faculty to learn new skills. Gene would've hated that. Paul used to call him a lazy dinosaur."

"But Gene's a decent man," Bethany objected. "I've known him for years. He cares about his students."

As if he hadn't heard her, Vince said, "Local yokel was another of Paul's tags for him. Son of a peanut farmer. I didn't think the last one funny. Crop farming is an important part of our Southwestern heritage. Peanuts help fund this university. Not every big donor got rich from gold mining."

He obviously referred to the original source of the Jarvisses' wealth. "My family mined gold and silver in the 1800s. Not these days," Bethany said mildly.

"Now, you Jarvisses live off your oil and gas revenues."

The conversation had veered off track. No point in mentioning her aunt's responsible oversight of the business or her father's management of the Foundation. "I'd better go."

"Hey, Bethany, I'm sorry," Vince said, sounding like he meant it. "New Mexico would be in a fix without the taxes on oil and gas."

Mindful of a tight squeeze between the tables, Bethany rose with as much grace as she could manage. "Good luck with the heritage festival."

"You'll get a call to help out again." He jotted something on his legal pad.

"I'll see if I can fit it into my busy schedule." On the street, she regretted the retort.

****

Pedaling home, Bethany stayed alert on the streets lacking bike lanes. Only when she reached her quieter neighborhood did she calm down and mentally replay the conversation with Vince. Why had he sniped at her family? Envy of inherited wealth, she supposed, coupled with an ignorance of the Jarviss Corporation's considerable investment in solar and wind energy projects and its firm opposition to fracking. Vince had made no mention of the Foundation. Maybe he thought, incorrectly, that the Jarvisses used it as a tax dodge.

Some other time, she'd educate Vince about her family's ventures. Slowing to prolong her ride, she considered what she had learned from him. Paul's divorce seemed like the single painful aspect of his otherwise charmed life. Had divorce created some sort of bond between Paul and Gene, as Vince supposed? Evidently, Paul hadn't respected Gene professionally; he'd ridiculed Gene behind his back. How might that have sat with Gene if he learned of it after supporting Paul's promotion? He would have been hurt and angry. Enough to kill?

Since Gene's divorce, on Sundays, he walked his dogs in the square block of city park across from his house. Bethany had run across him trotting behind a trio of fat Dachshunds. He had said, only half in jest, that he found the ritual dog walking more pleasant and more useful than the church services his wife used to drag him to. Tomorrow, it might be a good idea to look for him in

95

the park.

****

After she stowed her bike in the garage, Bethany flopped onto her couch and called Eleanor. "Vince said Paul and Gene might have bonded at the conference over talk about their divorces. Can you see them doing that? Complaining about their ex-wives?"

"Maybe," Eleanor said. "Did Vince tell you Gene's ex-wife attended the conference? She's married to a textbook salesman now, and both of them go to the major education events."

"Oh, my goddess! Vince didn't say that. Maybe he didn't know. Did Gene tell you she was there?"

"No, I don't think so. Maybe Kim Lamont mentioned it. She's new to conferences and remarked about their small-world nature."

Shifting her throw pillows to better support her back, Bethany mused out loud. "If Gene's ex attended the conference, maybe Paul commiserated with him about it. Poor Gene. Seeing her and the current husband must have been tough. Do you think if Paul showed Gene sympathy, Gene would have supported his promotion application?"

"Hold on a minute," Eleanor said. "I'm making almond biscotti. It's time to flip them."

Soon, she returned. "Okay, I have five minutes until they have to come out. Let's see. Male bonding can be a strong force. But I thought Gene supported Paul because although what he calls 'newfangled teaching methods' aren't for him, they benefit students."

"It would seem Gene had no motive for killing Paul. Unless he heard what Paul called him behind his back."

"What do you mean?"

"Vince said Paul called Gene names. A dinosaur. Son of a peanut farmer. Vince made them sound like nicknames kids taunt each other with. Ones that stick and hurt."

"I never heard those," Eleanor said. "Maybe Paul only used those terms with Vince. But let's say Gene found out. Would he have committed murder for schoolboy taunts?"

Bethany heard the oven door creak open and snap closed as her mother, a nervous baker, checked her cookies before the timer buzzed.

Seconds ticked by, then Eleanor returned. "Listen, I've learned something more about the murder. Someone drugged Paul's coffee, as we suspected. With a medication to lessen anxiety. I've taken such medication myself."

"Mom! When?"

"Three years ago. When your sister went through that bad time. Joni had almost stopped eating. If she tried, she only managed a morsel. You recall how the whole family worried about her. I couldn't sleep, which affected my teaching. I found it surprisingly easy to get a prescription for some pills from my doctor."

"Did the pills help? Do you still take them?"

"I have to get those biscotti out before the kitchen smells like burnt almonds."

Impatiently, Bethany waited, wishing she were a child on hand for a cookie fresh from the oven.

Back on the phone, Eleanor said, "I had the prescription for only a short time. I felt too relaxed, in a stupor. Then Joni went back to therapy, and I stopped worrying about her as much and didn't need the pills. Do you think I should tell the police I took them?"

97

"Do you have any left?"

"No, dear."

"Then I don't see why. Your pills had nothing to do with Paul's death."

"Certainly not!"

"By the way, Mom, I'd heard about drugged coffee figuring in the murder. Vince told me."

"Vince? How did he know? I heard it directly from Chief Marcos. That detail will be released to the press, but it hasn't been yet. I appreciated that she called me after she informed the president and the dean."

"Vince knows a campus cop. They play tennis together."

"How did someone drug Paul's coffee?" Eleanor mused. "I've been thinking about that. The police took the office coffeemaker—the can of coffee too—and haven't brought them back. I had Jereen replace them."

"You told me Paul didn't have a coffeemaker in his office, that he got his coffee from your department's communal pot."

"Like most faculty."

"Dosing the pot would've drugged other people. The killer must've slipped the drug into Paul's travel mug," Bethany said. "But how? He would've filled the mug and put the lid on it. The lid was on the mug you saw tipped over in his lap."

"He carried that mug everywhere," Eleanor said. "To class. Down the hall when he went to see other faculty in their offices. Even to the student center. He was a miser, saving a quarter there by using his own mug."

"I usually forget and pay the twenty-five cents for a to-go cup."

"Me too, dear. Then I feel guilty about the plastic lids, which can't be recycled, clogging the city's landfill."

Bethany appreciated her mother's attempt at levity. "Same here. Mom, I meant to tell you: I took your advice and visited with Meryl Darwood in the tutor center. She said she has no idea who murdered Paul, but it seems she suspects Charlotte."

"That's ridiculous. Charlotte is a nonviolent person, New Age to the bone."

"But you have to admit she could've viewed Paul as a threat to her projects, to the funding of them."

"True. But if that's a motive for murder, Meryl should count herself among the prime suspects."

"Nope. She believes that as the dean's wife, she could've warded off Paul's threats to the tutor center and literacy program."

"As the dean's wife?" Eleanor paused. "Meryl has an old-fashioned mentality. She may not realize wives don't have the influence they once did. Since Meryl doesn't have a doctorate, if Paul had been promoted, he might have made a fuss about the dean's wife holding a plum position at a center that needed modernizing. He might have made the president aware of his disapproval."

Bethany considered her mother's words. "You think Meryl has less power than she imagines."

"Possibly. If Paul had strongly pushed for changes in the space Meryl manages, the dean would have had to pay attention, especially if Paul had gained the support of other faculty members."

"Did you support Paul's ideas to repurpose the center? Or did you support Charlotte?"

"Actually, I could have supported both. I've looked at the rooms near the tutor center—a couple unoccupied offices and a storeroom. The college could have knocked out some walls and made room for the tech lab Paul wanted. We could have had a single front desk where students could sign in to either space. I haven't proposed it yet, but I may. I imagine the dean cutting a ribbon to the Paul Kiefer Memorial Technology Lab."

"You're joking!"

"Not at all. At some point, the dean will memorialize Paul's service to the college."

"Dad may want to award a Foundation grant for the renovation," Bethany said. "That would be ironic since I told Paul we wouldn't fund his research. What are you doing tonight? Seeing as Dad and Don won't be back."

"Freezing these biscotti. Phoning the guys and your sister. Have you heard from Nathan?"

"No, not yet. It's a long haul to Wyoming. I suppose he'll call when he takes a break."

Chapter 11

Just past midnight, Bethany's phone rang, waking her from a restless sleep. "Nathan! Is everything okay?"

"Temporary setback."

His truck had broken down on the outskirts of Denver, he said. He was spending the night with friends from his rodeo days. One of them had towed the truck to a cut-rate mechanic who would work on it in the morning, and Nathan hoped, get him back on the road. "Plan B is to rent a ride and come back for the truck on my way home. I should've sold the old beater before now, but I hoped she had a few good miles left in her. With what this repair job will cost, I'll have to keep her a while longer. She's a cunning old girl."

"Why do most men consider their vehicles female?" Bethany asked.

"'Cause like real ladies, they're a bundle of trouble. Present company excluded."

"I'm not actually in your company."

"Bet you're in bed wearing nothing but a smile."

She didn't mention that she wore her usual T-shirt, leggings, and socks. "You're making me blush. When do you expect to reach Wyoming?"

"Tomorrow, one way or the other. The rancher sounded ticked on the phone but still willing to meet me and show me the place. His wife planned to cook a special Saturday night meal. I said she shouldn't go to any trouble on Sunday night. He said, 'Don't worry, she won't.' Maybe I already lost the job, and they haven't even met me in the flesh."

"When they do, they'll see it's very nice flesh," Bethany said. "Tanned. Firm."

"One part is getting firm indeed," he said.

"Oh, really?"

"Yeah. So Nancy Drew, how was your day?"

She shared what she'd learned from various people, including how the dosed coffee figured in the murder. "Some people have motives, but I don't think they'd kill someone."

Nathan said not to be too sure. He'd once known a rodeo cowboy who killed a friend over five hundred dollars. "The money was stashed under a mattress in the motel room they shared. When it went missing, the guy knew his buddy took it. The two of them got into a fight. The guy who was robbed stabbed the other one in the gut. Then he called 911 and tried to stop the bleeding with his neckerchief, but the thief bled out. The fool's still doing time, I heard."

"That's not the same thing as drugging someone's coffee, and when they're out of it, swaddling their head in tape."

"Maybe whoever did that left prints on the cup. Or on the tape. Are the cops taking fingerprints?"

"Sure. And DNA."

"Yours?"

"Neither. Why would they?"

"You dated the guy. Or don't the cops know?"

That Nathan knew came as a surprise. "I doubt the police care about my social life. How did you find out?"

"You forget that your brother and I have a beer once

in a while."

"What did Don say about Paul?"

"That he wasn't the man for you. Don knew him mostly by reputation. A peacock, that's what he called him. Full of himself."

"Sorry I didn't mention seeing him."

"No sorry needed, I guess."

He sounded a trifle jealous. Of a dead man. "It was only a couple of times. Turns out he was after a research grant."

Nathan laughed. "I could use a grant too, for the repairs to my truck. Don't suppose the Foundation has a fund for poor cowboys?"

"Sadly, no."

"Then I better get that job, or if not, I better hightail it back to the Carters before they find out why I'm away."

"Hightail it! Haven't heard that one in a while."

****

In the morning, Bethany walked the three blocks, with a newspaper tucked under her arm, to the park across from Gene Waverly's house. A square space bounded on all sides by nineteenth-century houses, the park boasted a central gazebo built in the early twentieth century and trees sprouting fresh leaves. Bethany loved the compact park but usually drove right by it.

She watched Gene's house from a chilly wrought-iron bench, wishing she had worn more than a denim jacket and leggings for an eight thirty vigil. Ignoring her discomfort, she read the latest report on the murder. The police had revealed that Paul Kiefer's coffee had been drugged, and he had been smothered. They confirmed details that, like Vince, the media already had gotten wind of: that the drug was commonly used to treat anxiety, and the smothering had been done with packing tape.

After about forty minutes, wherein Bethany had browsed the entire newspaper, including the ads, and was now reading her email, she finally got lucky. Gene emerged from a side gate of his house with three yipping Dachshunds straining at their leashes. They dragged him across the sidewalk, edging the park to sniff and piddle on the sparse grass.

"Whoa!" he called as the dogs saw Bethany and ran toward her. She pretended to be absorbed in her phone, then feigned surprise. "Gene! Good morning."

"Morning, young lady. Looks like my pooches want to say hello."

The Dachshunds sniffed Bethany's sneakers and ankles. Trying not to get entangled in the leashes, she bent down to give each one a pat. The dogs' dark eyes bulged, and their tongues hung out as they panted hot, smelly breath in her face. "What are their names?"

"Harry and Mary, the two fattest, are the papa and mama of Moe. They were the wife's more than mine, but she left them behind when she moved out. She made the excuse that without them, I'd get in a funk and never leave the house except to teach. She might've been right. Can't say I like sausage dogs—we always had big mutts on the farm—but they keep me moving."

"Didn't she want them? If they were her dogs—"

"The guy she left me for hates pets." He didn't sound angry, maybe because the divorce must have been how many years ago? Two or three.

Newspaper in hand, Bethany strolled alongside Gene. "Have you read the story on Paul Kiefer's shocking murder, as the reporter wrote?"

"With my breakfast cornflakes," Gene said. "No big surprise his java contained a knockout dose of something. Otherwise, how would he have let anybody tape up his noggin? I went through my medicine cabinet as soon as I read the article. Sure enough, I found an old bottle of stuff to calm you down. My ex's prescription. Out of date, but still—"

"Indeed. What are you going to do with it?"

"Already did it. Flushed the pills. Ripped up the label and flushed that too. Not good for the city's sewer system, I know, but I didn't want the police to find those pills in my house."

Bethany stopped in her tracks.

Gene planted his heels, forcing the dogs to halt. "Don't look so shocked. What would you have done in my boots? Everybody knew I didn't cotton to Kiefer. I told you that."

"But you were in favor of him becoming a full professor."

"Told you that too. It's no secret."

The Dachshunds were examining the base of a tree. Moe moved to the right, the other two to the left.

"Hey, get your act together, doggies," Gene commanded.

The three Dachshunds ignored him.

"Wait a minute," Bethany said. She gripped Moe by the middle and turned him around while Gene tugged him toward the older dogs. This was not the best situation for a talk, but Bethany persisted. "It's the timing that seems strange," she said. "You never liked Paul, you admit, but from what I heard, after one education conference, you changed your attitude about him. Quite a turnaround."

The dogs had found another animal's droppings. Gene yelled, "Don't eat that!" and yanked on the leashes.

"Why did you do that?" Bethany asked.

"Because they'll get sick if they eat poop."

"No, I mean, why did you support such a young faculty member's promotion? Did something happen at the conference?"

"Oh. The bar talk bored me, so I listened to Kiefer's paper presentation. I already told you I never read his papers. When he gave that talk, I realized he knew stuff I'd never even heard of. He had ideas I never would've thought of. I had to admit he was smarter than the rest of us put together in the C&I department. If he didn't get promoted early, I figured he would hightail it out of NMU for a bigger and better school."

Hightail? He and Nathan should meet!

"We couldn't afford to lose a young guy like that. Plus, he taught those techie classes I can't and won't."

The mother dog stopped and squatted. Gene took a black plastic bag out of his back pocket, stuck his hand inside it, and scooped up a morsel of excrement.

"I heard Kim Lamont also attended the conference," Bethany said.

Gene tied a knot in the bag. "Now that's something worth checking out. Not that I want to get the gal in trouble. But I noticed she and Kiefer started out sharing a hotel room but ended up in separate ones. She switched rooms. Didn't come to his presentation or sit with him in the bar after that. She shifted to a group of females from different universities."

Interesting. "Do you know what happened between her and Paul?"

"Nope. None of my business. But I saw them pass each other in the hallway after that, and she shot him the kind of look my wife used to give me right before she filed for divorce."

"What kind of a look?"

"Like a woman who hates a man's guts."

"Your ex-wife attended the conference, I heard."

"Drat!" The bag dangling from Gene's fingers caught in the leashes. He clicked his tongue in irritation and untangled the bag as Bethany wrinkled her nose at the smell of doggie doo-doo. She followed him to a pet-waste receptacle.

"That must have been hard on you," she said. "Seeing your ex there."

"Not that hard." His voice lifted. "We're over the hate stage. Still friends. She gave me a nice wad of cash at that conference. Guilt money."

"For what? Leaving you?"

His weathered face crinkled. "For abandoning the dogs. She gives me money once in a while to make sure I buy them treats."

As they parted, Gene said, "Next time you want to talk, why don't you knock on my door? I watched you read the whole newspaper before I took pity on you and came out to see what you wanted." He tipped an imaginary hat and flicked the leashes. "Giddyup, little doggies!"

Chapter 12

Bethany set off at a jog. Gene had directed the conversation for the most part. What niggled at her brain? What hadn't she asked him?

A block from her house, she stopped, took gulps of air, and mentally smacked her forehead. The names Paul had called Gene. Son of a peanut farmer. Dinosaur. She hadn't asked Gene if he knew about those behind-the-back, hurtful words. He admitted having had pills in his house to treat anxiety. Would Paul's killer have mentioned that? He might have, to make her think him innocent of murder. That aside, Gene's story about Kim and Paul intrigued her.

She finished her outing at a slow pace. In her kitchen, she took a container of stew from the freezer and popped it into the microwave. Glass of water in hand, she called Eleanor to relay Gene's information. "Kim and Paul had some sort of breakup at that conference. I waylaid Gene this morning when he was walking his dogs, and he told me."

That news didn't surprise Eleanor. "I have to approve the faculty's travel expenses so they get reimbursed," she said. "I wondered what had happened between those two that they only shared a room two out of three nights, but I didn't ask."

Watching the container of stew revolve behind glass, Bethany wished her mother had been nosier.

"Mom, when I talked to Lenny Ortiz and Alma Gomez at Los Mariachis, Alma said rumor had it Paul and Kim broke up right before Valentine's Day. That wasn't long after the conference. Then Lenny heard Kim shouting at Paul. I think Paul upset her about something other than his scorn for Lenny's thesis topic or Paul's not wanting children right away."

"I can't imagine what it would have been."

"Do you think you could find out? Have a talk with Kim? She told me Paul liked younger women, students even. She didn't believe he slept with undergraduates, but maybe he did, and she found out."

"I don't want to believe that of Paul."

"Neither does Meryl Darwood. I wish Gene knew more about why Kim switched rooms. But he did tell me something interesting. His ex-wife left pills for anxiety in their medicine cabinet. He swears he disposed of them after the murder."

"Heavens! I wonder how many of us faculty have had access to that kind of drug. I wish I had a bottle of it now."

"Mom, don't even kid like that!"

"I'm not kidding. I dread going to campus tomorrow with Paul's murder unresolved. Meryl called me this morning, unusual on a Sunday, and asked my opinion."

The microwave timer dinged. "Wait, Mom. I'm thawing something." She stirred the still-icy stew and reset the timer. "Okay, I've added more minutes. Meryl wanted your opinion? About what?"

"Whether she was right not to let Gerald cancel their Spring Fling. You're going, you know."

"Yes, Meryl mentioned the party when I saw her yesterday at the tutor center."

"She's second-guessing her insistence on having it," Eleanor said.

"What did you say to her?"

"I didn't need to take a stand. In the end, she convinced herself to stay the course. I listened to her rationale that the spring party at their home is a tradition that shouldn't be broken. Meryl loves to entertain the entire college faculty and staff and quite a few donors. She believes the party will boost college morale. Gerald will play the congenial host. He doesn't do the prep tasks, you can be sure. It's all up to Meryl, but she manages beautifully. By the way, May Zeller will be there, in charge of the food."

"May! I haven't thought about her since she found Paul's body. Has she recovered from the shock of it?"

"Oh, certainly. May's a sturdy soul. She stopped in my office the next day, her usual self, to see how I was coping. I complimented her on having the presence of mind to come get me that night. People with weaker constitutions might have passed out at the sight of a murdered man, but not May. She said her job hadn't been that exciting since she saw a janitor slip on a wet floor and break a hip in the early 2000s."

Bethany imagined her mom's grin. Eleanor enjoyed talking to May Zeller.

"May told me something I didn't know," Eleanor continued. "That she was Paul's housekeeper. I knew she did cleaning jobs on the weekends, but not that her list included Paul's condo. She wondered if his parents will come from Chicago to pack his things. I said I didn't know. May asked me to tell Chief Marcos she's willing to help. We speculated about a funeral. I suppose it will be in Chicago, after his body is released. May's a thoughtful woman and loyal to NMU. Do you know that she and her partner, Sue, are raising Sue's two young boys? Sue's an assistant math professor who went through a divorce after she came out as gay. And May is pursuing a special-education degree part-time."

"I didn't know any of that." She wasn't surprised that the middle-aged custodian was also a student and a female professor's partner. The university's small-world, liberal culture was a fact of local life.

The microwave beeped. "My stew is hot, Mom. I'd better do some laundry over lunch." *And wait for Nathan to call.*

"I'd better finish prepping for class," Eleanor said. "By the way, Lenny Ortiz made an appointment to see me. I'm going to offer to serve as that young man's thesis adviser, and I'll get to hear his mariachi band. They're playing at the Darwoods' party."

****

As Bethany ate the spicy stew, she realized she hadn't asked her mother to talk to Kim Lamont about the belittling names Paul supposedly had called Gene. Local yokel. That was another one. She wrote in her journal for a while, making a note to see Gene again.

The day wore on. Bethany had an itch to call Nathan but didn't scratch it. Her cowboy would phone when he had something to report. Did she want to hear he took the job? He definitely deserved good luck. He coped with his injured hand without complaint. She'd seen his nearly illegible writing on a grocery list and on notes stuck to her door. She hoped the Wyoming ranchers didn't make him fill out a job application beyond what he'd written in an email responding to their ad.

The landline phone rang as she pulled blouses out of

the dryer in the kitchen nook. They would wrinkle if she didn't hang them up fast. She raced to answer and brought the handset back with her.

"I couldn't get you on your cell. I didn't get the job yet," Nathan said without preamble. "I made it here late, met the Hartshorns, and saw some of the place. They're full of plans. Tomorrow, we're going to ride around the ranch."

"By horse or ATV?"

"Good question. Josh and Mindy have both. They're only in their thirties, but they've taken over from his folks. Mindy plans to get more companies to have staff retreats here. Josh's parents mostly attracted families with kids. Mindy has bigger ideas."

Bethany put Nathan on the speakerphone and went back to smoothing blouses and sliding them on hangers. She transferred a wet load of clothes from washer to dryer as he told her about a barn converted into a dance hall. "It's as clean as a whistle and decorated nice and homey for drinks and barn dances."

"Would you be expected to dance with the single ladies?" Immediately, she regretted the question. It made her sound jealous.

"Didn't ask. I was thinking of you and me doing the do-si-do. I was quite the square dancer in grade school."

She pictured him wearing a bandanna and dancing with cute girls in swirly skirts. "I square danced as a kid too," she said.

"There you have it. We'd be a force on the dance floor. 'Course I might have to sweep it first. And that's the thing. It's another jack-of-all-trades job. But the pay beats what I get now, and there'd be no lack of action. I'd lead trail rides and show guests how to cast a fly.

Groom the horses and clean up after them."

"Work with the cattle?"

"Not as many head as I expected, but yeah, I guess. I'll find out more about that end of things tomorrow when we take a ride. It's beautiful country. The ranch has a trout stream running through it and hilly, rolling pasture land. Mountain views. I'd give my eye teeth to own a place like this."

Most cowboys would. But as the son of a single, working-class mother, Nathan never had a chance to own land unless he won the lottery. He had to be satisfied with being a hired hand.

"Enough about me," he said. "What have you been doing?"

Moving to the living room, Bethany said, "Talking to people about the murder. The faculty member Lenny mentioned, Kim Lamont, admitted shouting at Paul. She says she ended their relationship, but I wonder if he did. She pointed the finger at an old prof I've known for years. Paul ridiculed him, apparently. Then there's the matter of a drug used to make Paul woozy. Gene, the old prof, told me he had some pills his ex-wife left behind. He flushed them down the toilet. Turns out Mom had a prescription in the past."

"Well, your mother didn't kill the guy."

Bethany propped her feet on a footstool. Nathan's belief in Eleanor's innocence buoyed her spirits. "About anybody else in Mom's department might have done it."

"Didn't he have any friends?"

"One, a kind of sidekick. Beats me why a man would play second fiddle to a friend."

"Buddies are rarely equals," Nathan said. "On the rodeo circuit, we had the stars and the guys who admired them. I bet it's the same with profs."

Nathan didn't talk about his record, and Bethany hadn't looked it up. She'd assumed his rodeo days hadn't been easy. He deserved a decent life, and if that meant signing on with the Hartshorns, he should go for it.

The call ended with kissing sounds tickling her ear. Bethany kissed the air in return. Holding the phone, she wished he were sitting beside her. If he took the job, would keeping in touch be too much of a struggle?

****

Later, as she trudged upstairs with her clean laundry, she considered going to bed early but knew she wouldn't be able to sleep. She slipped on a jacket and went downstairs again to her compact backyard. She breathed in the scents of budding plants. In the distance, the traffic on Main Street droned on, a familiar sound she didn't mind.

Her whole life so far had been spent in Las Cuevas except for her college years. Since college, she'd had a few lovers but no liaisons of any longevity. Every relationship had started out with no expectations except having fun and someone in her life besides her family and a few female friends. When she turned thirty, she noticed most of the men she dated were divorced, and the still-single ones, Nathan included, tended to talk about past bad involvements. Nathan could tell horror stories about old lovers. The worst story was about getting dumped after he injured his hand.

"Mollie, her name was," Nathan had confided. "She wanted a hero to cheer for, not a wounded warrior." He mentioned Mollie the second time Bethany invited him into her bed. In the quiet moments after lovemaking, when he allowed her to trace the scars on his hand with her fingertips, he told the painful account of the breakup. "After the surgery, she stopped taking my calls. That was okay. She wasn't the one for me." He'd shrugged his broad, naked shoulders.

Am I the one? Bethany mused now. She rephrased the question. *Is Nathan the one for me?* The sky, sprinkled with stars, didn't give her an answer. With effort, she turned her thoughts to the question of who murdered Paul Kiefer. She didn't get an answer to that one either.

Chapter 13

On Monday morning, Eleanor remembered Bethany's request to speak to Kim Lamont as she saw Kim, with a worried face, standing by Jereen's desk. The secretary was nowhere in sight. From her office, Eleanor called to the junior faculty member. "Is there a problem, Kim? Come in for a minute."

Kim left the door open. In the visitor's chair, she crossed then uncrossed her legs. "I have class soon. Jereen should have left some photocopies in my mailbox, but she didn't."

Not a life-or-death problem. "Do you need them for class today?"

"Yes, so my students can read an article that's not online. That woman always seems to be absent when I need her."

"She's probably in the ladies' room," Eleanor said.

"Or outside sneaking a cigarette."

Eleanor guessed that Kim was right. "Either way, she should be back soon."

The young woman's lipstick wasn't as fresh as usual, Eleanor noticed. Nor was her upswept hairdo as carefully styled; too many tendrils escaped from it. "Kim, how are you holding up?"

Kim didn't fake confusion. "Students are whispering behind my back, speculating about Paul and me on social media. They know we were together and say he dropped me. They're sharing a cartoon of a woman being dropped out of an airplane. The pilot looks out the window and says, 'Oops!' One of my loyal students showed it to me."

The cruel cartoon made Eleanor angry. "I'll tell the dean. He needs to know."

Kim's eyes turned glassy. "Paul didn't drop me. I told that to your daughter, and I assume she told you. What is she doing poking around in people's private lives?"

"She's talking to people about Paul, for my sake, for all of our sakes. She's investigated murders before. Unofficially but successfully. She wonders if you told her the real reason for ending your relationship with Paul. Was it more than about him not being eager to start a family?"

Peering toward Jereen's still-empty desk, Kim said, "Oh, all right, I'll tell you. Paul essentially blackmailed Gene Waverly. That's why Gene suddenly supported Paul's bid for full professor. A despicable thing of Paul to do."

Stunned, Eleanor asked, "He blackmailed Gene? Over what?"

"An incident at the conference in January. Paul saw Gene and his ex-wife kissing outside of Gene's hotel room. Paul got Gene to admit they'd just had sex."

"But she's married to that textbook salesman now!"

"The salesman brought her to the conference. Apparently, Gene still has a thing for his ex, and it's mutual. Obviously, they didn't want her current husband to know. Paul threatened to tell the salesman unless Gene supported his application for full professor."

Eleanor put her hands over her mouth to curb a

laugh. "Sounds like an episode of a bad daytime drama. Not that I watch those shows."

"Nor do I," Kim said. "Not in the daytime. I record them to watch at night."

They grinned at each other. Then Kim said solemnly, "How awful of Paul to blackmail Gene, who's still in love with a two-timing woman. She cheated on Gene, and then she cheated on the new husband with Gene! That shouldn't become common knowledge. Can you imagine what the students would make of it?"

The secretary's voice from the front office interrupted them. "I'm back, Dr. Jarviss."

"I have to dash to class," Kim said. "I hope Jereen has my photocopies."

"Close the door, would you, please?" Alone, Eleanor sat thinking. *Gene has a motive for murder.* Her thoughts spun until her phone rang. Dean Darwood—not his administrative assistant—asked if she had time to come to his office.

"Of course." Taking the request as a summons, she pumped her chair to floor level.

****

The dean's reception area contained no politely smiling secretary, no administrative assistant. It was past noon; they would be at lunch. Odd that the dean, a man who liked his meals, remained in the building. Eleanor steadied her nerves as she rapped on his door.

To her surprise, he opened it rather than calling his usual hearty, "Come in" from behind his bulwark of a desk. "Eleanor, thanks for seeing me at such short notice. Let's sit at the table."

That he came from behind his desk and settled his big body into an armless chair signaled a need for a favor. She braced herself for what was to come, guessing it would be about the murder.

"Eleanor, I'm worried," he said. "I just got off the phone with a crime reporter from Albuquerque. She asked sticky questions about Paul. She knows more than she reported in Sunday's paper, more than the police revealed in the Saturday press conference. Evidently, she has sources who say he was wildly unpopular among his colleagues, hated even, for his brilliance. She asked if that was true, but I didn't comment. Then, she asked if I suspected that one of the faculty murdered him. I told her that such rumors are total nonsense and she'd better beware of what she writes. She snorted in my ear. An ugly sound."

Eleanor had an urge to laugh as she had with Kim, but the dean hadn't made a joke.

"Have you heard the same rumor?" He shifted side to side, then stopped, obviously realizing that—unlike his desk chair—this one didn't swivel.

"No, but I can imagine gossip running in that direction," Eleanor admitted. "I've learned about one troubling incident on social media." She related Kim Lamont's account of the cartoon. "I told Dr. Lamont I'd let you know. Perhaps you could put a stop to it."

The dean fingered the knot of his golf ball-patterned tie. *The poor man must wish he were teeing off right now.*

"I can issue a statement to students to refrain from that kind of foul messaging," he said, "but we all know social media is like a wildfire, often beyond anyone's control. Students have First Amendment rights to free speech. The university couldn't punish the culprits even if we could track them down. Wouldn't it be better to simply ignore a tasteless cartoon?"

Eleanor knew a rhetorical question when she heard it. And sure enough, the dean didn't wait for an answer. "In any event, the police might find out without our help," he said. "Chief Marcos said not to be surprised if the investigators on the city force want a look at our computers and emails and social media accounts. The university attorney advises we refuse to comply unless they produce the appropriate court orders. They might want to search our desks and even our homes for the kind of medication that's now widely known to have been found in Paul's body."

None of that should have come as a surprise. "The faculty will be up in arms, screaming invasion of privacy," Eleanor said. "I have nothing to hide, but I'd hate the police snooping through my emails and social media posts. And my medicine cabinet."

The dean nodded. "I, for one, don't take any medication except ibuprofen and statins. I don't use social media. Our campus PR folks chide me for not being in the loop that way with people. But you are, Eleanor. You could be my eyes and ears. You might learn something I could pass on to Chief Marcos to demonstrate that the college is cooperating with the investigation."

Ah, the favor. The reason for subjecting himself to the small, immobile chair. She could tell him things he didn't know. Should she mention what Kim had said about Paul blackmailing Gene? No, she wanted to hear from Gene first. "What you ask makes me uncomfortable, Gerald. It sounds like you want me to spy and snitch."

"Not at all. But as dean, I'm often the last to hear what's common knowledge among the faculty. Eleanor,

I know Bethany is involved. I left the scholarship luncheon at the first opportunity and saw her with the Gomez girl. And Meryl said Bethany came to see her and asked who had a reason to murder Paul. I think my wife believes Charlotte Kline did the deed."

What an old gossip! Despite the somber voice, the man enjoyed passing along his wife's concerns about Charlotte. Eleanor was glad the low chair enabled her feet to touch the ground. Planting them firmly under her, she said, "Charlotte would never hurt a fly."

"I realize she's your best friend, Eleanor, but are you sure she's innocent? Paul saw Charlotte as well-meaning but behind the curve regarding technology. He made no secret of coveting funding that Charlotte, and Meryl too, would have assumed to be safely theirs until he came along like a fox in the henhouse."

Henhouse! How dare the man compare Charlotte and his wife to barn fowl!

"Eleanor, I'd like to know what, if anything, Bethany has discovered."

She took a steadying breath, not caring about sounding frosty. "Bethany has learned of normal human conflicts. An essay supposedly not turned in online that resulted in a zero, the lack of enthusiasm for a thesis topic, the end of a love affair."

"Even I know about Paul's affair with Kim Lamont," the dean said eagerly. "I heard he ended it."

"Dr. Lamont says she did, but whichever is true, I don't think she killed him."

"I hope not, Eleanor. I like the young woman." His face contorted. "My back is giving me fits. I can't swing a club without feeling a twinge. Meryl told me she spoke to you about the college party. You know that I've considered canceling it. She's taken the position we should hold it as usual."

"Has her position prevailed?"

"My wife's position usually does." He sounded droll. "As does yours at home, I've heard from Wayne."

"Only when I'm right."

The dean rewarded her quip with a chuckle, followed by a cough. He cleared his throat. Everyone knew he had dry-mouth problems and that his assistant kept a carafe filled with water on his sideboard. He rose, poured himself a glass, and offered one to Eleanor, who shook her head. He drank thirstily, took a bottle of ibuprofen from the sideboard, popped three red pills into his mouth, and drank again.

He had no means to make coffee, Eleanor noticed. "What happened to your coffeemaker? Did the police take it?"

"Yes, they confiscated all of them in the building."

"I had Jereen replace my department's," Eleanor said. "The demand for caffeine hasn't slackened."

"If they don't bring back mine, I'm going to acquire one of those pod affairs that make one cup at a time." He refilled his glass. "Do you think Meryl is right in this instance? About the party?"

"Canceling will provide more grist for the rumor mill," Eleanor said. "Not canceling will show people that the college won't succumb to fear."

"Fear of one another, you mean."

"You don't want us hiding in our offices behind locked doors? Afraid to interact with other faculty?"

"No. But the fact remains that people suspect one another. They definitely suspect you. Paul's death makes your job easier. Of all the C&I faculty, Paul had to be the hardest to manage."

Eleanor got to her feet but tried not to raise her voice. "Manage? I don't manage my colleagues. I manage the department. There's a difference, Gerald."

The dean jiggled his glass, disturbing the remaining water. "You don't enjoy the little power you have, do you, Eleanor?"

"Power over what? Course schedules and classroom assignments?"

He smiled, revealing strong teeth he must have had chemically whitened since the last time she noticed. "Dear friend, I'm thinking more of tenure and promotion."

"What real power do I have over those?" Eleanor asked. "The departmental committee will meet and give a thumbs up or down on a candidate. If I disagree, I can say so in the report I send to the college committee. Then, that committee will make a recommendation to you. After that, you'll have a say, which likely will stand but could be overruled by the president."

"Your point is, like you, I'm a cog in the academic wheel. But unlike you, Eleanor, I enjoy my role in the process."

"Even in the case of Paul Kiefer?"

"Despite his enormous ego, Paul had the good sense to be deferential to me. He considered himself the brightest mind in the college, but he still called me 'sir' in formal settings. I quite liked that."

Bully for you. Gerald Darwood could be a likable man and friend outside of the university. But as a dean, he tended to be pompous. She consulted her watch, exclaimed at the time, and said she needed to squeeze in a quick sandwich before her afternoon class.

He spoke to her fleeing back. "Eyes and ears, Eleanor. Eyes and ears."

In the sanctuary of her office, she closed the door. She dropped into her chair, kicked off her shoes, and stared at her toes, wishing they weren't encased in pantyhose. She felt fine about not telling the dean about the argument Lenny had heard between Kim and Paul, and about Kim's shifting accounts of it. No reason to inform him that Kim had made several claims about why she'd ended her relationship with Paul: his scorn of Lenny's thesis topic, his reluctance to become a father, his blackmailing of Gene. If she had revealed Gene's motive for murder, the dean might have gone straight to the president or Chief Marcos. She would give Gene a chance to confirm or deny the blackmail. *If it was true, how had he dealt with it? Surely not by murdering Paul!* Eleanor clenched and unclenched her toes but couldn't relax her feet or her brain.

Chapter 14

By midday on Monday, Bethany desperately needed to get away from her minuscule home office. All morning, she had tried to concentrate on proposals to the Foundation, but her thoughts kept flicking to Nathan in Wyoming. Would he be offered the job? Would he take it? She willed him to phone. When he didn't, she drove to her stress-relieving go-to place, the Cuevas Café, a not-for-profit lunch spot supported by the Foundation and a handful of other charities. At the front counter, she paid a volunteer a set price, knowing anyone without money for a meal could put in an hour washing dishes or doing some other simple chore. The system had worked well for almost four years.

Today's meal consisted of a tuna casserole, a lettuce salad with carrots and dried cranberries, and a huge peanut butter cookie. A crowd filled the single room, but Bethany didn't mind sharing a table with two blond guys, who looked barely past their teens, with dusty backpacks propped at their feet. Seeing them wolf down their cookies, she offered them hers. One of them broke it in half and said a polite, "Thank you, ma'am." The other cast her a shy smile.

"Traveling the country?" Bethany asked.

"Headed south, ma'am," the first one said. "Aiming to see our shirttail cousins down in Sorrel. Never been there before. It's some sort of tourist town that might have summer work."

Bethany said she knew Sorrel well. "It's a beautiful mountain village but a long way from here. Are you hitching?"

"Yep. Bus costs too much."

Taking a business card from her daypack, she suggested asking at the Sorrel Lodge to do odd jobs. She wrote Joni's name on the card's flip side. "This is my sister. Tell her Bethany sent you."

The talkative one said they were Simon and Shawn Bisbee. "We worked in Clayton at a place that recycled tires, but it went bust."

"Too bad. I hope you find something else."

The café's manager, Zena, caught Bethany's eye and came their way. Zena wore a blue bandanna over her voluminous red hair and a green T-shirt bearing the café's logo—a crisscrossed knife, fork, and spoon. She leaned down to give Bethany a hug, then asked the two travelers if they would help unload a grocery truck before they left. "I'd appreciate it, gentlemen. Somebody out back can show you what to do."

Zena's freckles and slight build made her look waiflike, yet she spoke with authority. People tended to do her bidding willingly. No exception, the two young men hefted their backpacks. Simon tucked Bethany's card into a jeans pocket. "Thanks for the tip."

Shawn added, "Much obliged" to his boots.

"Check at the mercantile too," Bethany said. "They might need extra help."

As the pair moved off, Zena asked, "You know those boys?"

"No, but they seem to be decent types. They're on their way to Sorrel. Maybe Joni can give them temporary jobs at the lodge."

"You Jarvisses! Always doing a good turn. The other night, I told one of our new board members about the annual gifts and how the café wouldn't have gotten off the ground without your seed money."

"You wrote a dynamite proposal. Is that the new T-shirt?"

Zena twisted her torso in a modeling pose. "Like it? We'll make a decent profit at twenty bucks a pop. There's a pile by the coffee urn. Help yourself to a free one."

"I'd like one, but not for free." Bethany raised her empty coffee cup. "I'll take a refill, though."

"Stay put. I'll get it."

Zena traversed the tables of diners to an industrial-size coffeemaker and returned. Setting the refilled cup in front of Bethany, she said, "I can sit for a minute. How's it going at the university?"

An MBA graduate, Zena had finished the program soon after Bethany had begun hers.

"I'm slogging along in my night classes. But it's hard to concentrate on them."

Zena's freckled face showed concern. "With what happened to that professor. Your mother was his department head, right?"

Bethany nodded.

"The cops haven't caught whoever killed him?"

"No, not yet."

"Is your mother a suspect?"

"Like everybody who knew Paul Kiefer. Including me, I suppose, if the police get wind I dated Paul a couple of times."

"Really? Was he at least a good kisser?"

"Zena!"

"Well, was he?"

"I wouldn't know. We never kissed. He dated me for a Foundation grant he didn't get." Bethany blinked under Zena's intense gaze.

"But you're involved." Hastily, Zena added, "Not in his death of course. You're trying to figure out who did him in. To help your mother like you did Joni. You straightened out that mess in Sorrel in no time. Too bad the state police got most of the credit."

"That was fine with me." Bethany drained her cup. "Good coffee."

"Fair trade dark roast. Kiefer's coffee was poisoned, and he was smothered? Did the press get that right?"

"In vivid detail."

"Your mother discovered the body?"

"Actually, it was a college custodian."

"But your mother saw it too, I heard."

"It was awful for her."

"Have the cops told you guys anything since then? With your father's connections, he must be in the know…"

"He's staying out of it, at least I think he is. Zena, what else have you heard? Table talk, I mean."

Zena fell silent and surveyed her customers. Bethany couldn't tell who among them could afford a meal and who couldn't. Humans were skilled at camouflaging their problems. "Come on, Zena. Tell me what's being said."

"Okay… The academics tend to say they bet the killer wandered in from the street, but I don't think they believe it for a second. I hear some debate about whether the university should hire armed guards. Talk like that makes me thankful we don't have much trouble at the café despite half our crowd living on the streets."

"Trouble? You've had some?"

"Once in a while, somebody who can't pay skips out without doing a chore. But that's rare. I saw you give those boys your cookie. I can get you another."

"Nah, I'm full. I'd better get going."

Zena gave her a warm smile. "You're a good person, Bethany Jarviss, and—wait for it—a smart cookie." She winked. "If anyone can figure out who killed that prof, you can. We're about ready to close. I'd best see about cleanup." She adjusted the bandanna over her fiery hair and hot-footed it to the kitchen.

Bethany selected a medium-sized T-shirt and, on impulse, a large one for Nathan from a table near a window. The two hitchhikers, she saw, were unloading flour sacks from the grocery truck. At the front counter, she paid for the shirts.

On the way to her car, she passed the homeless shelter, where people rested on a sparse lawn. The city didn't fund the shelter; the municipal budget lacked the means for such a project. A group of churches kept it going on "a wish and a prayer" as the organizers liked to say. The Jarviss Foundation had been approached by the group to join them but ultimately had steered clear of the religious-based project.

Bethany's father had come in for considerable criticism by several church leaders later when the Foundation opted to support the Cuevas Café. Bethany watched him grow weary of defending his decisions to people who chose to believe the Foundation had unlimited funds. But he didn't let anyone outside the family see him in that state. Bethany doubted that she could ever develop his fortitude.

****

In Eleanor's afternoon class, her students had barely settled into their seats when one in the front row raised his hand. "What's up with the Kiefer case, Dr. Jarviss? My mom and dad keep calling to make sure I'm alive." Jason, the class joker, got a smattering of laughter from his fellow education majors. Eleanor gave him a deadpan look and swept the room with an encompassing glance. *These students deserve a frank answer.* She did her best, saying what had been shared with the public in the latest news conference.

"Kiefer was drugged," Jason said. "Or was he on drugs? I wouldn't doubt it."

The student next to him, Marla, poked him in the ribs. "Don't joke about it, okay? It's not funny."

"I heard Dr. Lamont did the dirty deed," Jason persisted, swiveling in his seat to face his classmates. "It's all over social media. With original artwork. He dropped her, so she offed him."

Eleanor let the babble of voices reach a crescendo, then asked for a show of hands. "How many people have seen the cartoon Jason referred to?"

From a middle row, a student asked, "The cartoon with the airplane?"

Eleanor nodded. "Raise your hands if you've seen it."

All but two students thrust their hands into the air. One had fallen asleep. The other, a middle-aged woman who rarely spoke in class, shook her head—to indicate no or in disapproval of the sleeper, Eleanor couldn't discern.

Straightening her spine, she led an impromptu

discussion about the appropriate use of social media. *I must sound like a disapproving old fogey.* Standing before the group, she felt her arches cramp. It would be a long class.

****

In the afternoon, Eleanor did a rare thing: she left campus before five o'clock. At home, she tried to nap in the master bedroom but couldn't doze off. In her silk cocoon, she considered Wayne's undisturbed side of the king-sized bed. She was more than ready for him to return today from his trip with Don, who would stay in Florida for another spring tournament. By phone, she'd kept Wayne up to date about the murder. When she'd told him about seeing Paul Kiefer's body, the dear man had offered to fly home immediately, but she'd said to remain with their son, insisting, "I'm not going to be murdered in my office."

Unable even to rest, let alone nap, she phoned Bethany, who answered on the second ring. "I have a few things to tell you, dear, but I won't keep you long."

"No problem, Mom. I'm working from home but about ready to call it quits."

Eleanor recapped the talk with Kim Lamont, the dean's summons, and the exhausting class discussion.

Bethany summarized, "Meryl thinks Charlotte is the murderer, but the students' money is on Kim Lamont. Naturally, though, they'd bet on Gene if they knew what Kim told you. If what she said is true, Gene withheld an important piece of information from me yesterday morning. He implied that he and his ex only shared a concern for those wiener dogs. Not that I would've expected him to say he had sex with her. Certainly not if he killed Paul to stop being blackmailed."

"I can't imagine Gene as a murderer. Or any of the faculty," Eleanor said, knowing she sounded like a looped recording. "We're good people at heart despite the petty jealousies and occasional squabbles that go with being academics." She felt her throat dry up like the dean's had. She turned her head away from the phone and coughed.

"Mom, are you okay?"

She cleared her throat. "I'm fine."

"Why don't I talk to Gene again? Maybe Paul saw Gene and his ex in a kiss for old times' sake after she gave him money for treats for those Dachshunds. Maybe Paul misunderstood what he saw. Or he made up the whole thing to entertain Kim, and she fell for it."

Eleanor pictured Kim's face. "Kim believed Paul. It's possible he lied, but I never found him to be untruthful. But if he lied about Gene and his ex-wife that must mean Gene told you the truth. Perhaps Gene did see Paul give an impressive conference presentation and threw his support behind him. I wish I'd been there. I might have noticed how Gene reacted to Paul's talk. As it is, I don't recall Gene mentioning anything about it."

As they ended the call, Eleanor reminded Bethany that her father was due home. "Come to dinner. And do see Gene again; he might say more to you than to me as department head." But Eleanor told herself she should speak to Gene too. She hoped Kim Lamont wouldn't go to the police in the meantime.

Chapter 15

Closing her laptop, Bethany considered phoning Gene to ask if what Kim had said about Paul blackmailing him was true. No, she wouldn't call; she'd surprise him and see how he reacted.

Her cell phone rang, startling her. *Not Nathan.*

"Ms. Jarviss?"

"Yes, this is Bethany."

"Ms. Jarviss, this is Alma Gomez. I'm sorry to disturb you. It's about my friend Roxanne and the pills, you see."

Not seeing at all, Bethany asked, "What pills?"

"Those pills she takes. The kind the police say put Dr. Kiefer to sleep."

"Tell me what's going on, Alma."

"Roxanne has lost a bottle of her pills. She called me, very upset. We are to meet in the Commons in half an hour. Can you come as well? Please, Ms. Jarviss?"

"Okay. See you in thirty minutes."

As she drove to campus, Bethany considered that anxiety was quite a problem for Gene's ex-wife, Eleanor, and apparently Roxanne. Late in the day, Bethany readily found a parking space. In the student center's sparsely populated Commons, she spotted Alma and Roxanne in a booth next to one of the chrome-and-glass walls. The two seemed oblivious to the scant flow of students outdoors or the mostly older crowd eating while studying before their night classes. With a jolt, Bethany realized that she should have been preparing for her classes. Work, Nathan, and the murder had consumed her time and energy.

She slid next to Roxanne in the booth. The student's head drooped like a wilted tulip, and her long hair needed combing.

Bethany spoke first. "Alma called me. Sounds like you have a problem."

"Tell her, Roxanne. She won't bite," Alma prompted.

At the command, Roxanne raised her head. "I take pills to help me not be so jittery and worried about school. Every morning, I take a pill before I go to class. But sometimes I forget, so I keep—kept—some pills in my bag."

She gripped the messenger bag beside her. "A while back, I took a pill at the water fountain in the education building. Down the hall from the C&I office." She dropped her head again.

"Tell the rest, Roxanne," Alma urged.

At the stern tone, Bethany frowned. "Take your time, Roxanne."

Roxanne took a shaky breath. "I might have left the bottle on the water fountain. It's not in my bag anymore."

"The terrible thing is that bottle had her name on it," Alma said.

"I used an old bottle with the prescription label on it. A little plastic bottle."

"How many pills were in it?" Bethany asked.

Roxanne shook her head. "I don't know. A dozen?"

"Enough to put a horse to sleep," Alma said.

Or a professor. The students had to be thinking it.

Firmly, Bethany said, "You need to tell the police."

"I told you Ms. Jarviss would say that," Alma said. "Roxanne, it is what you must do."

"Do you think my pills were used to knock out Dr. Kiefer?"

Probably. "If they were, his death isn't your fault. Someone did more than sedate him by drugging his coffee."

"They taped his nose and mouth and eyes shut," Alma said. "Imagine!"

"Stop it, Alma!" Roxanne leaped up, lost her balance in the narrow booth, and sat back down with a thump. She pressed her hands to her ears. "I don't want to think about it!"

At the raised voices, an older woman nearby shook her head in disapproval as she highlighted in a textbook.

Gently, Bethany touched Roxanne's back, feeling the girl's bones through her summery cotton dress. "Try to calm down, Roxanne. It will be much better to tell the campus police than continue to worry. You know that, don't you?"

Roxanne took her hands away from her ears. Mutely, she nodded.

"That is what I told her," Alma said. "Roxanne, I'll go with you. We can go now."

"Do you know where the police office is located?" Bethany asked.

Both girls nodded, Alma with more confidence.

Roxanne didn't budge. "Will I have to write something? My spelling is awful."

The corners of Alma's lips lifted. "No one will care about your terrible spelling. The police are not English teachers."

"As if you've ever given them a statement!" Roxanne said.

"True," Alma said. "I have not. Come on, Roxanne. Thank you, Ms. Jarviss. We'll tell you how it goes."

Watching the students leave, Bethany considered going with them. But they hadn't asked to be accompanied. Alma Gomez would provide the support Roxanne needed to get through an ordeal with the police. But why did Alma insist that Roxanne report losing the pills? To cast suspicion of murder on an innocent friend rather than on herself? Had Roxanne left the bottle on the water fountain, or had Alma stolen it and used the pills to drug Paul?

Two guys, carrying paper plates heaped with pizza, came straight at Bethany. When they reached her, they parted like a stream around a boulder. Pepperoni scent wafted in the air, awakening in her a keen sense of hunger. Her mother expected her for dinner, she remembered. It would be good to see her father, even though she had been short-changing her Foundation work as well as her classwork. If she hurried home, she could read more of the grant applications he would want to discuss soon.

****

As Wayne pressed a juicy steak with a spatula and fiddled with a dial on the deck's gas grill, Bethany remembered his delight with the new grill presented to him by the family last Christmas. He always fed them the best New Mexico beef he could buy. When he cooked, he preferred to chat about innocuous topics, not work.

"Don't want this baby to cook too fast," he said. "It's going to be exactly the way you like it, honey, with a touch of pink in the center." He hummed some made-up tune and gave her his hundred-watt smile. "It's good to be home. Look at that view."

The sun had set, but the sky retained a wash of pink blending into blue over the valley. Bethany admired the view as Wayne rambled on. "They didn't have pure air like this in Florida, and the humidity was unbelievable. Don sweated the entire tournament. And I mean literally. It hit him harder than golfers used to that climate. He did fine, considering."

At the table, Eleanor moved bowls around to make room for a fragrant green enchilada casserole, a family favorite. Bethany had expected her mother to serve the traditional welcome-home dish. Wayne often bragged that Eleanor made the best enchilada casserole in Las Cuevas. None of the Mexican restaurants could match its perfect spiciness, he claimed.

He brought the steaks to the table, and they sat down to eat. Tan and rested, and still wearing a golf shirt, he recapped Don's fourth-place finish. "His short game's improved. He has a real chance to bag a win this summer."

Bethany ate contentedly as her father analyzed Don's game. She had no idea if her brother would ever be a golf star. He often placed near the top of the pack but rarely won. This didn't bother Wayne, who noted that golfers couldn't count on winning game after game. "Look how many times the pros play versus the times they come out on top. Persistence is the key. You can't get discouraged."

"You taught Don that," Eleanor said. "The girls too."

Bethany relished her father's die-hard optimism. The world seemed a better place with Wayne Jarviss nearby. He had a contagious smile. When she looked in a mirror, she saw dark hair and eyes like his. As a child, she felt sure this six-foot-one man could protect her from harm. As an adult, she realized her father was shielded from a good many of life's problems. He led the Foundation effectively, but his job wasn't difficult, nor was hers. She never took much credit for holding a position for which she hadn't had to apply.

Wayne helped himself to a second serving of casserole. "Terrific dish, Ellie. But you didn't have to make it tonight. You look tired. Doesn't she, Bethany?"

"Mom's coping with a lot."

"I know. She's been filling me in on the phone. Not today, though. Anything new from the police? I suppose they haven't caught Kiefer's killer?"

"If so, they haven't informed me," Eleanor said, irony heavy in her voice.

Wayne cleared his throat. "Honey, your mom says she involved you in that terrible situation."

Eleanor carefully cut a piece of steak. "People are telling Bethany things they wouldn't say to me or the police."

Here it comes, Bethany thought.

"I wish you hadn't dated Kiefer," Wayne said. "Do the police know about that?"

Bethany squirmed under his direct gaze. "Probably not, and even if they do, what would it matter? Our dates came to nothing. I told you why he took me to dinner."

"Because of the Foundation. It's a nice part of the job, being wined and dined. When it happens to me, I enjoy it. But if you and Kiefer parted on bad terms…"

"We didn't, Dad. He didn't ask me out again after I told him, over a meal less delicious than this one, that the

Foundation doesn't fund research projects."

"Did somebody stop him from grabbing their piece of the college pie? Your mother fears one of the faculty killed him."

Eleanor's fork stopped midway to her mouth. "Wayne, I never said that." She chewed a bite of steak with vigor.

Bethany squirmed again at the growing tension between her parents but didn't intervene.

"No, Ellie, you didn't say that, but you and the press suspect somebody at NMU murdered one of your own," Wayne said. "Today, at the Lauderdale airport, I read a recap of the murder on my phone. Kiefer's murder wasn't a spur-of-the-moment act. Somebody who hated the guy knew what they were doing, drugging him before they killed him. I'd put my money on a colleague. Makes you wonder what kind of faculty NMU employs nowadays."

"People under stress like most mortals, Wayne."

"Who readily medicate for it," he said with a shake of his head.

Bethany glanced at her mother. Did her father know Eleanor had needed pills to help deal with her anxiety about Joni? Did their parents share everything about their lives? Maybe not.

No one spoke for a moment, then Wayne said, "Bethany, I know you have a knack for getting at the truth. I'll never forget how you helped your sister after those bones were found."

"And don't forget Bethany found out, in one day, the truth about that poor student's death in Albuquerque," Eleanor said.

"But neither of those experiences qualifies you to be

a homicide detective," Wayne pointed out. "And Ellie, you're a professor, not Sherlock Holmes."

"Holmes would have made a fine faculty member," Eleanor said.

Wayne patted his mouth with his napkin. "An eccentric one."

"A good fit at a university." She smiled sweetly and made assurances that she and Bethany would be careful.

Bethany recognized the family ritual of telling Wayne what he wanted to hear. *It makes him feel he's done his job as the patriarch.*

****

After dinner, Bethany helped clear the table while Wayne started a blaze in the deck's built-in fireplace. In the kitchen, she told Eleanor she hadn't had time to speak with Gene again. "I was thinking about it when Alma Gomez phoned." She explained about Roxanne's missing bottle of pills. "Alma and Roxanne agreed to go to the campus police. I didn't see the need to go with them."

"Another person struggling with anxiety. Poor Roxanne. She must be a bundle of nerves. I'm glad Alma reached out to you. You're someone the girls can trust."

"They could trust you, too, Mom."

"But I don't expect them to believe that. Students don't always trust their professors in normal times. As it is, like your father, they probably assume one of us is a murderer."

Eleanor rinsed the dinner dishes and handed them to Bethany to place in the dishwasher. They had done this so often as a team, they finished the cleanup in no time. Eleanor dried her hands and pressed the dishwasher's start button. "I hope the police don't treat Roxanne as a suspect." She tossed a hand towel to Bethany, who caught it neatly.

"Officially, the police might have to, Mom. And they'll inform the city police. Alma promised to let me know what happens." She took her phone out of her daypack. "No message from Alma."

"I'll check with Chief Marcos tomorrow," Eleanor said, then contradicted herself. "No, I'll contact her now. I'll tell her that I know about Roxanne's concern because the students talked to you."

"Of course, Mom. That's fine."

"I'll remind her of your connection to Alma through the Foundation scholarship."

Eleanor used the kitchen landline and had to leave a message. "I'll call again in the morning if she doesn't get back to me."

Her mother was a good person to have on one's side. Eleanor wouldn't forget to check on the students.

From the doorway, Wayne asked, "What's for dessert, Ellie?"

When she told him lemon pie, he licked his lips. Eleanor cut three slices, and Bethany put away her phone, willing herself not to worry. *Plenty of time left for Nathan to call tonight.*

****

After Eleanor sent Bethany home with a container of leftovers, Wayne added another log to the deck's corner fireplace and moved two lounge chairs in front of it. "It's good to be home. Sit with me for a while, Ellie."

He didn't recline his chair. She braced herself, expecting the topic to be the murder, so what he said surprised her. "Change is in the wind, Ellie. Can you smell it?"

"I smell wood smoke, Wayne."

"Good one! I should have said, 'Can you feel it?' You must. Don is on the cusp of a breakthrough with his game, Joni is antsy to get married, and Bethany is tiring of her job. And dare I say it? I'm tired of managing the Foundation."

He extended a hand. She gave it a light squeeze, let go, and said carefully, "But you get pleasure from the Foundation's accomplishments. It makes a difference in people's lives."

He turned toward her, but because neither of them had switched on the deck's floodlights, she couldn't see his eyes well. A knot of fear settled in her full stomach. "Wayne, are you okay? You're not sick? Did you catch a bug in Florida?"

"No, nothing like that. My golf game's rusty, but I'm fairly fit for sixty. That's the problem: I'm sixty but could go on doing the same things for years. Day after day."

"You make your life sound dull. What would you like to do about it?"

"Honestly? Pass on the major Foundation responsibility to Bethany. Not immediately, but in the next year or so. I'd play more golf, get back to fly fishing, take you places over spring break and in the summer. Fully retire at sixty-two. I'd like you to stop working when I do, but I suppose that's not realistic since you're such a spring chicken. When I'm sixty-two, you'll only be what?"

The man never remembers. "Fifty-seven, dear."

"Fifty-seven. Right. You'll probably want to stay on at the university for a few more years as department head. But I'd like to wrap up my professional role. I'd be around to advise Bethany, of course, if she needed me."

Eleanor's stomach throbbed, a shame after a good meal. "Do you assume Bethany would want to take over as director?"

Wayne went to the fireplace and prodded the logs. The fire flared. "We've never discussed it. Time goes by so fast. It seems she was our little girl only yesterday. Then a new college graduate, then a twenty-something with a few jobs before joining the Foundation. It's hard to believe she's been my right-hand gal for four years."

"Five," Eleanor said. "They've flown by."

Wayne set the poker on the tool stand. "She's ambitious, studying for an MBA part-time. When she completes it, taking charge of the Foundation will be a natural step in her career."

"Have you spoken to your sister about this?"

"No. I won't broach the subject with Elizabeth until after I discuss it with Bethany. No sense trying to sell an idea to my sister if the directorship is not something Bethany would want."

Eleanor rose and put her arms around Wayne's waist. Its circumference had grown over the years. She felt his chin press against the top of her head.

"Bethany is underutilized at the Foundation," Wayne said. "She does her job without complaint, but it's mostly reading grant applications and helping people with the forms. She gets out some, but as director, she'd do more ribbon cuttings and follow-up visits. More responsibility would satisfy that brilliant mind she inherited from you, Ellie. But she shouldn't involve herself in matters best left to the police."

Eleanor extricated herself from his embrace but stayed by his side. "In each case, she's had a natural reason for getting involved. And this time, I do too."

"I wish neither of you had to set foot on campus again until someone is arrested for Kiefer's murder. Gerald Darwood must be under tremendous stress running the college. Tomorrow, I should call him."

"Don't do that, Wayne. You'll see the Darwoods Saturday at their college party. That will be soon enough."

He didn't press the point, but Eleanor's stomach gave a sharp pang as he said, "The other thing I worry about is Bethany's relationship with Nathan Fuller."

She crossed her arms. "He's a nice young man, Wayne. You like him."

"I do, but look at his life. I know about the Carters. They don't run that many head of cattle anymore. Like me, they're about retirement age. If their youngest kid amounted to anything, they wouldn't need Nathan. That's not a good situation for our daughter's potential husband."

"She hasn't talked about marriage. Besides, Nathan could get other work if he and Bethany were to marry."

"He might drag her off to the middle of nowhere to live. We'd lose her and the Foundation would too."

Was he psychic? It was tempting to spill the beans about Nathan's potential job in Wyoming, but she held back. Let Bethany mention it if and when Nathan accepted an offer.

She gave Wayne a nudge. "Stoke the fire. It's burnt to embers. And don't worry about Bethany and Nathan. Or at least, don't tell her you do. I worry too, but she's thirty-two and can take care of herself."

"Thirty-two. Let's hope she doesn't jump at the chance to marry that cowboy because she hears her biological clock ticking."

Eleanor laughed. "Must I remind you that we adopted two kids? Bethany has choices in life. If she doesn't have biological children, she might follow in our footsteps and adopt. Or opt not to be a parent."

Wayne picked up a piece of kindling, then dropped it back onto the woodpile. "That's enough fire for tonight." His voice changed to an Old West twang. "I'm bushed, as the cowpokes say. Time, my girl, to hit the hay. Join me?"

Eleanor's stomach settled down as she said yes.

Chapter 16

In her daypack, Bethany's phone sounded as she drove home. She pulled over on a dark residential street a few blocks from her house, hoping to hear from Nathan. But Alma was calling about the ordeal with the campus police.

"We both had to make reports. It was a little scary."

"You don't sound too upset."

"The police cared more about Roxanne's story. They did ask me if I knew Dr. Kiefer. Naturally, I said yes, I took a class from him. They didn't know about my essay, and I didn't tell them. Should I have, Ms. Jarviss?"

What would she have done in Alma's shoes? Kept quiet and felt guilty about it? "If they find out from another source, you might be questioned again. If that happens, tell them all you know. But what about Roxanne? Did she give a report without any problems?"

"To a police officer not much older than us. Roxanne's hand jerked like it had a jumping bean inside. He told her spelling and punctuation mistakes didn't matter. He barely spoke to me. He took her statement to an older officer we could see through an inside window. Then, the young one came back and said we could leave."

Alma seemed miffed that the officer hadn't paid her special attention. As a beautiful girl, she undoubtedly had expected it. Bethany thanked Alma for the call and encouraged her to keep in touch. "Tell Roxanne she did the right thing."

"Do you think the police will learn about my dispute with Dr. Kiefer?"

Her patience fraying like a rope about to snap, Bethany said, "I don't know. Try to get a good night's sleep. If you're troubled in the morning, go back to the station and add to your statement."

"Yes, Ms. Jarviss. Thank you." Alma didn't sound grateful.

****

Prone on her couch, Bethany considered Alma Gomez. The student had a knack for setting the cat among the pigeons. Because of her, Lenny mentioned overhearing the argument between Paul and Kim, which cast suspicion on Kim. Alma pushed Roxanne into reporting losing her pills. But Alma kept quiet about her missing essay. What if she had failed to turn it in on time? Maybe she was an accomplished liar. Had she expected, after Paul's death, that the police would check the professor's records and find a zero for the assignment next to her name? That could still happen, Bethany supposed. If so, would Alma expect Bethany to vouch for her? *I'd have to say Alma told me she submitted the essay on time, that she worried the police would suspect her, an innocent student, of her professor's murder.*

Imagining Alma in her high heels and high-piled hair, Bethany saw a young woman who relished the spotlight. *A drama queen.* Bethany appreciated a good drama, but on a stage or screen.

In the kitchen, she made a cup of black tea in the microwave. As she took milk from the fridge, her landline rang. She snatched up the handset. "Nathan!

I've been waiting for your call. How's your day been going?"

"Perfect now, hearing your voice. How's yours?"

"Fine. I had dinner with the folks. Dad's back, all charged up about Don's tournament."

She mentioned that Don had finished in fourth place. "It's a respectable outcome in a big field of contenders. But enough about that. How'd it go with the Hartshorns?"

"They offered me the job."

"Wow." She hesitated. "Are you going to take it?"

"Dunno. Depends."

"On what? The salary?"

Nathan's laugh boomed in her ear. "The salary's what it is. Typical cowboy pay."

"What then? The work?"

"Some of that, yeah. There's more meet-and-greet with the guests than I expected.

"They need a pretty boy with the gift of gab to represent the authentic West. They get people who've never been to our part of the country before, who will go 'Gee whiz, are those real spurs?' when I wear them over my old boots. The Hartshorns want me to wear a neckerchief too, and do rope tricks for the kiddies. The rope tricks might not be a cinch with my hand the way it is, but with practice I guess I could do 'em. On the hunts, I may have to show some of the guests which end of the gun to point at the deer and elk."

"Will you like doing all that?"

"Don't know. For the corporate retreats, I may be called to grill the meat and pour on the barbecue sauce. Do whatever it takes to make the customers happy. That's the ranch motto."

"At least they won't have you lay tile or hem curtains."

"Don't be too sure about that."

She imagined his rueful smile. "What about working with the horses? Will you give riding lessons and lead trail rides?"

"Yeah, and muck out the stalls with my buddy Harvey. He's not as pretty as me. He stays close to the barns most of the time. But in a pinch, even old Harv might have to dance with the ladies and teach kids how to whistle with a blade of grass."

Bethany dunked her teabag, removed it from the mug, and added milk. She wished she could see Nathan's face. "You sound disappointed in the job."

"It's the best I can expect, I guess. A bunged-up fella like me can't rodeo or do the heavy lifting on a big commercial ranch."

"Heavy lifting? I thought most ranches had machines to do the heavy work."

"Don't think that. Cowboys wrestle their share of cows. Branding, ear tagging, and so forth. But even if I wanted a regular ranch gig, I don't know of one being advertised. And to be fair, the Hartshorns are honest about what their enterprise involves. Without the guests, they couldn't hang onto their place. They don't own as much acreage as I expected. They lease quite a chunk of public land. But it's a beautiful spread, valley and forest combined."

"Did you get to see it on horseback?"

"We took a trail ride along the flats. Then they drove me in their truck higher up, along some old logging roads. The views are something to write home about. You'd love it here. The air is so sweet you could spread it like honey on toast."

"Sounds like there are pros and cons to working for the Hartshorns. Where would you live?"

"In a room in a bunkhouse. It's basic but rent-free. Free meals too. Not a bad deal. But there's one huge drawback that makes me think I should say no and goodbye."

Bethany swallowed a sip of tea, hoping she knew what he would say. "Something worse than doing rope tricks?"

"Yeah, the distance from you."

"A long day's drive."

"You'd come visit?"

"I might sign up as a paying guest. You know I'm not great on a horse. You could give me riding lessons. Or would Harvey do that?"

"I wouldn't let him. Anything a man can do for you, I'd do myself. I guarantee it."

Sharing a laugh felt good. This was a guy to keep in her life. "Do you have to give the Hartshorns an answer right away?"

"Harv says I'm not the only cowboy who's applied. If I don't say yes tomorrow, they'll interview the next guy. They need to get the place fully staffed. They're hiring a housekeeper too. Want to go for that?"

Physically active work had its appeal at times, but surely he joked. "I'd better stick to my guns here."

"Working for your papa or solving murders?"

"Both, but I'm not doing either well. I'm behind in my Foundation stuff and getting nowhere with the murder investigation. I should talk another time to the professor I mentioned. Gene Waverly."

"Why him?"

In brief, she brought him up to speed, trusting him to keep what she said to himself. He chuckled about Gene's sex with his ex. "Most guys would brag about being attractive to an ex-wife."

"You don't get it, Nathan. I think Gene loves his ex enough to care about their one-time fling ruining her second marriage."

"Do you know it was only the once? Could be an ongoing thing."

"Good point," Bethany said. "If it's an ongoing affair, he definitely wouldn't want her husband to find out."

"Nooky without husband duties. A lot of guys would kill for that."

Bethany groaned and said, "The way you put it, Gene should be my prime suspect. I should see him again and the two students, Alma, whom you met, and a friend of hers, Roxanne." She summarized the story about Roxanne's lost pills and how Roxanne, with Alma's support, informed the campus police.

"It's a tricky business," Nathan said.

When they eventually said goodnight, she didn't know if he would take the job or if he should. She dumped out the dregs of her tea, regretting the caffeine coursing through her veins.

Upstairs in bed, she tried to soothe her nerves by calling to mind Nathan's clean-shaven face, his strong chin, his expressive blue-gray eyes. Was he also staring into the darkness? Would he be wooly-headed in the morning and say yes to the Hartshorns because that's what they wanted to hear? She worried about him making a hasty decision he'd regret.

Unable to sleep, she put in an hour of Foundation

work in her office. Then, in an act of pure will, she began an assigned class reading. She awoke face down, literally with her nose in her book, at 2:30 a.m. and hauled her body back to bed. What would her parents say if she announced she might drop out of grad school? She burrowed under the covers to consider that question.

Chapter 17

Bethany started the new day with a plan to get to the Foundation office by nine o'clock after a quick stop to see Gene Waverly. She parked in his short driveway, and hoping he hadn't left for campus, stepped up to a covered porch. As she knocked on the front door, she heard a chorus of yapping. She had never been inside this nineteenth-century home across from the park. She'd never had a reason to visit Gene's home before now.

She could hear him admonish his dogs. "Pipe down, you three." Moments later, he peered out at her. "Bethany Jarviss? Not a sight for sore eyes. Seems we just saw each other."

"You did invite me to see you again."

"Yes, I did. Come on in. Don't mind the ankle biters."

"Ankle sniffers." The Dachshunds examined her feet and lower legs. She gave each dog a pat.

"Let's go out back," Gene said. "I'm having my morning coffee. Interest you in a cup?"

"No thanks. I've had mine."

She followed him through a homey living room and kitchen to a porch filled with marigolds and geraniums ranging from white to pale pink to red. The potted plants covered a patio table, the porch railings, and most of the floor. The Dachshunds fitted themselves into tight spaces among the greenery and lay panting.

Gene drew out a chair for Bethany. Across from her, he drank from a purple mug stamped with a worn NMU logo.

"It's nice out here," Bethany said. "Your flowers are beautiful."

"The wife's. Like the sausage dogs."

"You take good care of them."

"The plants or the doggies?"

"Both." Bethany relaxed in the peaceful surroundings. "Know what, if it's not too much trouble, may I have a cup of coffee after all?"

"'Course you can. Back in a sec."

He rose from the chair in a quick, startling motion. A spry old guy in his red suspenders and faded jeans, the man in the flesh didn't fit his lazy-prof image. *People must underestimate him.*

He returned with coffee in a worn mug that matched the first one. Bethany imagined Gene and his wife sitting here with their coffees year after year, the mugs' lettering fading with repeated washings. Apparently, their marriage had faded as well. She felt sorry for this man left to lovingly care for the ex's little dogs and her flowers.

Bethany hesitated to say what she had come to ask. Instead, she said, "Good, strong coffee. Do I taste peanuts?"

Gene thumbed a suspender and stuck out his chest. "That's right. I grind some from the family farm in Portales with the coffee beans. People like hazelnut coffee. I figured why not try putting in peanuts."

"Clever," Bethany said. "Delicious."

Past the porch, the fenced-in backyard held bushes and trees as healthy as the potted plants. Gene was a farmer at heart; he didn't neglect the living things on his property.

"You're obviously good with animals and plants, Gene. Why didn't you become an ag prof or county agent? Why choose education?"

"Because of my mama. She said kids needed more men teachers. If I was an education prof, I could be a role model for guys considering majoring in it."

"Are you?"

"I guess. In my college days, hardly any guys majored in ed. Since I started teaching at NMU, and that's over thirty years ago, we've gone from almost none to about twenty-five percent male ed students. It's not fifty-fifty, but it's a heck of a change from my mama's day. I've had a hand in boosting the numbers. But you didn't come to hear about my illustrious career. Why'd you stop by?"

"To talk more about the murder."

His chest deflated. "Ah. As I thought."

Bethany dived right in. "Paul Kiefer knew that you had sex with your ex-wife at the conference in January."

Gene tugged on a droopy earlobe. "You mean Kiefer told somebody before he died and that somebody told you? Who was it?"

"I don't want to say."

"Let me think. Meryl Darwood? She went to the conference. But Paul wouldn't have told the dean's wife. He would've told somebody who would keep it to themselves. I guess Kim Lamont while she was still his girlfriend."

He let go of the earlobe to point a finger at Bethany like a kid aiming an imaginary pistol at an enemy. "You think I killed Paul to keep it a secret that my ex and I rekindled a flame from what we thought was a dead ember?"

He slapped the table, jiggling the plants. The youngest Dachshund stretched and trotted to his master's side. Gene rubbed its head. "That's a good one, Moe. I killed a guy to stop him from ruining my reputation."

"Your wife's reputation," Bethany said. "She wouldn't want her current husband to know about you two. I think you still love her and don't want her to get hurt."

Gene picked up Moe and propped him in his lap. The dog gazed at Gene lovingly with deep brown, bulging eyes. Moe had a silly face; he might have been making fun of Bethany's information. But she pushed on. "At the conference, after Paul caught you and your ex kissing—like more than friends—outside your hotel room, I suspect he asked you to support his application for full professor. He didn't have to spell out a deal: He would tell no one what he saw if you dropped your opposition to his promotion. And lo and behold, after the conference, you did."

"Then why kill him? The way you figure it, we both got what we wanted."

"I don't know," Bethany admitted. "Maybe he wanted more. Maybe he expected you to support his ideas to force change to programs you think should be left as they are. I know he wanted the tutor center turned into a tech lab for his research. Not only that, he aimed to get his hands on the funding for Charlotte Kline's projects that most faculty see as beneficial. Or you killed him for making fun of you behind your back. That might have been the last straw."

Moe wouldn't settle down, so Gene set the

wriggling dog on the floor. Moe's long body moved down the porch steps like a coiled-wire toy. The dog nosed around an oleander bush, lifted a stubby back leg, and relieved himself.

"Good boy," Gene called. "Water the bushes."

Bethany stayed on track. "Paul called you cruel names. You must have heard some of them."

Gene shrugged. "The old fossil. The department's dinosaur. Mister green jeans, even though my jeans are blue. I know he didn't respect me or the farm country I come from. He didn't believe I should've been a prof, let alone a full prof. One time, he complained about my getting what he called 'preferential treatment.' Said I should've taught more classes and him less because of his heavy research load. I laughed in his face. He wasn't my boss."

"And only an associate professor."

"When he first called me a dinosaur, he was an assistant prof, if I remember right. But then he speed-raced to associate and agitated for full."

"It must have galled you to be disrespected by such a young man."

"Kiefer rubbed most of the faculty the wrong way. He called Charlotte Kline a flower child gone to seed. He dubbed Eleanor lady bountiful and the queen mother. He called his buddy Vince the sidekick."

"I've viewed Vince Morrison as a sidekick," Bethany admitted. "He gave me the impression he considered himself one."

"Vince is a realist despite all his fanciful notions about how the West was won."

"Do you think Vince could have killed Paul?"

"I doubt it. If Kiefer was killed with a six-shooter, I

might've fingered Vince for the deed." He formed his hand into a pistol again, fired an imaginary shot, and blew away invisible smoke. Nonchalantly, he fished in his shirt pocket for his cigarettes. "Little lady, did you tell Eleanor what you heard about me and Janet?"

Her cheeks had to be blazing. She was glad he didn't look at her as he lit up. "Your ex-wife's name is Janet? Yes, I told Mom. I've told her everything I've found out that might relate to Paul's death. But she hasn't said anything about you to the police. She agreed to let me talk to you first."

"She'll want to have a confab with me. She'll push me to tell my story to Chief Marcos. My ugly mug will wind up marked *suspect* on a whiteboard, along with a picture of Kiefer's pretty face. I've seen those boards on cop shows."

Gene stuck a cigarette into the corner of his mouth and consulted his watch. The watch's gilt, like the letters on his mug, had mostly worn off. "Time to get to school. Can't say I'm happy we had this little talk. But you have pluck—I give you that—knocking on my door like I told you to. I hoped you'd come for my help, not to get me to say I'm the guilty party. You don't seriously think I'm the killer, do you, Bethany? Otherwise, you wouldn't have had a cup of my coffee."

Chapter 18

Did Gene hold out hope for his ex-wife's return? Bethany pondered that question as she parked near the university behind the restored 1890s business hotel housing the Jarviss Foundation. Usually, she didn't give the familiar lobby a thought, but with Gene's home still in mind, she paid special attention to the décor. Potted palms flanked upholstered easy chairs. Newspapers and magazines lay scattered about on varnished coffee tables. Ceiling fans slowly circulated no matter the season.

Gene might appreciate the historic atmosphere. For he was a man firmly tied to the past. Living in the house he'd shared with his wife for decades and taking care of her dogs had to constantly remind him of his married life. After the brief liaison with his ex at the conference, had he expected more lovemaking? Did he kill Paul not only to stop the blackmail but to stop Paul from spoiling his chances of getting his ex-wife back? If Paul had gone public with what he'd observed, Janet would have been humiliated. Her second marriage might have ended, and rather than return to Gene, she might never have spoken to him again.

From behind the front desk, a staffer in a crisp, white shirt bobbed his head at Bethany. She waved, then ascended the broad stone staircase. She rarely took the slow-moving elevator. Instead, she climbed past two floors of guest rooms, and one floor of offices rented mostly by attorneys and CPA's, to the Foundation's top-floor suite overlooking the city.

The lobby held no visitors. Through a glass panel, Bethany spied her father's assistant, Felicia Delgado. Beyond her, the director's door stood ajar. "Dad's in already?"

"You look as surprised as me," Felicia whispered. "In fifteen years, he's only done that a half dozen times." She raised her voice. "He wants you to go directly in to see him. Looks like he missed you while he was in Florida."

"That can't be it. I saw him last night at dinner. Thanks, Felicia."

"*De nada.*"

As Bethany passed Felicia's desk, she caught a whiff of the expensive perfume Felicia's husband lavished on her for every birthday and Christmas. One of the classiest women in Las Cuevas, today she had fashioned her silver hair into a low bun and wore hoop earrings, a red blouse, and a black silk suit. Felicia inspired Bethany to dress professionally, not show up in jeans. Bethany complied, partly to avoid the older woman's scrutiny.

Felicia never disapproved of Wayne Jarviss's choice of apparel; it reflected the day's agenda. This morning, he wore a Western shirt and bolo tie for his monthly lunch with a group of local businessmen. When the Bolo Boys met, Wayne dressed like the others. He said he was honored to be included, not being a true local but having moved from a few counties away to Las Cuevas when Eleanor began teaching at NMU. Today's tie featured a chunk of New Mexico turquoise that matched the stones in his watchband. Wayne wasn't a Las Cuevas native, but he was a New Mexican through and through.

"There you are, honey," Wayne said, rising to hug her as if he hadn't seen her in years. He shut the door and returned to his desk. The closed door signaled he meant to discuss a touchy topic.

"Felicia said you wanted to see me first thing. What do you need, Dad? I intended to work for an hour before we talk about the proposals."

"That's fine, Bethany. We can meet when you're ready. First, I want to tell you something I told your mother last night."

That I shouldn't be investigating this murder?

He cleared his throat. "The thing is, I'm considering my future and the future of the Foundation. I'm thinking of retiring." Her face must have registered astonishment because he hastened to add, "In a year or two. Not right away."

"Wow, that's a surprise, Dad. The Foundation is doing so much good, I assumed you'd want it to continue indefinitely."

"Oh, I do. But I don't intend to lead it forever. I'd rather be free to watch that brother of yours play golf, take your mother on vacations, cook more steaks for you, and go see Joni more often. It's hard to believe I'll turn sixty-one soon. Won't be too long before I can collect my Social Security."

He didn't need the government pension, but being almost eligible to file for it had to be a sobering fact of life. When did her middle-aged father start getting old? She struggled to stay calm. "Okay. It's good you're thinking of the future. You deserve to spend your time any way you want."

"Aren't you going to ask the obvious question?"

Bethany thought for only a heartbeat. "Who will direct the Foundation?"

"Exactly. And what do you think is my answer?"

She met his amused gaze. "You'll contact a headhunting firm and hire someone?" As she said it, she realized he didn't want that response.

"No need for a headhunter," he said. "My natural successor is in this room."

"Me?" Fear gripped her solar plexus and seemed to freeze her brain. "I can't think why you'd say that. I'm not prepared to lead the Foundation."

"You will be. I'll give you all the training you'll need. You'll have that MBA soon too, a useful credential. If you continue to support the worthiest causes, you'll be fine."

"You make it seem simple."

"Giving money away to help folks? Simplest job in the world."

Not with a slew of competitors vying for grants. "Dad, I don't know…"

"Think about it. That's all I ask for now. With the directorship, you'll get a hefty raise. You can pay off your mortgage, buy yourself nice things, join me at some of Don's tournaments. There's one in Maui a year from now, same week as Eleanor's spring break. You could come along with us."

Abruptly, he stopped like a winded runner. "Whoo. I'm babbling. Not something I usually do." He leaned back in his chair and tented his fingers like when he listened to her make a case for funding a project.

"You've blindsided me, Dad. You said you told Mom."

"Of course."

"Aunt Elizabeth?"

"Not yet."

"She'll be as surprised as I am and will try to convince you not to retire. She gets satisfaction from the Foundation's good works without involving herself in them. She won't appreciate anyone else in charge, certainly not me, with only a few years of experience here."

"Are you done with the excuses?"

"Not excuses. Points of argument."

"Flimsy ones. Your aunt knows you're a capable young woman. Elizabeth would happily employ you if you wanted to live on the east side of the state."

"No way. That country is too flat. I need to see the mountains."

"I think we agree we wouldn't want to live anywhere else than Las Cuevas. What better job can you get in this town than managing the Foundation?"

As she opened her mouth to speak, he held up a hand. "Know what, in the next few weeks, I want you to take trips around the state I normally would, meet with the top contenders for new or renewable grants—the mayors and city councilors and state legislators who seek our support. Then let's see if the directorship interests you. Fair enough?" He gave her a smile that meant *discussion over.*

"That's fine, Dad. I can travel more. But can we deal with the business at hand? Let me get to my office. Give me an hour before we meet about the proposals?"

"Come back when you're ready." He went to the sliding glass door to the rooftop patio and opened it. "Ah, the air smells sweet."

It smelled like ordinary city air to Bethany.

163

****

In her office, she realized she'd never considered taking on some of her father's burdens. She'd been too busy falling in love with a cowboy. Her father didn't want to live anywhere else than here. Did she feel the same? What if Nathan accepted the job in Wyoming and asked her to move there to live with him? Would she consider it?

It would be lovely to be up in the mountains, smelling air scented by pine and juniper. What a tangle her life had become, with both Nathan and her father pursuing change while she wanted her routine life to continue. Or was she kidding herself? If she desired a simple, uneventful life, she wouldn't meddle in murder investigations. A part of her craved mental stimulation that she didn't get in her job or MBA studies.

Through her doorway, she saw Felicia greet the office intern, a student majoring in business at NMU. With her hair in its customary ponytail, she could be taken for fifteen. *She'd think I'm plenty old enough to be the boss.*

For the next fifty minutes, Bethany kept her mind on grant proposals. The applicants deserved to learn if their projects would be funded. She needed to make recommendations to Wayne before his Bolo Boys lunch. If she took the Foundation's reins, would that group make her their first female member? They could rename themselves the Bolo Lunch Bunch. She could borrow Wayne's ties, no problem.

Chapter 19

Foundation matters sorted to Wayne's satisfaction, Bethany checked her messages. Nothing from Nathan. She pictured him on horseback with the Hartshorns. At one o'clock, ignoring her empty stomach, she polished off a batch of correspondence, informing the winners and encouraging the others to try again. At two o'clock, she clicked send on the last email. Time to forget her day job and go to campus.

Finding a parking space proved to be the usual challenge, but after circling like a buzzard, she scored a spot after another driver vacated it. In the flow of foot traffic, she marveled at the normal campus scene as if the murder hadn't happened. As she went around a slow-moving female group, one made a remark that elicited a laugh from the others. Bethany envied their cheerfulness.

She took a seat under one of the largest trees on campus, an ancient ash. This favorite place couldn't dispel a glum feeling about her going-nowhere murder investigation. The more she learned, the more she suspected everyone and no one in particular. She'd had luck investigating in the past without formal credentials. This time, she had discovered aspects of people's lives the police might not know, but nothing screamed, "Killer!"

Plus, she couldn't deny that her father's urge to retire had knocked her for a loop. If Nathan phoned right now, would she share Wayne's announcement? And how would Nathan's decision to take or decline the Wyoming job offer affect the answer she gave her father?

She jiggled her jaw to release tension. A student walking by, a carefree undergrad by the look of him, glanced at her with sympathy. Rummaging in her daypack, she discovered a package of peanuts. Chewing the stale snack, she wished she'd gone home for a decent meal and to change out of her office clothes. Then she thought of her mother, who without complaint suited up each day to manage the C&I department. *It would be so good to see her.*

On impulse, Bethany made for the education building and took the stairs two at a time. As she passed Paul Kiefer's office, she noticed the crime scene tape had been removed. *People must be relieved.*

In the C&I front office, Jereen insisted on phoning Eleanor, who'd asked not to be disturbed. But Eleanor opened her door immediately, looking cool and in command in a cream jacket and toast-colored sheath. She waved Bethany into a chair and joined her at a table covered with samples of brochures promoting the department.

"I have to choose one of these designs. University Communications needs the go-ahead to print fresh brochures. Recruiting students never stops, which I didn't realize until I became department head." Her mother stopped the small talk. "You look drained, dear. Have you eaten lunch?"

"A snack. I can get something more at the student center. I'll go there to study before class, but I had an urge to see you. Dad told me he wants to retire and put me in charge of the Foundation."

"Yes, he sprang it on me after dinner last night. But I've suspected for some time that he's been thinking about it." The office phone rang, but Eleanor didn't move. "Jereen can take a message. There, it's stopped."

"Dad blindsided me. I didn't see it coming." Eleanor nudged a box of tissues toward her, but Bethany ignored it. "It's hard to think Dad's old enough to retire or that he'd want to. I expected he'd be in charge of the Foundation for another twenty years. It's his life."

"His family is his life." Eleanor said it softly.

"He did mention wanting to do more things with all of us." Bethany felt her mother observing her as she took a tissue and blew her nose.

Eleanor went to her sideboard and filled two water glasses from a vintage cut-glass carafe. "Here, drink this. You don't want to get dehydrated."

Like a child, Bethany did as her mother asked. She couldn't recall drinking water since the early morning.

"Bethany, you don't believe the only reason Wayne wants to retire is to have more free time, do you? He's thinking of you as well. He sees how easily you handle any task he sets for you. And I agree with him. You're ready for a bigger challenge."

"Is that why you asked me to investigate Paul Kiefer's murder? For the challenge of it? Because my job isn't challenging enough? Not because you needed my help?"

Eleanor sipped water, gazing into the bottom of her glass like a gypsy reading tea leaves. "It was—is—to help me, not to shake up your daily routine. But look how you jumped at the chance to question people and report what you've discovered. You never talk much about the details of your Foundation job."

"My glass seems to be empty. May I have more water?"

"Of course. Help yourself."

She carefully handled the carafe passed down on the maternal side of the family. "Mom, will you retire if Dad does?"

"Heavens no. I've barely started as department head. Although if I were booted out of this position, I might."

"Booted out?" Bethany dropped into her chair.

Eleanor sighed. "There's faculty gossip to the effect that I should step down. Some say that departmental conflicts, which I should have dealt with, led to Paul's death. That in a sense, his murder is my fault."

"That's so unfair, Mom!"

"Is it? How can I know? Paul's killer hasn't been caught. We don't know that person's motive."

Bethany set down her glass with a bang. "Sorry, Mom. I don't want to break one of these. And I'm sorry to be getting nowhere, even though people tell me interesting things."

"You can stop looking into the murder. Give up."

She recognized Eleanor's strategy with her children. A feud with a school friend seemed impossible to solve. "Give up," Eleanor would suggest. A math problem too tough? "Give up." Their father besting them at chess? "Stop playing."

Bethany felt sheepish. "You know I won't quit. And I should stop complaining, right?"

"As should I," Eleanor said. "Faculty gossip about my leadership is nothing new. It started the day I became the first woman to lead this department. And the first head to face such a crisis. How it's resolved will affect all of the faculty and possibly determine if I can continue in this role."

Her mother looked so troubled that Bethany vowed, "And I'll keep talking to people about Paul. By the way, did you hear from Chief Marcos about the two students?"

"Yes, she called me back today. I told her I knew about Roxanne's claim to have lost some pills. I couldn't tell if Roxanne was a murder suspect. The chief kept her cards close to her vest."

"Her padded vest," Bethany said. "I imagine her in full SWAT gear."

The quip fell with an almost-audible thud between them. "Sorry, Mom, I shouldn't joke."

Eleanor forced a smile. "It's fine. Joking will keep us sane. We have a lot to contend with. Have you heard more from Nathan? By the way, I didn't mention to your father that Nathan is in Wyoming."

"Good," Bethany said. "No sense telling Dad if it turns out that Nathan doesn't take the job. He called to say he'd been offered it."

"But he hasn't said yes?"

"As of last night, no. I'm waiting for him to phone again."

"You must be on pins and needles. Listen to me, I sound like your grandmother."

"It's an apt expression, Mom. Waiting makes my body ache like I'm being pricked with sharp objects. If Nathan moves to Wyoming, it will change our relationship in ways we can't predict. But I want what's best for him. And for Dad. And you."

"Concentrate on what's best for you, my dear daughter."

"Like I know what that is. How about we change the

subject? Please?"

Eleanor furrowed her forehead and nodded. "That's fine."

"I saw Gene again," Bethany said. "This morning at his house. I told him what Kim said about Paul blackmailing him."

"You did? Bold of you. How did Gene respond?"

"He didn't deny the blackmail, but he denied killing Paul. According to Gene, he and Paul both got what they wanted. Gene supported Paul's bid for full prof, something Paul deserved anyway. In return, Paul didn't spread the story about Gene's sex with his ex."

"Gene actually felt Paul deserved the promotion?"

"I don't know," Bethany admitted.

"It's more likely that Gene succumbed to Paul's threat. Gene takes the easy paths in life. It's hard to respect him. I wouldn't be sorry to see him retire."

"There's something else," Bethany said. "I noticed the crime scene tape is gone from Paul's door."

"Yes, Jereen watched the campus police take it away. I'll have to arrange for Paul's office to be cleaned out and his possessions sent to his parents, I guess."

"Who will pack it all up?"

"The campus facilities office could send someone. No, I don't want that. I'll do it myself in time. When Chief Marcos gives her permission. Oh, I feel sorry for Paul's parents. I'll have to find out if they want his academic materials."

An idea occurred to Bethany. "Do you have keys to all the offices in the department?"

"One key. A master that opens everyone's door. It comes in handy when faculty lock themselves out. The doors automatically lock behind them."

"Hmm. Mom, what do you think about me taking a look in Paul's office?"

"Invade his privacy?"

"The deceased have no right to privacy. I want to get into that office for a good reason—to find clues to why Paul was killed—not to snoop."

Eleanor propped a fist under her chin. "The police were in there for ages. They must have gone over Paul's office quite thoroughly."

Bethany picked her daypack off the floor. "Could be I'll see something they missed."

"Don't think that you'll find Paul's office very interesting. It's not filled with personal items, and the police took his computer."

"Even so, why don't I look right now? I won't let myself in if anyone's around, and I'll phone you when I'm done. You can make sure the coast is clear before I come out."

Eleanor bit her lip. "Okay, I won't budge from here until you call. But be careful. If someone sees you, it may get awkward." She went to her desk and brandished a ring of keys. "Some of these are so old, I have no idea what they open. By trial and error, I found that this one should do the trick. Here, take it. Go, before I change my mind."

Bethany hugged her. Looking down at the top of Eleanor's head, she saw gray hairs in the part of her stylish blonde do. Eleanor had been coloring her brown hair for years. *By now, brown mixed with gray must be her natural color.* Bethany let go as the desk phone rang again. She slipped out the door.

Chapter 20

No one passed by in the hallway. Bethany glanced to the left and right as she unlocked Paul Kiefer's door. A gray metal desk, a leather swivel chair, a straight-backed visitor's chair, a pair of file cabinets, and a bookshelf crowded the small office. Venetian blinds blocked the daylight, so Bethany flipped on the fluorescent lights. What she assumed to be fingerprint powder adhered to her thumb. The police had left other traces of powder here and there, but since they had cleared the crime scene, Bethany didn't worry about touching things.

Paul hadn't dressed up his office with framed awards, family photos, or knickknacks like most faculty. A cactus with one yellow bloom sat on the desk. A realistic fake, it fared fine without sunlight.

Besides the cactus, the desk held only a beige phone, pencils and gel pens in a clear holder, and a pad of sticky notes, all arranged around an empty space, probably where the laptop confiscated by the investigators had sat. Bethany opened the desk's top drawer to find more ordinary items: a roll of mints, a nail clipper, lip balm, and an opened packet of stale-smelling crackers. The other drawers were empty.

A toy basketball hoop hung low on a wall over a wastebasket half-filled with balled-up sheets of printer paper. Bethany unfolded the sheets and saw that they

172

were blank. She rolled one back into a ball and tossed it through the hoop. Paul probably did that while pondering knotty, scholarly problems. Or when he was bored. A printer on a stand lacked paper; maybe Paul only used paper for his basketball shots. The office screamed Paul's passion for a paperless society. She recalled that on their first date, he had championed his feelings on the subject when the waiter presented oversized, glossy menus. "What a waste of trees. We could've accessed the menu on our phones." Paul's complaint had embarrassed her.

The few shelved books leaned at crazy angles or lay flat, obviously disturbed by the police search. Ironically, most of the books were about teaching with technology. A purist publisher might have stuck to e-books. She pushed the books aside but found nothing hidden behind them.

One file cabinet held only dust; folders crammed with education journals filled another. As she pushed the folders apart, she encountered resistance. At the back of the drawer, she found a photo in a metal frame of Paul with his arm around a pretty, dark-haired woman. The ex-wife? The couple must have been in their twenties in the casual shot in front of a barbecue grill. Bethany put the photo back, feeling that maybe a dead person's privacy could be violated despite laws to the contrary.

A corkboard displayed nothing but an NMU calendar, still opened to January, which pictured the engineering building. A mirror about a foot square hung at what would have been Paul's eye level. Here, he could check his teeth and run a comb through his hair before class. Seeing fingerprint powder on the mirror's edges, Bethany looked behind the mirror as a police officer no doubt had done. Nothing was concealed there.

Any secrets Paul harbored might have been on his laptop or on the so-called cloud. No, in neither of those places, she guessed, but filed in his brain's neat compartments.

She tried out the dead man's fancy chair. Paul hadn't been satisfied with the desk chair the university provided. She imagined him unconscious in this seat, with coffee spilling onto his lap as someone wrapped his head in tape. Had there been a roll in the desk, or had the killer brought it in a briefcase, backpack, or pocket— perhaps a roomy cargo pocket?

From the hallway came a periodic shuffling of feet and muffled talk. Bethany eyed the artificial cactus; a real one wouldn't have needed much of Paul's attention.

She took out her phone to call Eleanor, turned toward the door, and saw a gym bag hanging on the back. The bag held a pair of white shorts, smelly white tennis shoes, a dirty tennis ball, a container of three new balls, and an empty water bottle. A tennis racquet in its case was propped by the door. Paul's life had involved more than his career. But Paul's tennis playing revealed nothing about his murder. He hadn't been beaten to death with a tennis racquet.

Bethany gave one last look around the plain vanilla office as she phoned Eleanor. "Mom, I'm done. Get me out of here!"

In under a minute, Bethany heard a pattering of feet and Eleanor saying hello to someone. Then, Eleanor lowered her voice. "The coast is clear. Come on out."

When Bethany emerged, Eleanor said in relief, "Let's go outside."

They found seats near the Mexican fountain in the

Old Quad. Watching water flow from tier to tier, Bethany breathed slowly to calm her heart. She handed Eleanor the master key and described the fruitless search.

"I found one interesting thing, but it probably doesn't relate to Paul's murder," Bethany said. "He kept a photo of himself and a woman, probably his ex-wife, but hidden in a file drawer. What do you think that meant? That he still loved her?"

"Could be. Or maybe the woman was someone else. His sister?" Eleanor slipped off her high-heeled sandals and wiggled her nylon-clad toes. "Ah, that feels good. You should try it."

Bethany slid her feet out of her pumps. It was going to be a long afternoon and evening on campus. "I don't think the woman was his sister. The way he had his arm around her said lovers. They looked happy, all smiles. Paul never smiled more than politely at me."

"He'd mastered the social smile," Eleanor said. "His smiles never reached his eyes. I think his divorce permanently damaged him."

At the edge of the fountain, sparrows flitted and settled, took turns drinking, then flew up to the blue sky. The spring day felt almost summery with students populating the grassy quad. In one group, a student lay with his head on his backpack, apparently asleep.

"That guy's going to miss class," Bethany said. But another student nudged him awake.

"Saved by his friend," Eleanor said.

The group moved off, among them a young woman in a straw hat decked out with artificial flowers.

"Paul didn't personalize his office," Bethany said. "The only decorative item on his desk was a fake cactus."

"I asked Paul about that cactus," Eleanor said. "A friend gave it to him, a colleague at his previous university who knew he was notoriously bad with plants. Paul's wife had given him one plant after another, but they all died from lack of water."

"That doesn't speak well of him, does it?"

"Or the ex-wife," Eleanor said.

"What do you mean? Oh, she should've known not to give him a living thing to care for. We know he wasn't eager to have children."

"At least he didn't pretend to be," Eleanor said. "I'd better get back to the office. And you should eat something before your class."

Bethany felt the gentle pressure of her mother's petite hand on hers. "I will, Mom, at the student center. While I skim the reading for tonight."

****

Waiting in line with much younger students at the food court, Bethany heard no mention of Paul's name. But then, most students had never met him.

She chose a table and tucked into a turkey wrap without enthusiasm. Mayonnaise oozed out and dripped onto the tabletop. Wiping up the mess, she noticed a middle-aged woman scanning the crowd for a place to sit. It took a moment to recognize the campus custodian, May Zeller. Instead of her shirt-and-jeans uniform, she wore a white gauze top and short denim skirt. Her hair stood erect in gelled spikes. Bethany recalled Eleanor mentioning that May took classes toward a special education degree.

Seeing Bethany, May came over, smiling sympathetically. "Hi, Ms. Jarviss. Sloppy things, these wraps." She held one of her own. "I always grab extra napkins. Have some."

Bethany took the napkins gratefully. "Want to join me?"

"Sure, why not?" May propped her elbows on the table and commenced to eat.

An awkward tension grew between them. Up to now, they'd mostly said quick hellos in the education building's hallways. Between mouthfuls, they agreed the end of the school year couldn't come soon enough.

"How's Dr. Jarviss?" May asked. "Since you-know-what happened?"

"Since you found Paul Kiefer's body. She's okay."

"I think about it all the time. I can't help myself."

"That's understandable, but it must be tough."

Setting down the half-eaten wrap, May stared at her work-worn hands. Her bony fingers contrasted with her sturdy legs. Maybe hands thinned from physical labor while legs gained muscle?

May went on without prompting. "I didn't mind all the hoopla. That makes me feel guilty and ashamed of myself. The police talked to me, and I liked it. My partner, Sue, wanted to hear every detail too. Other people ask me to describe what I saw, and I do. I tell them about the spilled coffee and the tape around Dr. Kiefer's head. I say I'm a tough old bird; I didn't freak out. But I got out of his office lickety-split. Sick, isn't it, that I keep telling that story?" She finished the wrap and used a napkin.

Watching May, Bethany said, "No, not really. I can relate."

"You, Ms. Jarviss?"

"Call me Bethany, please. Unless you like being called Ms. Zeller."

May hooted with laughter. "I'm plain May to everybody from the dean on down. When I have my special ed degree, I'll have my students call me May too. But what do you mean, you can relate?"

Wiping her fingers, Bethany said, "It's human nature, after something shocking happens, to tell the story of it repeatedly." She recalled her past encounters with murderers. Talking to her family and Nathan had helped her shake off the heebie-geebies.

"Sue keeps bad stuff to herself," May said. "Like a closed oyster. But I can never keep my mouth shut. And I'm nosy as all get-out about everybody. I keep asking myself who killed Dr. Kiefer and why they did it. To be honest, it's made my life more exciting."

"Mine too," Bethany admitted.

"Your life's not exciting?"

"The most excitement I had lately was presenting a scholarship."

May's head bobbed. "To Alma Gomez. It's good that young woman was rewarded for using her brains. Another one with her looks would get by on them alone. I see guys panting after her in the hallways. One time, I saw Dr. Kiefer staring like he wanted to eat her up. Men can be such pigs!" She scrunched up her nose.

Bethany giggled at the porcine face until May's expression returned to normal.

"I'm terrible, right?" May asked. "I come from a long line of folks who've had to make their own fun. What's it like handing out money all over New Mexico?"

"My father does the bulk of that. I mostly read and rank grant applications."

"My job is pretty much routine too," May said. "But it's honest labor."

"Do you put in much overtime?"

"Not at the university. I'm helping raise Sue's two kids, so I take jobs on the side. I cleaned Dr. Kiefer's condo."

"My mother told me. Did you know Dr. Kiefer well?"

"Nah. After the first time I cleaned, he made himself scarce. Handed me a key to keep and left cash on the table. I never saw him there again."

A key! "I suppose you gave the key back. Gave it to police, I mean."

"Nope. Nobody asked me about a key. The police probably don't know Dr. Kiefer hired me."

"When did you last clean for him?"

May rummaged in her backpack. Bethany expected her to produce Kiefer's key, but May brought out a tin of mints. She popped one into her mouth and offered one to Bethany, who took it with a "thanks."

"Let's see," May said. "I cleaned at his place for the last time about a week before he died. I'd go to his condo twice a month. He didn't need me more often. He kept the place neat." She cocked her head. "Why do you ask?"

Under the table, Bethany crossed her fingers. "May, I'm going to tell you something. It's not a secret, but what I'm going to ask of you will have to be."

"Huh?" May leaned forward so their minty breaths mingled.

"Like you, May, I do some work on the side but not for pay. Seems I have a knack for investigating suspicious deaths." She explained about the previous cases she'd solved. "Mom asked me to look into Dr. Kiefer's murder."

As Bethany spoke, May's deep-blue eyes widened.

"To find out whodunit, like they say in books. Some people think she did. Sorry! I shouldn't have told you."

"That's okay. Mom is innocent, and she wants the truth to come out. I've been speaking with people who knew Dr. Kiefer, but I'm getting nowhere. That's why it occurs to me—"

"You want a look-see inside his condo, and I have a key."

"Nailed it in one, May. Would you consider letting me take a peek?"

May leaned closer. "On one condition."

How much is this going to cost? "What's that?"

"I go along to open the door."

Relieved, Bethany said, "For the excitement of it. You can stand lookout."

"When do you want to go? I can't right now. I have a class in a while."

"Me too. An MBA night class. How about afterward?"

"Tonight?" May asked.

"Before I chicken out."

"You won't," May said staunchly. "What do you think you'll find?"

"No idea. Can you give me the address?"

They set a time to meet at the condo and exchanged phone numbers.

"I'd better not tell Sue," May said. "She'd stop me in my tracks. Will you tell Dr. Jarviss?"

"Mom? Sure. After the fact."

Chapter 21

In her office, Eleanor noted that by the computerized faculty schedule, Gene should be finishing his office hours. No time like the present to call him. After several rings, he picked up, sounding drowsy. Guessing he'd been asleep, she asked him to come see her, not caring if she sounded bossy.

He ambled into her office and sat opposite her. "I must be in trouble by the look on your face, Eleanor."

She folded her hands on her desktop. "I know that Bethany spoke with you at your home. She filled me in on that visit, so I'm aware Paul Kiefer saw something startling at the conference you both attended. You and your ex-wife kissing outside your hotel room door. He concluded you'd had sex with her and wouldn't want her current husband to find out. Forgive me if I ask: Would you have supported Paul's application for a full professorship if he hadn't been blackmailing you?"

Gene hooked a thumb under a suspender and puffed out his chest. "Blackmail? That's a strong word." He snapped the suspender. His hand moved to the shirt pocket holding his cigarettes. *How badly the poor man must want to light up.*

"Kiefer gave a fine presentation at the conference," Gene said. "Until then, I didn't see the young man's strengths. What most people see as the future, he talked about in the present tense. He made good points about

181

what our students need to know about tech stuff before they start teaching. I could see why he called me a dinosaur behind my back."

"But you must have resented that, Gene."

His hand again strayed to his bulging shirt pocket as if he were about to recite the Pledge of Allegiance. "Before the conference, sure I resented his attitude. But his speech made me think. I am a dinosaur, although I'd rather be called an old stallion. But that romp in the hay was a quickie, a one-off. A way of making up and deciding to be friends. Afterward, Janet and I mostly talked about the kids and grandkids and how I'm taking care of her doggies."

"Still, you wouldn't have wanted Paul Kiefer to tell Janet's husband about that fling or broadcast it to the world."

"No. But I didn't only support Kiefer because he saw Janet and me lip-locked. The man made good sense about what this college needs. It'll be hard to fill his boots. But maybe Vince Morrison can do it. He's an intelligent young guy. Without Paul's looming shadow, Vince might step up to the plate and teach a tech class or two. Or Kim Lamont could. Either one of 'em is young enough to know their way around computers and social media and all. They grew up with high-tech stuff."

"True," Eleanor said. "But they're not experts."

"They know loads more than the pair of us, Eleanor."

Deliberately, she gave him a steely gaze. "You'd be surprised how much I've learned through trial-and-error and professional development opportunities. It's a struggle to keep up with technological innovation, but it's vital to do so." She didn't mind the stern tone. She wouldn't let Gene portray her as a fellow dinosaur.

"Bully for you." He took the cigarette pack out of his pocket. "Thanks for the chat. Next thing, you'll tell me it's time I retire. The trouble is I'm not ready to sit on the back porch and watch my pooches pee on the bushes. I can still teach college kids a thing or two. And no, I didn't kill Paul Kiefer to keep him from telling the world about me and Janet. I didn't think he'd do it. It would've made him look like a petty SOB."

"You need to tell Chief Marcos about what Paul saw," Eleanor said.

"Or what? You'll squeal to her?"

"No, but someone else might."

He shook out a cigarette, stuck it behind an ear, and marched out of the office.

"Do the smart thing, Gene," Eleanor called to his retreating form.

The ensuing silence felt deafening. Eleanor left her door ajar to clear the air of Gene's spicy aftershave. Did he kill Paul? She fervently hoped not. *Give him time to talk to Chief Marcos.*

She couldn't settle her mind and get on with the tasks at hand. She swiveled her chair and stared out the window at a clear sky for several minutes until her office phone rang.

Charlotte Kline sounded flustered. "Are you doing anything, Eleanor? Anything important?"

"I should be, but actually, no."

"Could you meet me for coffee? Off campus. Before you go home."

"Sure, what's up?"

"I just had a meeting with the dean. He called me into his office. He got the idea from Meryl that I murdered Paul. She's supposed to be my friend!"

Eleanor recalled her conversation with Gerald. He'd said Meryl suspected Charlotte, but he hadn't hinted he would say that to Charlotte's face. "I can get away for coffee in a couple of hours." Eleanor dropped her voice to a stage whisper. "Earlier than that, and Jereen will give me the evil eye." Charlotte didn't laugh. Clearly, the meeting with Gerald Darwood had agitated her.

****

Eleanor found Charlotte on the patio at Campus Coffee Roasters, swirling a swizzle stick in a lidless to-go cup of something yellowish. Eleanor set down her coffee and a blueberry scone as she scrutinized her friend. Charlotte's head drooped so that her massive hoop earrings nearly reached her chest. With obvious effort, she looked up and gave a weak smile.

"So... Bad meeting with the big guy," Eleanor said.

"When he summoned me, I had no idea why. At first, he hemmed and hawed, praising my dedication to teacher training and my projects. He said that he and Meryl will always support literacy efforts. I'm eager to read her newest novel, I told him, but he didn't want to talk about that. He let me know they think I'm a killer."

"He actually said that?"

"In that deep voice, he said, 'Charlotte, if you hurt Paul, you must tell me.' And that he and Meryl could understand why I'd do it. I was speechless! He didn't act like Gerald, our friend, but the DEAN in capital letters. I think Meryl pushed him to confront me."

"Did you defend yourself?"

"When I could get the words out, I insisted I'm no murderer. Then, he asked if I had an alibi. I admitted to teaching only part of the day Paul died and spending some time in my office. 'Alone?' he asked, like I was on trial. I had to say yes." Charlotte shook her head like a tinnitus sufferer. The hoops swung under her fluffy hair.

"Did Gerald say anything else?"

"Something that made my mind whirl like a dervish. 'You were attracted to Paul, am I right?' He spoke in that irritating just-between-friends tone he uses when he gets personal."

"Attracted to Paul? Where did Gerald get that idea?"

"From observing us in college meetings. From seeing my face while Paul spoke to me. Gerald said my cheeks got shiny."

"For goodness' sake! What an odd thing to mention."

Charlotte sipped her drink. "When Paul addressed me in meetings, I could hardly reply sensibly. He got under my skin."

"That young man could be blunt and offensive. He got in everyone's face at one time or another and enjoyed making his divisive points. He liked to hear himself talk."

"He had a beautiful voice." Charlotte said it dreamily.

Eleanor thought she had misheard. "Did you say beautiful?"

"Captivating. Mesmerizing even. And he was so handsome. The only attractive male in our department. Who else is there? Milquetoast Vince? Farmer Gene? Paul was our only sexy man, and he knew it.

"But not long before he died, he said something like, 'You're a nice woman, Charlotte, with a kind heart. You believe all of our students will make fine teachers, no matter how much they flounder in class.' He'd seen me

185

talking with Roxanne Vale. I took it as a compliment but then realized it was a back-handed one. He said Roxanne shouldn't be pursuing a bachelor's. He considered her community college material. Said she would make a decent nanny but not a teacher. He patted my arm like you'd pat a puppy on the head. I'm ashamed to admit his touch flustered me so much I didn't stand up for Roxanne."

Eleanor flicked a glance at the other customers. She spoke quietly. "You were sexually attracted to Paul Kiefer?"

"I couldn't think straight around him, couldn't argue my case when we had opposing views. Another time, he stopped in my office after a meeting and told me I'd gotten flustered because I knew he was right. 'Breathing life' into the department would lead to 'a wave of change.' "

Charlotte's lavender-polished nails cut into the sides of the paper cup. Eleanor pushed the blueberry scone toward her. "Despite what Paul said, you found him attractive?"

"That time in my office, I tingled to my toes. He said, 'You smell delicious, like an exotic flower. You're the only woman professor around here who dares to wear perfume.' I told him I didn't wear it and please leave. I would have slammed the door behind him if it didn't have that metal doohickey at the top. I was aroused and infuriated, like in high school with certain boys who were out of my league and knew it. He probably smelled candle scent clinging to my clothes and hair. Eleanor, tell me honestly. Do I smell like I wear perfume?"

"You smell of vanilla like you've been baking."

Charlotte gave her a sheepish look. "I keep a vanilla

candle on my desk. I burn it pretty often." She took a drink, made a face, and set the pockmarked cup down. "Chamomile. Stone cold. Why did I order it? I should've had a coffee, but it gives me the jitters in the afternoon."

Eleanor nudged the scone closer to Charlotte. "Have some."

Charlotte broke off a piece and ate it. "Ah, that's good. I need the sugar." She eyed Eleanor's coffee. "May I have a sip of that?"

"Finish it. I've had too much today."

"You're a special friend, Eleanor. Part of my support system. I have a good life at work and at home. Friends, my teaching, and my Jerry. He loves coaching football at Cuevas High even though it's hard for him to stay as fit as the younger coaches. Jerry and I feel our age. Neither of us regrets having Toby and Theresa when I was thirty-nine. Sometimes, though, I feel out of step with the younger mothers of twelve-year-olds. And those moms find my style strange. Even Jerry finds me too ethereal. He's no romantic, so I create fantasies of being with younger men who make love to me. In vivid detail." Charlotte stuffed more scone into her mouth and moaned with pleasure.

Amazed and amused, Eleanor said, "You've fantasized about Paul?"

"Not now that he's dead, but in the past, yes. In a spring garden with songbirds and fragrant blossoms. And a fountain like in the Old Quad."

Perspiration dotted Charlotte's cheeks. She waved a hand in front of her face. "I'm going through menopause as if you can't tell. I need to get help with these hot flashes. I confided that to Meryl, and I hope she didn't tell Gerald." She laughed uncomfortably.

The coffee shop's patio contained a mostly young crowd. Eleanor sympathized with her friend. Charlotte, a vulnerable fifty-one-year-old, faced the fact of aging with trepidation. The much younger Paul must have sensed it. "You didn't have sex with Paul?"

The question caught Charlotte off guard. She sputtered, "In real life? No! Of course not!"

A twenty-something woman nearby removed her earbuds.

"Shh," Eleanor cautioned.

"Let's go," Charlotte said. "I'll tell you the rest where it's more private."

"Good idea."

As they walked to their campus parking lot, Charlotte said, "If I were a full professor, I think Paul might have slept with me to get my support for his promotion. But he knew I'm only an associate prof and don't have a vote."

They reached Eleanor's car as Charlotte continued her tell-all. "I swear things didn't progress beyond his awareness of his effect on me. Before he died, I came to my senses. A few days ago, I saw Paul come out of the dean's office with a smug look on his face. He said they'd had a 'highly satisfactory' meeting and that I should learn to promote myself and my projects directly."

"Directly? You think he went over my head to the dean?"

"Yes, to get full prof and that research and teaching lab he meant to establish. He didn't say as much, only that I should look for funding from other sources. 'You ought to apply to the Jarviss Foundation,' he said, 'since you and Eleanor are such good friends.' "

"How did you respond? If you did, that is."

"Oh, I responded all right." Charlotte's voice shook with anger. "I told him the Foundation partially supports the literacy program but not the books project for third graders. I could have bitten my tongue for telling him something he didn't know. He said, 'You'd better go to the Foundation before the college's funding for those books dries up.'"

Eleanor, distracted by a honk, recognized a faculty member from another department and waved. Charlotte didn't appear to see the man.

"I had an urge to kick him or myself, Eleanor. I made the mistake of saying you're not involved in Foundation grants. 'Then go to Eleanor's daughter,' he said. 'Bethany turned a deaf ear to my projects, but she's bound to be on your side.' He said personal relationships make or break us as if I don't know that. A woman probably killed him. He must have upset a lot of women and not only older ones like me."

"You mean Kim Lamont?"

"Or one of his students."

Alma Gomez. "Charlotte, you've taken over Paul's class that Alma Gomez attends. She told Bethany that he claimed not to have received an essay she uploaded by the deadline. Did she mention that problem to you? Did you check to see if the essay is in the system?"

"She did come to me about it, all upset. I tried to calm her, but she said she needs to know how her grade stands." Charlotte winced. "To tell you the truth, Eleanor, I haven't contacted the computer services folks to get access to Paul's class records. I haven't had the time. That's no excuse, I realize."

Seeing Charlotte's chagrined expression, Eleanor

Rita A. Popp

didn't tell her friend to get her act together. Instead, she said, "I've given them your name and the names of the adjuncts teaching Paul's online classes. Get into the system with their help and set your own password. Find out and let me know if Alma turned in that essay by the deadline."

"Okay," Charlotte said. "If she did, I'll read and grade it. Why do you want to know if it's there?"

"To find out if Paul lied to Alma. If he desired her sexually and she didn't respond to him, might he have pretended not to get the essay and suggested she sleep with him to wipe out a zero? Instead, maybe she killed him."

"That's appalling!" Charlotte said, her earrings gyrating.

"It's farfetched," Eleanor said. "I don't like to suspect a student of murder. But it has been in the back of my mind since the scholarship luncheon. I saw an odd expression, anger or disgust, on Alma's face as the dean spoke about Paul. That reaction was so strange I asked Bethany to talk to Alma after the meal. Alma told Bethany about the problem with her essay. Please keep this between us, Charlotte. If you hadn't assumed responsibility for Paul's class, I wouldn't have mentioned it. Don't tell anyone, not even Jerry."

"I won't. And Eleanor, don't tell anybody about my stupid feelings for Paul, okay? Tell Bethany that the Darwoods suspect me of murder. They'll owe me huge apologies when Paul's killer is found."

"Are you all right, Charlotte? You're shaking."

"I'm fine. It helps to unload on a friend."

Charlotte hugged her tightly, and Eleanor again smelled vanilla.

Chapter 22

At 9:00 p.m., Bethany parked at the condominium complex where Paul had lived. She chose a slot a few doors down from his address and waited only minutes for May Zeller, who drove up in an aged panel truck. As they approached Paul's front door, they set off a motion-activated overhead light.

"I don't know about this, Ms. Jarviss," May said, forgetting that they were on a first-name basis. "What if somebody sees us?"

As soon as May said it, a teenage girl passed within feet of them. But with her eyes on her phone, she didn't glance their way.

"Open the door, May," Bethany said in a hushed tone. "Hurry!"

The condo's interior smelled stale, like unwashed socks. "Pee-yew," May said. "I'll open some windows. It's really warm in here." She reached for the cord of a gray drape.

"No! Don't do that." As May whipped around, Bethany added, "Sorry. I didn't mean to shout. Let's keep the drapes and windows closed. But we'll turn on the lights."

"I'm upping the air conditioning." May tapped a wall-mounted control panel. "There, you can hear it kick in."

They had stepped into an entryway. Traces of

fingerprint powder had been left on the edges of a mirror and a small table. "The police came here," Bethany said.

In the living room, she saw more powder residue. But that wasn't what she noticed the most. A massive abstract painting almost filled a wall above a gray sofa. Someone had applied acrylic paint in swirls of fuchsia, aqua, lime green, and orange to the edges of the unframed canvas.

May grinned at Bethany's surprise. "A bizarre thing for Dr. K to have, huh?"

"Why do you say that?"

"It's too happy and too loud. I wouldn't have thought Dr. K even liked color. He always wore such dull clothes."

Charlotte's bright outfits came to mind. Gene's red suspenders. *They might have appreciated this painting, but Paul? Odd.* Bethany skirted the sofa to take a closer look at the artwork and saw a signature: *Laura.*

The living room held nothing else of interest. Gray upholstered chairs matched the sofa. One of them, a recliner, faced a wall-mounted TV.

They surveyed the kitchen. The refrigerator held a minimum of items: bread, milk, eggs, condiments, and a take-out container from Wok World. Someone should rid the fridge of spoiling food soon, Bethany thought. "Where's Paul's bedroom?"

May led her down a hall and opened a door. Bethany found a wall switch that operated a black metal lamp on a bedside table dusted with fingerprint powder. Two walls held abstract paintings, one in green and blue and the other in orange and gray, both signed *Laura.* Here, too, the drapes were closed. A navy blue bedspread covered a queen-sized bed. Bethany felt a twinge of sadness at seeing that Paul had made his bed so neatly on the last day of his life. In the bedside table's single drawer, she found a photo in a tarnished silver frame. Paul was pictured in a suit and bow tie with the same woman as in the photo he kept on campus. Here, she wore a strapless white gown and veil. The couple beamed happiness at the camera.

At Bethany's elbow, May said, "The poor guy. He kept his wedding picture. He must've still carried a torch for his ex."

Bethany agreed. "But he didn't display this photo. I'd like to know if her name is Laura."

"I bet it is," May said. "Just shows you."

"Shows you what?"

"That profs have problems with love like everybody else."

Sure, they do. Bethany imagined a solitary Paul taking out this photo to moon over. What emotions and memories had it stirred in him? She put it back and closed the drawer.

A quick check of the closet yielded nothing except the man's wardrobe—sports jackets, shirts, khakis and jeans, tennis togs, two suits, various shoes. Bethany moved on to examine a chest of drawers' contents.

"The police rummaged through his top drawer," May said.

"How do you know?"

"His tighty-whities are jumbled. They should be folded."

That got Bethany's attention. "And you know this how?"

May opened a laundry hamper half filled with dirty clothes. "He had me do his washing while I cleaned. I put everything away for him."

"I hope he paid you well."

"Enough, I guess. I'll miss the extra cash."

"Did I see a door to a second bedroom?"

"His office."

"Show me." Here, too, Bethany found traces of fingerprint powder. Another abstract painting, this one in swirls of purple, silver, and gold covered most of a wall. Bookshelves lined the other walls. The tech-obsessed professor—who kept few books in his office and only accepted students' essays online—had amassed an impressive home library. The bookshelves contained education textbooks as well as books on history, math, and science. Classic novels in hardcover and paperback filled an entire shelf, science fiction another. The man had collected at least fifty books on tennis, from biographies of world-renowned players to books on how to improve one's game.

In the middle of the room, a tall stack of publications sat atop an antique wooden desk. There was no desktop computer or space for one. The desk drawers held the usual office supplies. The desk chair appeared well used; a pillow covered a dip in the seat. *Paul must have sat here reading. For hours probably.*

A buzz sounded at the front door. "Oh no. Somebody's out there," May said. "What should we do?"

Bethany's heart pounded. "Let me think. Answer the door and tell them you're the cleaner."

"Cleaning for a dead guy? At night? Who'll believe that?"

"Go on! Improvise. That's probably a neighbor. If they noticed us and nobody answers the door, they might call 911." She gave May a firm look as the buzz, like the drone of an electric razor, came again.

May disappeared from view, and the buzzing stopped. Bethany heard a woman's muffled words and May's distinct reply: "The family asked me to deal with the garbage, ma'am, and tidy up."

The woman at the door spoke again, and May said, "None of 'em live local."

May is buying me time. Bethany shifted her stance and gasped as the stack of publications toppled to the floor.

"What's that noise?" the stranger asked, distinctly this time.

Bethany dropped to a crouch and held her breath.

"Air conditioner probably," May said. "Coming on, it makes that thunk."

Good improvisation. What May said next, Bethany didn't hear. At her feet lay a number of Meryl Darwood's paperback novels for literacy learners and five-by-eight-inch academic journals like the ones Paul had secreted in his college office.

May returned and looked at the mess on the floor. "That's what thunked. Nosy neighbor's gone, but you'd better hurry in case she calls the cops."

As they picked up the items, Bethany skimmed the journals' tables of contents. Each table listed an article by Paul or a fellow educator, including Eleanor, Vince, and the dean. So Paul had kept track of his colleagues' written output, even Meryl's non-academic work. But why keep all this here rather than in his campus office? *Of course! He didn't want people to know he read printed publications. What a hypocrite!*

Rising, she brushed off her knees and gave the abstract artwork another glance. *Did Laura know about*

Paul's death? That he had displayed her paintings after their divorce?

The insistent sound of her phone cut into her thoughts. *Nathan! Bad timing.* She answered and asked, "May I get back to you? I can't talk right now." She heard a puzzled "okay" and turned to May. "Would you reset the air conditioner? We'd better get out of here."

In the parking lot, she thanked the housekeeper and gave her a twenty-dollar tip.

May didn't refuse the cash. "That didn't help, did it?"

"But worth a try," Bethany assured her. "You never know; something we saw might turn out to be significant."

****

After May took off in her panel truck, Bethany drove to a nearby apartment complex and returned Nathan's call. "I'm in the car on my way home."

"Talking to me while you're driving? That's not safe."

"No, I stopped by some apartments. Should we talk now, or can you wait 'til I'm home?"

"I took the job. I wanted you to know right away."

Bethany's teeth snapped together. It literally hurt to ask, "Are you excited about it?"

"Don't know. Are you happy for me?"

"You seemed on the fence the last time we spoke."

A couple parked in the next space but paid no attention to Bethany sitting in the dark.

"Seems I hesitated long enough for the Hartshorns to sweeten the offer," Nathan said. "They added ten percent to the salary. They'll give me a decent amount of time off as long as it isn't prime tourist season or during one of the hunts. Guess I'm a desirable hire."

Her mouth dry, her teeth zinging, she said, "They're lucky to get you. You'll do great." Did she sound robotic? "When are you coming back to New Mexico?"

"Tomorrow. I'll drive to the Carters' place in one long haul. I'll give them two weeks' notice. Not much, but the Hartshorns need help fixing up the guest cabins for the high season. A bunch of families are coming after the schools let out."

Bethany could hardly endure listening to his plans. But hadn't she expected this decision? Didn't she want the best for Nathan, no matter how it affected her life?

"Bethany? Are you still there? Can you hear me?"

"I'm here."

"Hey, don't be sad. I'm coming to Las Cuevas soon, remember? To go to that hotsy-totsy affair with you."

"The Darwoods' Spring Fling. Don't call it hotsy-totsy. The invitations say *Business Casual*. That means you in pressed jeans and a nice shirt, me in a dress and sandals. Expect a cross between a cocktail party and a fiesta. You met one of the mariachis who will play. Lenny."

"The grad student."

A young man got out of a two-seater convertible, spoke into his phone, then hopped back into the car and drove off. People went in and out of the apartment buildings. How many of them, like her, were dealing with heartache? She shifted into drive but kept her foot on the brake. "You take care on the road."

"Sure thing. We'll talk more tomorrow, darlin'."

Fisting her eyelids to suppress tears, she mulled the fact that nothing in life is a sure thing.

****

At her house, Bethany ran a hot bath, her tension releaser of long practice. She sat in the tub with her back against a pink inflatable pillow she'd had since childhood and brought Nathan to mind. His sandy hair usually needed a trim. She imagined caressing his face and sliding her fingers through that hair. She set the fantasy in a spa with an in-room Jacuzzi rather than her ordinary white tub.

If only they could get away together soon, but he wouldn't have time. He'd be reporting to his new job. But he'd be at the Darwoods' party on Saturday. That commitment surely meant he didn't intend to stop seeing her.

The bath water gone cold, she stepped out of the tub and toweled briskly. In her bedroom, she dressed in leggings and a white T-shirt. She vowed to stop fretting about the future. Worrying would do her no good.

In the kitchen, she popped open a can of sparkling water and took it and a bag of tortilla chips to her backyard. The night birds called to each other, and the traffic hummed on Main Street a couple blocks away. She closed her eyes to think about the search of Paul Kiefer's condo. The guy had collected all those books and journals where he could read them in private. He saw those abstract paintings every day. Was Laura the ex-wife? If so, had Paul displayed those paintings to torture himself? Didn't he want to heal after the divorce? Would Paul's friend Vince Morrison know?

She and Vince had exchanged phone numbers. She went inside for her cell phone, returned to the patio, and called Vince. *No luck.* She left a message, then lingered outside until the cool air penetrated her ready-for-bed clothes. Time to get some sleep.

****

When Vince returned her call, Bethany surfaced from a dream of wandering barefooted in a maze of college corridors. She struggled to register Vince's apology for phoning at 11:00 p.m. "But you sounded like it was important," he said.

She snapped to attention. "I've been thinking about Paul's ex-wife. Do you remember her first name?"

"Why? I doubt Laura knows anything about Paul's death."

Laura. Yes! "I'm still curious about her. Did you know that May, the college custodian, cleaned for Paul?"

"No, but what's that got to do with Laura?"

"Did Paul ever invite you to his condo?"

"Once or twice. Bethany…"

"What was it like?"

"Like? A guy's condo. Modern."

"Sure, but what else? How did he decorate it?"

"I get it. You mean with Laura's paintings. How do you know about them? From May?"

"I don't like to say."

"From May, obviously. She's making trouble for a decent, innocent woman."

Bethany took note of his defense of Paul's ex-wife. "Forget about May. You've met Laura?"

"Yeah. She might still be in town."

"In Las Cuevas? Wasn't Paul divorced when he came to NMU?"

"Separated. Then he and Laura tried to patch things up. She joined him after he moved here. They lived together in his condo for about six months. Paul said she did some painting there. Then she moved out to live with another guy. Paul got a divorce but kept the paintings.

199

Did May tell you what they look like?"

He didn't need to know May let her into the condo. "They're abstracts. Large ones."

"Yeah, that's right. Paul said they were the kind of art he didn't mind on his walls. Realistic subjects distracted him from concentrating on his research or coursework. He wouldn't have been able to work surrounded by the Western scenes in my home office. He said Laura's mindless art suited him."

"Did Laura know Paul called her work mindless?"

"No idea."

"Do you know the guy she left him for?"

"Nope. Paul didn't mention her after they split. Oh, wait, he did say he saw her on the street one time, about a year later, and that she'd gotten a better job."

"Better job? Better than what?"

"Oh, I guess you wouldn't know. She's a grade-school art teacher, but when she moved here, she could only get a job as a teacher's assistant. When Paul bumped into her, she said she'd nailed a full-time teaching position and was going for a master's degree. But maybe she left town."

Eager to be alone with her thoughts, Bethany thanked Vince for the information. She stayed up until midnight. Had Laura not minded leaving those paintings behind? Or had Paul refused to let them go? If she hadn't left Las Cuevas, had something happened recently that prompted her to drug his coffee and swaddle his head in tape?

Chapter 23

Eleanor's digital clock's red numbers flipped to a new day. She hadn't managed even to doze on her side of the king-sized bed. Wayne slept peacefully, as usual, in the middle, his body pressed close to hers. Events and information she hadn't shared with him weighed on her mind. She hadn't mentioned giving Bethany access to Paul's office, or Paul's blackmailing of Gene, or Charlotte's attraction to Paul. She hadn't said Bethany's Nathan might take a job in Wyoming.

Wayne had enough to deal with. The urge to retire had unsettled him. He took pride in the Foundation. He devoted much more of his life to it than the Jarviss oil-and-gas business and the newer solar enterprise. Could he pass his Foundation role on to Bethany and become a camp follower at Don's tournaments, a guest at Joni's B&B? Or would he take on another charitable cause as a volunteer or board member? Eleanor shifted the covers and lay flat on her back, listening to his breathing. Usually, it lulled her to sleep, but it didn't do the trick tonight.

Should she speak to the dean again? Ask him to dismiss his and Meryl's suspicion of Charlotte? No, that would lead to a discussion of Charlotte's motives, her reputation for being disorganized, and perhaps never destined to make full prof. Gene was a much more likely suspect. He had admitted to being blackmailed, a juicy morsel of information Gerald would relish hearing. But Gene had flatly denied being a killer.

Alma Gomez's missing essay nagged at Eleanor's consciousness. She made a mental note to make sure Charlotte followed up and reported back about it. Turning on her side, careful not to wake Wayne, she stared into the darkness.

****

Eleanor was attending to departmental business Wednesday morning—reviewing course schedules and pondering how to replace Paul—when Bethany phoned. Eleanor filled her in on her meetings with Gene and Charlotte without mentioning the delicate matter of Charlotte's feelings for Paul.

"Charlotte must be so upset after meeting with Dean Darwood," Bethany said. "Poor woman! And poor Gene too. Mom, I called to tell you about something I did last night."

Eleanor listened without interrupting to an account of the search of Paul's condo.

"You took quite a risk, Bethany. Paul's death canceled May's right to enter his home."

"Well, we did it. You should have seen May. She's a quick thinker. She fended off a nosy neighbor."

Bethany described knocking over the pile of publications. "A guy fanatic about a paper-free society kept all that printed material at home. He had some of Meryl's novels and a boatload of academic journals that published articles by him and other people at NMU, including you, Mom."

Unable to sit still, Eleanor paced the office, shoeless. "It doesn't surprise me that Paul paid attention to what other faculty published. He considered colleagues his competitors and would have assessed our work."

"But Meryl's novels? They aren't in the same category as research papers. Surely, he wouldn't view her publications as competition for his own?"

"No, but he considered the tutor center and literacy program as competitors for funding. I'm not surprised that he wanted to see what Meryl wrote. Or maybe, because Meryl is the dean's wife, Paul had to satisfy his curiosity about her books."

"I guess. I saw something else in Paul's condo. In his bedroom."

Bethany had done a thorough job of snooping. *Thank goodness she wasn't caught.* "What was that, dear?"

"A wedding photo. Of him and the woman in the picture in his campus office. He kept the photo in a drawer of a bedside table. And there were huge abstract paintings on his walls. Signed *Laura*. I phoned Vince Morrison and found out Laura is Paul's ex-wife's name. Vince told me Laura lived there with him for a short time. I'd wrongly assumed Paul was divorced when he came to NMU."

"Is it relevant?"

"I don't know. Did you ever meet her?"

"Once, at a reception. His wife had hoped to teach in one of the public schools, but they had no openings for art teachers because of budget shortfalls."

"Naturally, the arts programs took a hit," Bethany said. "Vince knew that Laura settled for being a teacher's aide. After a few months in town, she left Paul for another man. You must have heard gossip about the breakup."

Eleanor thought back to that time. "I heard some talk

among the women faculty. Speculation about who might mend Paul's broken heart. I haven't thought of his wife in ages and couldn't have told you her first name."

"Vince said she may still live in Las Cuevas. She might be teaching or in a master's program."

"If she were pursuing a master's in education, I think I'd know that. Why does she interest you?"

"Because according to Vince, Paul called her paintings 'mindless.' He left them on his condo's walls because they didn't distract him while he worked."

Eleanor's dislike of the man cranked up a notch. "What a mean thing to say! If he said that to his wife's face—"

"Indeed. Did that make her angry enough to kill him?"

"But she's been out of Paul's life for years."

"Has she? We don't know that, Mom."

"True. Tell me about those paintings." Eleanor closed her eyes as Bethany described the large abstracts.

"They're not generic prints people buy to fill wall space," Bethany said. "Laura might've wanted them back to sell. Paul might have refused. Maybe he kept them to ridicule her. That would make any artist see red."

Eleanor's eyes flew open. "Enough to kill?"

"Okay, I'm brainstorming. Let's say Paul and Laura crossed paths recently. He could've infuriated her enough to wipe that superior look off his face."

"You remember that look?"

"Too well. From our dinner dates," Bethany said. "He assumed I'd hang on his every word about his amazing career. His plans and goals."

Agreeing, Eleanor said, "Paul expected to advance in his career without a hitch."

"I'd like to talk to Laura," Bethany said. "I paid for a rudimentary online search for her and checked the schools and university directories. Zip, zero, nada."

"Some people find Las Cuevas too small. We can assume she came here for her husband's sake, like so many wives, not for her career. She probably went back to where she came from."

"Went back! What if she went back to using her maiden name? Or if she never went by Kiefer? She could be in town, but I wouldn't have found a listing for her."

"But still, she must have had nothing to do with Paul for years."

"Like I said, they might've come across each other not too long ago. Mom, if Jereen isn't too busy…"

"You'd like her to try to track Laura down? That would make Jereen curious, don't you think?" Eleanor rubbed her neck. She would not succumb to a headache before noon.

"Tell Jereen you want to offer your condolences. These days, it's not unusual to send a sympathy card to ex-partners."

"I won't need to involve Jereen. I have contacts of long-standing in the grad school and the school district, people who will be discreet. But first, I have to attend to my own tasks."

Eleanor returned to her desk. She slipped on her shoes to make herself get down to business. She'd deal with the fall semester schedule, then try to locate Paul's ex-wife.

****

Grant applications kept Bethany busy until noon. She stretched her arms overhead and did her jaw exercises. When would she learn to take breaks? To not let deskwork overwhelm her? As part of her relaxation routine, she gazed at the artworks on her walls: two rural New Mexico scenes—one with a red truck dwarfed by the landscape—four close-ups of flowers and a monochrome photo of a cloudy sky over a harsh, beautiful desert. Each presented a striking take on reality.

Laura's art bore no resemblance to the iconic prints. But like these works, Laura's paintings had integrity, Bethany judged. Admittedly, she was no art expert. She had only taken a couple undergraduate art history classes. A business student, she had been more buttoned up than the expressive, free-spirited art bunch. Most lived for the day rather than preparing for financially profitable careers. But Paul's Laura had been practical. She had become a teacher. By now, she may have acquired a master's in education. *But why assume education? Why not a Master of Fine Arts from the College of Arts and Sciences?*

Bethany searched the NMU Department of Art website. No help; graduate students weren't listed, and the faculty listings contained no Laura. The department's homepage promoted the annual spring exhibition of student work, set to open Friday in the university's art gallery. Bethany had attended shows in the rambling building's annex. *Might be worth it to stop by the department to see if anyone knows a local artist named Laura.*

****

An odor of paint and something else—grit from the ceramics studio?—permeated the art building's interior. Seeing the front office locked at lunchtime, Bethany followed voices coming from the public gallery. Two guys, presumably students, walked a sculpture toward a pedestal under the watchful eye of a man in a hands-on-hips supervisory stance. The sculpture consisted of a bird cage containing a globe of the Earth resting on crushed beer cans and plastic drink bottles. *Statement art.*

The students set the piece under two mobiles dangling from a high ceiling. One was composed of electrical cords and discarded cell phones, another of leafless tree branches and small animal skulls and bones strung on fishing line.

The older man said, "The exhibition doesn't open until Friday. You can see we're installing it." He spoke politely but made it clear he considered her an intruder.

He couldn't be called handsome, but Bethany liked his wiry body and craggy, forty-something face. "I'm trying to find an artist who might be a graduate student," she said. "Laura Kiefer. Although she might go by another surname."

One of the students cut in, "Professor Dooley, what do you think?"

"Looks good, Noah."

"Yes!" Noah high-fived the other guy.

"Jeb, is your piece ready?"

"Yes, sir, I think it's dry enough."

"Go check, gentlemen."

The two raced off without glancing at Bethany. But the professor gave her a sharp once-over that didn't feel sexual. He might have been an alert airport security guard.

"Why are you looking for Laura?" he asked. "Are you interested in her art?"

Bethany's pulse quickened. "Yes, I am." *Sort of a true statement.*

"Come take a look then. Our graduate students'

pieces are farther back."

He led the way past artworks in a succession of partitioned areas that reminded Bethany of the troubling dream of being lost in a maze. Each area contained more sculptures until they reached a wall hung with paintings.

"Here's Laura's work." He pointed to a trio of collages, each about five feet square. Up close, Bethany saw the same signature as in Paul's condo. On top of abstract paintings of various hues, Laura had pasted faces cut from snapshots, snippets of handwriting, portions of postcards, bits of lace, dried flowers, and other items.

"Intriguing, but I don't know what to make of these," Bethany said.

"Laura has yet to post an artist's statement. What she writes will put the triptych in context. Tell me, how do you know her?"

Honesty. The best policy. "I don't. I knew her ex-husband, Paul Kiefer."

Startled, he stepped back but recovered quickly. "Terrible how he was killed. It's been all over social media. I find it hard to believe a murder happened on our campus."

"Do you know if Laura is around? I'd like to talk to her."

The professor's scrutiny intensified. "And who might you be?"

"My mother was Paul Kiefer's department head. Eleanor Jarviss."

"Hello, Eleanor."

"No, that's my mother. I'm Bethany. Bethany Jarviss."

She extended her hand. He clasped it with cool

fingers. "Dr. Jason Dooley. Dooley to all and sundry. So why are you here?"

"I'm helping my mother."

"To do what?"

Improvising, she said, "To extend the department's sympathies."

"To Laura? Why? She and Paul were divorced."

So he knows that. "Nevertheless, his death must affect her. It's affected my mother's entire department."

"Which department is that?"

"Curriculum and instruction. In the education college where Paul Kiefer taught."

"Do you teach there too?"

"No, I'm with the Jarviss Foundation."

Dooley's face expressed a sudden interest. "I know of the Foundation. Too bad none of your grants have been to this department." His smile softened the sting in his words but quickly vanished. "But why did you come instead of your mother?"

Bethany thought fast. "I'm an MBA student with classes not far from here. I volunteered to look up Laura. If you have her number, perhaps you could give it to me."

He considered the request, reluctantly, it seemed. "I could phone and ask if she's willing to see you. She might be in the building." He turned away to make the call.

Waiting, Bethany scrutinized the three collages. In the central one, she noticed a heads-only portion of the wedding photo she'd found in Paul's bedroom. The smiling couple might have been decapitated.

Chapter 24

Behind Bethany, a woman said, "The collages represent my life experiences."

A brunette about Bethany's height stood beside the professor.

"This is Laura," Dooley said as he put his arm around her. He kissed her cheek. "Laura and I live together. I'd call her my girlfriend, but she doesn't appreciate that word."

Why didn't he mention they're a couple?

"He's right," Laura said. "I don't like girlfriend or wife or partner. Or any term that sounds possessive. They're always used with a 'my' in front of them. Dooley said you're a bearer of condolences. From Paul's department head. Your mother."

"She and her colleagues are so sorry about his death."

"Condolences aren't necessary. That's what I told the campus police officer when she called. And the two city cops who showed up in the painting studio and questioned me in front of other grad students."

As she spoke, she stepped away from Dooley's embrace. "By the way, my last name is Vansetti. I never took the name Kiefer. I kept an identity apart from that of wife."

Bethany admired Laura's blunt-cut hairstyle, a shorter version of her own. Dark-haired women definitely had been Paul's type. Bethany saw elements of herself in this thinner, prettier woman who wore no discernable makeup.

"You must have met Paul," Laura said. "Did he ask you out?"

Startled, Bethany admitted, "We had dinner a couple times a few months ago."

"Only twice?"

"He didn't ask a third time. I didn't give him what he wanted."

"You refused him sex? That must have thrown him!" Laura puffed out her well-shaped lips.

"No, no. He was after a grant for his research."

Dooley said, "Bethany is with her family's charity, the Jarviss Foundation."

"You don't fund projects at NMU?" Laura asked.

"A scholarship and a literacy program. Mostly, we support community projects. Day-care centers and senior centers in remote towns, and the Cuevas Café."

"You weren't going to fund Paul's computer lab?"

"You knew about that? Had you seen him recently?"

Laura glanced at Dooley. "He came to see me the other day when I was finishing my pieces for the exhibit."

"You didn't tell me!" Dooley said, astonished.

"It wasn't worth mentioning. He only stayed a few minutes."

"What did he want?" he asked, saving Bethany from posing the question.

Laura addressed them both. "To brag. To tell me he was about to be made a full prof years before the usual time."

Dooley assumed his hands-on-hips stance. "But you

weren't in contact with him. How did he know where to find you?"

"He'd seen a flyer about the student show and asked in the art office if I would be exhibiting. He acted surprised that I have an assistantship. He used to scoff at my paintings."

"Her work is complex," Dooley said. "Her adviser has the highest praise for what Laura produced this semester. And no, I'm not her adviser. We met in my class but didn't get together until after I posted the grades."

"TMI, Dooley," Laura said with a shake of her head.

Privately, Bethany agreed. "If I may ask, how did Paul react to your collages?"

Laura laughed. "He saw the abstract paintings underneath and said, 'Good use for them. You didn't have to invest in new canvasses.' "

"You didn't tell me any of this!" Dooley said. "I hope you spat in the bastard's face."

"Why? Paul didn't understand the first thing about art. Or me. I ordered him out of the studio."

She faced Bethany. "For about one second, I felt like killing him. He looked me up to brag about himself and tried to get under my skin. But I didn't let him." She spread her arms before the triptych. "Paul saw that I've moved on."

"I'm eager to read your artist's statement," Dooley said.

"Paul's name won't be in it. I don't want to have to talk to the police again."

Dooley moved toward Bethany. "Did you come here with the idea that Laura might be fitted up for Kiefer's murder?"

Bethany's jaw tensed. "That's ridiculous."

"As is any thought that Laura might have done it. Now, please excuse us, Ms. Jarviss. You've conveyed your mother's condolences and seen my…" He stopped short of saying girlfriend or partner. "Seen Laura."

"I'll walk Ms. Jarviss out," Laura said.

Bethany felt Dooley's gaze drill into her back. They passed the students she'd seen earlier, this time with the other's sculpture: a ragged, white-flocked Christmas tree decorated with children's play money and piggy banks painted red, white, or blue.

"You finished it, Jeb. Good for you," Laura said in passing.

When they reached the lobby, Bethany asked, "What are your duties as a grad assistant? Do you teach classes?"

"Art history. And I supervise the undergrads' painting studio. Somebody has to make them clean up."

"You used to be a public school teacher?"

Laura frowned. "Yes, my parents were teachers and assumed I'd be one. I taught while Paul worked on his doctorate in Chicago, but here, I could only get a job as a teacher's assistant at first. I considered going for my MFA, but he didn't encourage me to do it."

"He had big plans for himself but not for you."

"I shouldn't talk ill of him. He didn't realize he was a sexist. He believed I left him for another man, but I did it because he didn't take me seriously as an artist."

"You didn't leave him for Dooley?"

"Dooley? No! We met well after that." She checked the lobby for listeners and, with no one else close by, said, "Everyone is talking about how Paul died. The police went through the desk I share with another grad assistant. They asked if I used packing tape. Not in my art, I told them, but if I ever sell a piece and have to mail it, I might. They didn't laugh.

"Ms. Jarviss, you may think I wished Paul harm, but I didn't. We had some good years together. Then, I got sick of being his support system, of having to proof and praise every little thing he wrote. One time, he said I should be glad he wrote his own papers."

"Why'd he say that?"

"Because he knew a doctoral candidate's girlfriend who did most of his research and even drafted part of his dissertation. I told Paul not to think I'd do that for him. I had my hands full teaching and starting on a master's."

"You began an MFA before you came here?"

"No, an MA in education, but I had to drop out to move here with Paul. Turns out this is a better program for me, the MFA. Since it's a terminal degree, I'll be able to teach at the university level. I'll be expected to produce my own art, a good challenge. When you teach art in the public schools, nobody much cares if you're an artist if you keep the kids occupied. Not that I don't like kids!"

"Did you and Paul plan to have children?" Immediately, Bethany thought the question too personal.

But Laura didn't take offense. "I wanted kids, but Paul said we should wait. For me, there's still time." With Dooley or another partner, she didn't say.

She consulted her paint-flecked watch. "I'd better finish my statement about the triptych. Tell your mother I appreciate the condolences, but other females must be mourning Paul's passing more than me."

"His students?"

"Females in his classes always had crushes on him,

or so he said. And he might have had a thing for a student or two."

"Dark-haired students?"

Laura's cheeks dimpled. "Paul always went for brunettes. But even if he lusted after an undergraduate, he would have kept it in his pants. He wouldn't have allowed his lust to interfere with his professional plans."

Remembering their dinner dates, Bethany said, "He did seem focused on his research."

"Not as much as on his self-image," Laura scoffed. "For a long time, I felt lucky to be chosen by such a brilliant man. That seems ages ago."

"Now you know your worth."

"I sense that you do too." Laura said goodbye without commenting on their physical similarity, but surely, by mentioning brunettes, she'd noticed it.

What a strong woman! She'd found her niche after the divorce. Had she gotten over Paul, or was she lying about that, maybe to herself as well as to the world?

Outdoors, away from the paint and dust odors, Bethany reached Eleanor by phone. "Mom, I tracked down Laura. Her surname is Vansetti; she never went by Kiefer. I talked to her for about fifteen minutes. This is the first chance I've had to call you. I hope you didn't try to find her."

Eleanor said not to worry. "I did, but I can call my contacts again and say I have what I need. Tell me about this woman!"

Bethany summarized meeting Laura and Dooley. "Professor Dooley tensed up at the mention of Paul."

"Could he be the killer?"

"Maybe…" Bethany said.

"But you doubt it."

"Paul posed no major threat to Laura or Professor Dooley, as far as I can tell. At the worst, they might have barred him from the gallery opening."

Nevertheless, she wouldn't eliminate the artist couple from her suspects list. She had only Laura's word about what happened during the recent encounter with Paul.

Chapter 25

Bethany sat near the Old Quad's fountain, wishing she were as happy in her graduate program as Laura seemed to be in hers. Wayne often bragged that she had "a head for business." He heartily approved of her pursuit of an MBA, and usually, the classes posed no problem for her. But she didn't look forward to an intense summer class she'd signed up for; she could use a break from the grind of grad school. *The grind.* A telling word choice. She sighed.

Her phone buzzed. *Mom again. Why so soon?*

"Charlotte called," Eleanor said. "Since she took over the class Paul taught that Alma is in, I had her check to see if Alma's essay is in the online system."

"Smart of you, Mom. Is it there?"

"Charlotte couldn't find it. She contacted the computer folks. They've had no glitches in the system."

As Bethany mulled over that interesting news, students streamed past. Several classes must have let out. "Maybe Alma never turned it in, or Paul deleted it and denied receiving it."

"Equally troubling scenarios," Eleanor said. "If Paul deleted it, he might have done so to make her beg to be allowed an extension of the deadline."

"Maybe in exchange for having sex with him," Bethany concluded.

She heard a "hmm," then: "Alma didn't say he

pressured her for sex, correct?"

"Only that he favored pretty girls," Bethany admitted. "But if Alma murdered him, she wouldn't mention everything that went on between them. I assume Charlotte will tell Alma the essay isn't there."

"Yes, but I don't know what Charlotte will do about it. Unfortunately, we only have one side of the story. Paul isn't alive to tell his side."

"If he were alive, we wouldn't be having this conversation. Catch you later, Mom."

Bethany tapped her phone's weather app, which predicted clear sailing on Nathan's route. Unfortunately, no app could predict if his rattletrap truck would make it to the Carters' ranch.

Her thoughts pinged back to Charlotte and Alma. What did Charlotte make of the student? And was Charlotte still shaken up from practically being accused by Dean Darwood of murder? Or had she exaggerated the dean's comments? She had a dramatic, emotional temperament. She might need some friendly support.

Bethany made tracks for the education building, but Charlotte's office door was locked. As she read Charlotte's posted schedule, a passing student offered, "Dr. Kline's behind the building, taking it easy." She grinned and moved on.

From the vending machines in a nearby nook, Bethany bought a bottled water and a granola bar. She found Charlotte sitting on the ground, her back to a freshly leafed-out tree, her tie-dyed skirt spread over her legs. She waved half a sandwich. "Bethany! Want to share? The twins made my lunch."

"I'll join you, but I brought something of my own." Bethany plopped down, hoping not to get grass stains on her wheat-colored slacks. *Oh, well.* In the relaxing spot, she found it hard to care.

"I lunch out here when the weather permits. To soak up the earth's energy." Charlotte took a bag of red grapes from a small cooler. "Have some. One of the twins washed them. I saw it with my own eyes."

They munched grapes companionably, and Bethany nibbled on the granola bar.

"Did Eleanor send you to cheer me up?" Charlotte asked.

"No, but she told me the dean called you into his office and what he said."

Charlotte narrowed her gaze. "I've been visualizing his comments rolling off my back and soaking into the bark of this tree."

Poor tree.

As if she had heard the thought, Charlotte leaned away from the trunk. "I imagine the dean's words as pure energy that can cause no harm. Do you believe he as much as said Meryl thinks I killed Paul?"

"That must have hurt."

"It did. I think he suspects me, too, but he didn't say that. It's just like Gerald to hide behind his wife's skirts. And before you ask, no, I haven't confronted Meryl. I'm not that assertive."

"I'm sorry you're going through this, Charlotte."

"And I'm sorry that Eleanor has to lead our department while we're all murder suspects. Maybe we all did it, like in that Agatha Christie book." Charlotte sipped bottled tea. "This tastes like pee. I keep drinking horrible-tasting things. Why do I do that?"

"Have some water?"

"Bless you!" She drank from Bethany's bottle and

handed it back.

"The killer isn't necessarily in your department," Bethany pointed out. "It could be anyone on or off campus. By the way, Mom said you didn't find Alma Gomez's essay in the computer system."

"After I spoke with Eleanor, I emailed Alma to give her until 5:00 p.m. today to submit it to me directly by email. If she did the work, the deadline should be no problem."

The ethereal Charlotte could be a hard-headed pragmatist, Bethany thought. But then she thought again. "If Alma didn't turn in the essay originally, Paul's death gave her extra time to finish it."

"True." Charlotte stowed the residue from her lunch in the cooler. "Submitting it now won't prove her innocent of the murder."

Bethany watched a glum Charlotte head back to her office. On the way to her SUV, Bethany checked her phone. *No message from Nathan.* She drove back to the Foundation, as glum as the older woman.

****

At five-fifteen, Charlotte called Bethany. "Alma emailed me her essay. I informed Eleanor, and she asked me to tell you. Alma admitted she revised parts of it. I asked to see the original version, but she said she didn't keep it. She revised the file on her computer. She hadn't made a printout of the original because Dr. Kiefer frowned on killing trees."

"Do you think she failed to meet his deadline?"

"No other students had trouble submitting their essays electronically, according to the computer center folks."

"Mom told me you contacted them."

"Bethany, I'm worried. Alma sounded almost too happy, like she'd pulled off something sneaky. Since she emailed me that essay, my brain's been racing like a gerbil on a wheel. But she might have sounded excited simply because she's going to a birthday party for a young cousin tonight. At Los Mariachis. Bethany, could you—"

Bethany finished the sentence. "Have a word with Alma at the restaurant."

"Would you? Expect it to be noisy. Alma said they'll have a piñata. Another cousin's mariachi band will be playing."

"Lenny. I've met him. By the way, did you read Alma's essay? Or would telling me breach faculty-student confidentiality?"

"I suppose, but my intentions are pure. I've skimmed the essay. Alma should earn her usual A."

"What's it about?"

"How students do better academically in schools with high-tech classrooms. She didn't emphasize enough that those schools tend to be in higher-income neighborhoods where students have their own computers, plenty to eat at home, and parents who can afford tutors. Still, the essay is sound undergraduate work, with a list of sources that includes articles by Paul."

"Alma wrote that paper to flatter him. He would've welcomed her topic," Bethany said. "I wonder what's bothering her. I'm always in the mood for Mexican food. I'll talk to her."

"Thanks, Bethany. Can you let me know what she says? And enjoy the food."

"I will. On both counts."

Too distracted to work, Bethany's thoughts spun like Charlotte's. Had Alma failed to submit the essay to Paul? Or had he deleted it from the system? Had either scenario led to his death?

Chapter 26

In Los Mariachis, Lenny's band competed for attention with kids in party hats blowing noisemakers. Someone had decorated one side of the restaurant with balloons, a cat-shaped piñata, and a banner shouting, *Happy 10th Birthday, Alicia!* At the head of a line of tables, the birthday girl, in a frilly dress and glitzy tiara, faced a pile of presents. Bethany didn't see Alma Gomez among the throng.

Bethany told a server in an off-the-shoulder Mexican blouse that she hadn't come for the party. The server ushered her to a table away from the action and plunked down a menu. "I have to warn you. The service is sort of slow tonight."

Bethany didn't check the menu; she ordered a combination plate. As she waited, she watched the band and tapped a foot in time to the music. Lenny caught her eye and spoke to his fellow players. The music stopped, which seemed to intensify the party group's roar. Lumbering toward her, Lenny mopped his face and tattooed neck with a rumpled handkerchief.

"Hello, Ms. Jarviss," he said respectfully. "Looking for me?"

"For Alma. I heard she might be here."

"For the birthday party? Yeah, it's for one of our cousins."

"You and Alma are second cousins, right?"

"That's right." He placed a hand on a chairback. "Can I join you?"

"Of course."

The chair squeaked under his weight. "I won't bother you for long. We're not supposed to be on break." He lowered his voice. "Did you talk to Dr. Lamont?"

"Yes, I did. She disapproved of the way Dr. Kiefer dealt with your thesis topic."

"Did she say why she called him an evil bastard?"

"She doesn't recall using the word 'evil,' but it looks like you witnessed the end of their relationship."

"I bet he didn't treat her right. Male members of the species can be bastards to women. Not me, though. I'm nice to the ladies." He rubbed the tattoo as if it bothered him. "But I didn't used to be."

"You must be a role model for your high school students. I bet they're impressed you're going for a master's."

"*Absolutamente*, as we say in *español*. Thanks a bunch if you had anything to do with Dr. Jarviss saying she'll supervise my thesis."

"No thanks needed. I knew Mom planned to call you. I'm glad that's working out."

"She's all for my topic. Mariachi clubs help keep teens in school. I'm going to prove it."

The server brought chips and salsa and two glasses of water. He drank and wiped his mouth with the back of his hand. His gaze followed the server's swaying hips as she moved off.

"A cousin?" Bethany asked.

"*Gracias a Dios*, no. She's a pretty one, but too young for me, only a freshman at NMU. But college girls mature fast." He wiggled his eyebrows. "Hey, there's

Alma and her friend."

Alma and Roxanne, in skimpy dresses, paused at the room's entrance. Then Alma led the way to the party table and added a gift to the pile. There were no empty chairs for the students. As they scanned the room, Lenny stood up, and Bethany gestured to her table. Alma and Roxanne came toward them reluctantly.

On the stage, the mariachis resumed strumming their guitars. Lenny kissed Alma on the cheek and said hello to Roxanne. As they seated themselves, he said, "Wish I could stay, but those *hombres* sound lame without me. Excuse me, ladies." He downed the rest of his water and returned to his fellow musicians.

Bethany asked Alma, "What did you bring the birthday girl?"

"A book about horses," Alma said. "Alicia is horse crazy. Her *padres*—parents—are giving her riding lessons."

A Spanish tune blasted them, but neither student paid attention to it. Alma smiled woodenly, but Roxanne only looked nervous.

"Roxanne, Alma told me you two went to the campus police." Bethany let the statement hang in the air.

"We haven't heard anything since," Alma said.

"If you gave an accurate report, you shouldn't have problems." False assurance. Bethany had no idea what the police would do with Roxanne's information. She turned to Alma. "So you cleared up the issue with your essay."

Alma's heavy lashes fluttered. "How do you know that?"

Not exactly answering, Bethany said, "Because

anything that might relate to Dr. Kiefer's murder interests me. Surely, you both want to see his killer caught."

"We do," Roxanne said. She cast a pleading look at Alma.

Alma ignored her friend. "But my essay has nothing to do with the murder."

"Dr. Kline said you improved the essay before you emailed it to her," Bethany said.

"So?"

"Other students didn't have extra time. You had an advantage over students whose papers Dr. Kiefer graded."

"They could ask Dr. Kline to let them revise their essays."

The server brought Bethany's meal and offered two more menus. Alma gestured to the noisy group across the room. "We are birthday guests. We will eat over there."

Bethany didn't drop the subject at hand. To Roxanne, she said, "How did you do on your essay, if I may ask?"

The girl hugged herself as if for warmth. "Dr. Kiefer gave me a B."

"A good grade," Alma said.

"Super good for me," Roxanne agreed. He usually gave me a C."

Abruptly, Alma said, "Alicia is opening her presents. I want to see if she likes mine. Roxanne, let's go watch."

Bethany felt Alma's rebuff as keenly as if a door had been slammed in her face. She watched as chairs were found for the two students and meals brought. Alma took one ladylike bite after another, but Roxanne picked at her food. As Bethany ate her own meal, she wished she knew what troubled Alma's companion. Not a B grade when she expected a C.

Bethany's phone buzzed. *Nathan, finally!* The birthday commotion made it hard to hear him, but she got that he'd returned to the Carters' ranch after a long, uneventful drive.

"Can you speak louder, Nathan? Did you give the Carters notice?"

"Nah, not yet. I kind of hate to. They're such decent folks. But I will. I can't wait to get back to Wyoming. It's beautiful country. Hey, I never asked if you've been to Laramie."

"Once, a long time ago. On a family car trip."

"It's still small, like Las Cuevas. But the university has huge, cool buildings. I walked around the main part of it."

"Think you might take classes there?"

"Don't know what I'd study or if they'd want an old guy like me."

Bethany watched Alicia rip the gift paper off the book from Alma. The little girl blew Alma a kiss and snatched another gift from the pile.

"Any university has mature students," Bethany said. "Mom's told you that."

"I should've tried to get into NMU. But the two hours to Las Cuevas would've worn me out. I'll only be about an hour from Laramie."

"Convenient."

"Yep, the Hartshorns' guests aren't isolated. If they get tired of the ranch, they can go into town and hit the shops and the bars."

Bethany lost her appetite as Nathan talked. He

planned to rent a trailer for the move. "I own more than fits in my truck."

"Your trophies alone would fill it," Bethany joked, then worried about referring to glory days Nathan could never repeat.

But he took the comment in stride. "Heck, my boots and hats would do that."

Alicia, done opening the gifts, jumped up as a man produced a pink bandanna and plastic wand with streamers. Kids crowded around the papier-mâché cat. The man waved the bandanna in the air, then blindfolded Alicia.

Meanwhile, Bethany faintly heard Nathan lament the cost of trailer rental. "Louder, Nathan! I'm at Los Mariachis. There's a birthday party going on, and it's piñata time."

"That explains the screaming kids. How 'bout I call again tomorrow? I'm bushed."

"Good idea. Get some sleep."

"Night then."

He hadn't asked why she was at the restaurant again. But he had big things on his mind; she needed to cut him some slack.

The mariachis punctuated the piñata action with musical notes. Alicia struck out with the wand and hit air three times. The next child in line looked like a preschooler. Not much chance of him breaking the piñata. If all went well, every child would get a turn before a lucky one emptied the cat of candy.

Roxanne seemed to be the only person in the party group not having fun. She produced her wallet, obviously to pay for her meal, but Alma shook her head and resumed watching the children. Unnoticed by Alma,

Roxanne made a quick exit.

Bethany tossed cash onto the table and trailed her. In the early evening daylight, Roxanne was hoofing it toward NMU. Bethany dashed to her car. She drove until she caught up with the student, then pulled to the curb. "Can I give you a ride? I'm going past campus."

A horn sounded behind them. Bethany motioned the driver to go around and got a second, angry honk in response. "Jump in!"

Roxanne looked uncertain but got into the SUV. *A compliant type, this young lady.*

"Thanks, Ms. Jarviss."

"You left that fiesta early."

"I love kids, but they were going so crazy, my head hurts. It was sweet of Alma to invite me, though."

"You and Alma are good friends, aren't you?"

"She does a lot for me." Roxanne fingered her purse strap.

The seatbelt buzzer sounded. "Better buckle up," Bethany said.

"Oh, right."

Bethany tried to sound casual. "What else does Alma do for you?"

Roxanne hugged her purse as if it were a comforting stuffed animal. "Nothing special."

"You said she does a lot. A lot of nothing special?" She tried to make light of the words.

"That came out wrong. Mostly, she helps me with my homework."

In a flash, Bethany understood. "She helped you with that essay for Dr. Kiefer."

"Yeah. She saved me."

"Did she write it for you?"

Roxanne shook her head in an emphatic no. "I would never have someone write a whole paper for me. I'm not a cheater."

"Well then, what did she do?"

"Some editing. And she helped me with my sources. We have to document everything and be careful not to plagiarize. I'm awful at what you call citing sources. Alma's a whiz, and she likes to show people how to do it. She could charge for it, but she doesn't."

"So what's the problem?"

"The problem?"

"You seem troubled. Is it about the help Alma gave you?" Seeing an open street-side parking space, Bethany took it. "Roxanne? It'll help to talk about whatever it is."

"Alma fell asleep. In my room on my bed while I was fixing my sources like she showed me. I finished them, submitted the essay, and put my head down on my arms. Next thing I knew, it was hours later. Alma hadn't finished her own essay. She'd planned to only help me for an hour and then go back to her place."

"Then what happened?"

"Nothing! She missed Dr. Kiefer's deadline because she stayed with me too long. He never accepted late work unless we asked for an extension beforehand."

Bethany absorbed Roxanne's story. "Alma lied to Dr. Kiefer. She told him she had submitted the essay."

"Yes, but he didn't believe her. He said students had given him that 'song and dance' before. Alma said he used those exact words: 'song and dance.' "

Softly, Bethany asked, "What did Alma do then?"

"I don't know!" Roxanne wailed. "I don't like to think about it!"

"Did she tell Dr. Kiefer she'd helped you, then fell

asleep? Did she admit the truth?"

"She couldn't do that. He might have suspected, like you kind of did, that she wrote my essay for me. One time, when a bunch of us did badly on a quiz, he said some students weren't fit to be in college. He isn't, wasn't, I mean, a fan of the tutor center where I go all the time. Alma couldn't tell him about helping me. He might've given me an F, and for sure he would've given her a zero for missing the deadline. If he hadn't died." Roxanne brushed tears from her pale cheeks.

"You worry that Alma killed Dr. Kiefer, don't you?"

"No! Yes, maybe. Could she have taken my pills, Ms. Jarviss? But if she did, she wouldn't have called you about my problem, right? She wouldn't have gone to the campus cops with me. Oh, I wish I hadn't lost that bottle!"

"Why did you tell her about losing it?"

"She's my friend. She's easy to talk to, like you. What should I do, Ms. Jarviss? I don't want to cause her trouble. She's always good to me. Tonight, she paid for my meal even though I would've been glad to."

"Paying for you seems fair. She invited you to that noisy party."

Roxanne responded with a wan smile.

"I know that Dr. Kline took over your class," Bethany said. "When does it meet again?"

"Tomorrow. For an hour and a half."

"I'll stop by at the end. We can take Alma aside and ask her to tell Dr. Kline the true story about the essays. Does Dr. Kline teach another class after yours? Do you and Alma have other classes?"

"We don't, and Dr. Kline has her office hours."

"Great. Let's see if Alma will tell the truth."

"But what if Dr. Kline gives her an F?"

"Dr. Kline is a sympathetic person. But even if she penalizes Alma, your friend's conscience will be clear, and you can stop worrying. Perhaps Alma should come clean to the campus police too, but first things first."

"And if Alma isn't willing to talk to Dr. Kline?"

"Then you should tell her, and I'll support you."

"Okay." Roxanne didn't sound relieved, but the tears had stopped.

"Good. I'll drop you off on campus."

Bethany thought furiously as she signaled and joined the traffic flow. "Listen, Roxanne, I haven't exactly been straight with you. Dr. Kline told me Alma had submitted the essay and would be celebrating her cousin's birthday at Los Mariachis. She suspects Alma didn't meet Dr. Kiefer's deadline. I'd like to let her know I spoke to you and Alma, but not what you just told me. I'll suggest waiting for you two after her class."

"That's fine, Ms. Jarviss. Like you said, Alma's conscience has to be bothering her. She seems sort of brittle to me."

"Brittle?"

"Yeah, cheerful in a fake way. Alma is a good person. She doesn't usually tell lies."

Roxanne directed Bethany to a residence hall parking lot. Hugging herself, Roxanne ran into the building. The night had turned too cool for that skimpy dress.

****

At home, Bethany put the Kiefer murder on her mind's back burner and switched her thoughts to the unsatisfactory conversation with Nathan. What would she have liked him to say, that he was torn between accepting the Hartshorns' offer and remaining with the Carters, only a two-hour drive to see her? He had been visiting her about every other week. How often would they see each other after he moved? Neither of them would relish the long drive and inevitable Denver traffic jams.

On her phone, she traced the route north along a virtual line. She wished Nathan had planned to call tonight, but he needed his rest and would get in touch the next day. She'd had the same kind of yo-yoing thoughts about boyfriends since her teens. Love didn't get easier with age.

Chapter 27

Thursday morning, Bethany called Charlotte to tell her to expect Roxanne and Alma to ask to meet with her after class. "It's best if I don't say more now. They should tell you themselves."

Charlotte didn't probe for details. "All right. *Namaste!*"

****

Bethany waited outside Charlotte's door as the morning class ended. She met Roxanne and Alma as they emerged with their classmates. Roxanne clutched a spiral notebook to her chest, and her messenger bag knocked against a hip. Seeing Bethany, she whispered into Alma's ear. Alma flashed Bethany a glance, her expression like a Halloween princess mask—big eyes and red lips frozen in a plastic smile. She turned tail and clicked down the hall.

"Alma, wait!" Bethany called. The student looked back, then continued weaving among the glut of young people. "Come on, Roxanne!" Bethany commanded.

They followed Alma to the end of the hallway and through the exit. On the outdoor landing, the door closed behind them with a soft hiss.

"Let's talk," Bethany said. "Please, Alma, just for a minute."

They had a third-floor view of treetops filled with cooing doves. Human chatter floated up from ground level. "Roxanne told me some things last night," Bethany said, "which you should tell Dr. Kline. She thinks something isn't right about your story about the essay."

Alma glared at Bethany. "You put that idea into Dr. Kline's head!"

"No, I didn't. Dr. Kline suspects you lied about your essay." Feeling Roxanne's hot breath on her neck, Bethany shifted so the students faced one another. She willed Roxanne to summon the courage to speak.

"We have to tell Dr. Kline you didn't get your essay done because you helped me," Roxanne begged. "You've been feeling bad ever since you said you turned it in on time."

"Your conscience must be giving you fits," Bethany said.

Alma's eyes slewed to the side. "I thought about telling Dr. Kiefer the truth. But then he died, and I was so relieved. I didn't have to see him in his office."

"In his office?" Bethany asked. "Why did that bother you? You said he gave pretty girls plenty of his time."

A trio of young women burst through the exit and clattered down the metal stairs. The interruption gave Alma time to compose herself. "I will tell you something about Professor Kiefer. That man looked at me like the big bad wolf in the children's story. I could feel the little hairs stand up on the back of my neck."

Roxanne gasped. "A wolf? No way."

"You couldn't see his true nature after that bicycle accident. He picked you up and fussed over you, so you saw him as your hero. You had a passion for him!"

"I didn't!"

"At the end, you came to your senses," Alma said.

"You saw that he disrespected your struggles to learn. But before that, you were in love."

Roxanne blushed. She pressed the notebook harder against her chest.

Bethany asked, "How about you, Alma? Did you have what you call a passion for Dr. Kiefer?"

Alma smoothed the bun atop her head like a dark-headed bird preening itself. "The professor lusted after me, Ms. Jarviss. I did not care for him."

"He had a thing for you?" Roxanne wailed. "How could you tell?"

"Because soon after the semester started, I went to see him during his office hours. I did not need help, but I know professors like students to do this."

The cunning girl! "What happened?"

"We didn't talk much about the class. Obviously, I am from Mexico. He wanted to know from where exactly. I told him Ciudad de Chihuahua. And he asked where I live in Las Cuevas. I said with my *tios*, my aunt and uncle. He asked if I had a boyfriend, and I said no."

"That doesn't seem strange to me," Roxanne said.

"Then he said a pretty girl should have a boyfriend. The way he said it made me nervous. I asked a question about the homework and left as soon as possible. I didn't go to see him again."

"Let's see if I have this right," Bethany said. "Alma, you told Dr. Kiefer you'd submitted the essay online when you hadn't. You probably expected him to say no problem, to submit it again. But he didn't."

Alma tucked a stray hair into her bun. "He invited me to his office to discuss the problem privately. He made the word privately sound dirty."

"As if he wanted to have sex?" Roxanne asked.

"Yes. In exchange for accepting my essay late."

"I can't believe it, Alma. He wasn't that evil!"

Bethany wondered about that. Kim Lamont reportedly had called Paul evil to his face.

Alma's chin quivered. "I didn't see him privately again, so I will never know. Then Dr. Kiefer died. That is the truth."

Shifting gears, Bethany said, "You didn't tell the truth to Dr. Kline either. You said you submitted the essay to Dr. Kiefer."

"We have to tell Dr. Kline everything," Roxanne begged. "I want her to know how much you helped me with my essay. Too much maybe."

Kindly, Alma said, "You did most of the work and have nothing to fear. I am the one who might fail the course or lose the nice scholarship. The university might expel me."

Bethany tried to calm her. "Don't expect the worst. Go see Dr. Kline during her office hours."

"Do I tell her how Dr. Kiefer looked at me? Like my problem would go away if I let him touch me."

"No! You might've imagined it," Roxanne said.

"What do you think, Ms. Jarviss?" Alma asked.

"I'd stick to the essay situation. Say you're sorry about lying. Do it for Roxanne as well as for yourself."

Roxanne gave a tiny nod. "My conscience is bothering me too."

"I know," Alma said. "I am sorry, Roxanne. Ms. Jarviss, will you also speak to Dr. Kline?"

"Afterward, if you need my help. But first, meet with her, all right?"

With the exit door locked, they trooped down the stairs. Wishing them well, Bethany left campus feeling like a spare tire gone flat. The flat feeling worsened as she noted that Nathan hadn't phoned.

****

At the Foundation, Bethany ate a soggy vending-machine tuna sandwich. At five-thirty, Wayne stopped at her doorway. "Felicia went home, and I'm on my way out. You should call it a day too."

"I went to the university for a while. I'm making up my time."

He cocked his head. "We don't punch a clock. Is something the matter?" He sank into a visitor's chair.

"I'm fine, Dad."

"What took you to campus? The Kiefer affair?"

"Indirectly. I nudged two of Paul's former students to go see Charlotte Kline about an essay situation. They're in a class she took over." She massaged her jaws as he loosened his tie—a striped silk today rather than a bolo.

"Your mother called me this afternoon," he said. "A city detective and a uniformed officer paid her a visit. Gerald had warned her the police might confiscate her computer, but they didn't. The detective questioned her about her relationship with Kiefer while the other guy took notes. He asked point blank if she and Kiefer had been having an affair, which of course she denied. And he asked if Kiefer had been after her job."

"Poor Mom! What did she say to that?"

"That many young faculty aspire to lead departments eventually."

"Did that satisfy the detective?"

"No. Your mother believes he went fishing for a murder motive, and she gave him two. Unrequited love and a threat to her academic position. She tried to make

238

light of his questions, but I could tell the detective upset her."

"The police must be clueless like I am. Mom has confidence in me, but I'm no detective."

"What have you learned?"

"Some not very nice things about Paul's interactions with other faculty, his students, and his ex-wife. But nothing crucial. I hope his killer is arrested soon. Otherwise, decent people, Mom included, will remain under suspicion."

"I can see that's weighing on you, honey. Eleanor is sorry she asked you to get involved. She said you have a personal issue to deal with. Might it have to do with your cowboy?"

He spoke in the sympathetic, fatherly voice that often loosened her tongue. "You might as well know, Dad. Nathan has accepted a job offer. From the owners of a guest ranch in Wyoming."

"Wyoming! A long ride in the saddle!"

She managed a smile. "Dad, he has a truck."

"And you have an SUV. But it's still quite a haul from here to there."

"I know. Part of me, the selfish part, wishes he'd refused the offer."

He slapped a knee. "Let's meet Ellie for a drink. It'll cheer up the both of you."

"Good idea." She shut down her computer.

"Is Los Mariachis okay?"

"Sure." Her father enjoyed the best margaritas in town, and she was becoming a regular at the place. "We can sit on the patio."

Chapter 28

They drove separately to Los Mariachis. Avoiding the dining room and the dark, almost-empty bar, Bethany went out to a patio filled with white wrought-iron tables and fenced in by lattice-work panels covered with budding red roses. The décor had remained the same as long as the oldest patrons could remember. By the summer, rose scent would hang heavily in the air. Bethany relished memories of wedding receptions and anniversary parties here.

Seeing her father in line at the drinks counter, she nodded as he mouthed, "Margarita?" She could never say no; he wouldn't believe she didn't like tequila or the salt rimming the wide-mouthed glasses. She would have preferred white wine.

Finding a table posed no problem on a Thursday among the usual mix of town and gown folks. The hard-core drinkers would hang out later in the bar lit by beer signs.

When Wayne brought the margaritas, he raised his glass for a ceremonial clink. "*Salud!*"

She echoed the wish for good health. "*Salud!*"

He gave a friendly nod to two men who, like him, wore business suits but no ties. He'd obviously shed his tie on the way over. She'd seen him do it in the past with a flourish, driving one-handed.

"Life is good," he proclaimed. Nearby, a woman

wore a T-shirt imprinted with that apparel company's slogan.

She grinned. "Right, Dad."

"Or isn't it? Your cowboy…"

"Nathan, Dad."

"He accepted a job offer, you said. In Wyoming. Tell me about it."

She recounted Nathan's description of the duties on the guest ranch. "He won't be bored like at the Carters' place. He'll work with horses, but he'll have to entertain the guests too. Do rope tricks and dance with the ladies." She sipped her icy drink. "It'll probably work out okay."

"Are you in love with the boy?"

"He's not a boy."

"He's younger than you by what, five years?"

"Three. What difference does that make? We're mature adults." She felt her father sizing her up to decide how much criticism she could take.

"Look at you compared to him," Wayne said. "You have a job to be proud of, and you're making progress toward your MBA."

The MBA. Not the time to say she might not take that summer class and at times considered quitting the program.

"Don't fidget like that, Bethany."

"Like what?"

"Like you want to tell your old dad to mind his own business."

"That's not what I was thinking."

"So it's a tad bit of praise that's making you squirm?"

"No, but don't say Nathan isn't good enough for me. He's a fine person who's had a rough time since his

241

rodeo accident."

"Sure, but what if he hadn't gotten injured? What kind of future can rodeo cowboys expect? Ones whose daddies don't own ranches?"

"He might go to college. In Laramie part-time."

Wayne made a move to adjust the tie he'd shed and instead patted his chest. "Good, because there's no decent future for a hired hand at somebody else's dude ranch. He may be a fine guy, but is he the right one for you in the long run? Guess you'll have to see. Now, how about another margarita?"

"I'm still working on this one."

"Keep at it. I need a second one." In passing, he kissed the top of her head as if she were a little girl. The gesture, meant to be comforting, annoyed her. Nathan was decent, kind, and loving. Would Wayne prefer her to date a man like Paul Kiefer, who'd had a resumé a yard long and only cared about himself? A man willing to blackmail Gene Waverly and possibly ruin a student's GPA if she didn't sleep with him? Bethany's mind raced along those lines until Wayne returned—with two margaritas.

"Dad, I said I didn't want another drink."

"It's not for you. Here comes your mom."

Eleanor adeptly maneuvered through the growing late-afternoon crowd.

Wayne kissed her on the lips. "Sit yourself down and have a sip of this."

She said a warm hello to Bethany and shed her tailored jacket. She had apparently refreshed her makeup but looked washed out nonetheless. Bethany pressed her lips together. When had she last applied lip gloss or combed her hair? At home in the morning? She couldn't recall. *No matter.*

A lone, elderly mariachi edged his way onto the patio, strumming his guitar and singing in Spanish.

Wayne slid close to Eleanor. "How's the police's prime suspect?"

Eleanor eyed him over the rim of her salt-edged glass. "Bethany, your father exaggerates. But I'm a likely suspect, I realize." If she noticed Bethany's mostly untouched drink, she didn't comment on it.

The businessmen that Wayne had acknowledged looked his way. "I should say hello to those fellows."

"Sure. Go ahead," Eleanor said. With Wayne out of earshot, she asked, "Would you like a glass of wine or a sparkling water instead of that margarita?"

"No, I'm fine. Did the police give you a hard time?"

Eleanor took a deep drink of margarita. "They treated me less civilly than the night they interviewed May Zeller and me."

"In what way?"

"They asked probing questions about my relationship with Paul and his with the other C&I faculty, even the adjuncts. They didn't seem to know about Gene Waverly and his ex-wife, but they pressed me about Kim Lamont. They'd learned she dated Paul. I pointed out that as a couple, they didn't break any university rules since neither supervised the other. The officers' intrusive manner worked against them. I said as little as possible. What a tiring hour!"

"I'm sorry, Mom."

"By the way, Charlotte called me. She met with Alma Gomez and Roxanne Vale. She said you prepared her to hear their 'confessions,' as she put it, and that you nudged them toward the confessional."

"How did it go?"

"Fine for both students. Charlotte had already decided to accept their essays as written if they came to see her. She's not making a fuss over Alma lying to Paul Kiefer since Alma has turned in the essay. She told them to concentrate on studying for the course final. Then she dismissed Alma and encouraged Roxanne to get tested for learning disabilities."

"Meryl told me Roxanne may not be able to afford the tests, but financial help may be available."

"Meryl has discretionary funds. Incidentally, I told Charlotte she needs to clear the air with Meryl before the college party."

"Do you believe Meryl actually suspects Charlotte of murder?"

"I don't know. I haven't broached the subject with Meryl."

"Maybe you should. I bet Charlotte won't; she's not that assertive. Look how easy she's being with Alma Gomez. I'd have her write a new essay."

"With the semester nearly over?"

"Sure. She's your department's top student; she could've pulled it off. It might have done her good to face the pressure."

Eleanor shook her head. "Woe be it for your students if you ever teach. You'd be hard on them."

"Not on all of them. I realize Alma helped Roxanne, which led to the missed deadline. But Alma is an admitted liar. I'd put her feet to the fire—in her high-heeled sandals." She pushed away her margarita and ignored the ancient mariachi angling for attention.

Eleanor frowned. "Charlotte appreciates Alma's help with the third graders. That's probably why she went easy on her. I get the impression you don't like her."

"She reeks entitlement."

"That's not true, dear. Alma is not from a rich family. Without financial aid, she wouldn't be at NMU. She stays free of charge during the school year with her aunt and uncle. The aunt is her mother's sister from Chihuahua, who married a Las Cuevas man she met when he was backpacking in Mexico. Their two boys share a bedroom so Alma can have one of her own."

Bethany shrugged. "Alma mentioned telling Paul Kiefer she lives with an aunt and uncle. But by entitlement, I don't mean in a financial way. She's smart and beautiful, but Roxanne isn't. I wonder what Alma could get Roxanne to do to stay in her orbit."

"You're suggesting Alma had Roxanne murder Paul Kiefer? Over a grade?"

"Not a grade. But maybe for a sexual reason. Kim Lamont said—bitterly, it seemed to me—that Paul liked his girlfriends young. His ex-wife, Laura, said essentially the same thing. They didn't think he had affairs with students, but maybe he couldn't resist Alma. If they had an affair that he regretted and ended, she might've retaliated. She could've stolen Roxanne's pills to drug Paul. It's possible Roxanne didn't leave that bottle by a water cooler. Or maybe they conspired to commit the murder."

"Dear, you don't believe any of that?"

"I'm just brainstorming." She switched gears slightly. "Did the police say if they're making progress?"

"I didn't ask, and I haven't heard from Elisa Marcos."

Waync, Bethany saw, was on his way back to them,

carefully carrying a laden tray. With a flourish, he distributed three more margaritas, chips and salsa, and a stack of cocktail napkins. Waving a five-dollar bill, he drew the aged mariachi to their table.

Dipping a chip, Bethany listened as the mariachi set forth with gusto. Hearing the Spanish words *muchacha* and *playa*, she gathered that he sang of a girl on a beach. Wayne, always the romantic, put his arm around Eleanor and hummed along. Bethany couldn't stay miffed at him for his attitude toward Nathan. Admittedly, she also worried about Nathan's career prospects, but she deep-sixed those thoughts in his charismatic presence. She wished he would call. Why hadn't he?

As the mariachi strolled to other tables, Wayne suggested ordering dinner.

"Not for me. I want to get home," Bethany said over his objections.

Eleanor said mildly, "Have a good evening, dear." She squeezed Wayne's upper arm, a familiar signal to say no more.

Bethany left the second margarita unsampled. Her parents wouldn't touch it. They limited themselves to two drinks when each of them had to drive.

Chapter 29

Journaling in her bedroom, Bethany listed everyone she or Eleanor had spoken to in the last few days about Paul Kiefer: faculty members Charlotte, Gene, Vince, and Kim. Meryl and Gerald Darwood. Alma, Roxanne, and the grad student, Lenny. May Zeller. Paul's ex-wife, Laura, and her lover, Dooley.

It seemed Gene and Alma had the strongest motives for the crime. Gene must have dreaded the sex with his ex becoming common knowledge. Alma must have feared losing her 4.0 GPA. Both had access to pills that, in excess, would make a man so drowsy he couldn't defend himself.

But journaling got her nowhere. She needed to de-stress. She took her cell phone into the bathroom, where she pried the seal from a bottle of bubble bath, a stocking stuffer from Eleanor last Christmas. She turned on the taps, poured a dollop of the lotion into the tub, and breathed in the scent of carnations. Settling into the frothy water, she recalled soaking in an antique, claw-footed tub a few months ago in the course of a previous murder investigation. Like then, she ached for Nathan.

Now, she lay with her eyes closed, picturing Nathan and herself as the only couple on a dance floor, he in a tuxedo and she in an ivory satin gown. She held a bouquet of carnations and scarlet roses as he took her free hand to commence their first wedding dance, ringed by family and friends. Playing the scene in her mind, she wondered how she would respond if Nathan ever asked her to marry him. Unsure, she shivered in the cooling bath and let the fantasy dissolve.

****

In bed, from a fitful sleep, she awoke to the insistent sound of her phone. She grabbed it and flipped on her lamp.

"Apologies for calling so late," Nathan said. "This is the first chance I've had."

Noticing the time, she said, "It's after 1:00 a.m. What's up?"

"I would've called earlier, but I had to drive all over hell and back, hunting down Mickey and his friends."

Bethany rubbed her eyes. "Mickey, who?"

"You know. The Carters' boy. The sixteen-year-old. He went out partying—on a school night, mind you—with some other kids. The older brother of one of them bought booze and took them for a drive."

"Don't tell me they had an accident?"

"No, not that." Nathan launched into an account of his quest for Mickey after a barmaid, who had grown up with the Carters' daughter, phoned them. Through a drive-up window, she'd sold a "crazy amount" of beer and whiskey to a twenty-one-year-old in an extended-cab truck. He had several boys along for the ride, Mickey among them. An anxious Mrs. Carter begged Nathan to go looking for them. Eventually, he found them in a popular meeting spot in a remote canyon, sitting around a bonfire—drunk, high, and unfit to drive.

"I used tough-guy language to commandeer the extended cab," Nathan said. "I took them all home. The older guy still lives with his family. A sister drove me back to collect my truck."

"Did Mickey get into trouble?"

Nathan chuckled. "He will. I had to carry him to his bed. His folks are fit to be tied. Tomorrow, they'll read him the riot act after he's slept it off."

Bethany didn't think the episode all that funny. "Why did you get involved? Couldn't Mickey's parents have phoned him?"

"Mrs. Carter tried, but there's no cell service in that canyon. Mickey's dad was off playing cards. The missus didn't want to interrupt his night out; it's only once a month. She asked me to go instead."

"Is the boy usually this much trouble?"

"Nope, that's the thing. He was helping another kid study for a test. That kid got sick of doing math and convinced his doofus big brother to take all of them for that ride."

"You're a hero, Nathan, but I wish you would've called me earlier." She didn't disguise her frustration.

"I am truly sorry, Bethany. Lordy, am I beat." He yawned in her ear.

Was that a hint to let him hang up? If so, she ignored it. "Did you give the Carters notice?"

"Not yet."

"Are you having second thoughts about leaving them?" Silence. "Nathan, are you still there?"

"Yeah. Thinking. The Carters are decent folks. The missus says I'm a good influence on their boy. I've taught him a few things."

"Like how to lay tile?"

"Yeah, that." He chuckled again. "I'll give notice tomorrow once the dust settles over Mickey's escapade. So how was your day?"

She had a desire to tell him that her father wanted to retire and saddle her with the job of Foundation director. To say the police had hassled her mother. To bemoan her lack of progress with her informal murder investigation. But not in the wee hours of the morning. "My day? Complicated. How about if we talk tomorrow?"

"Okay. Apologies for wrecking your sleep."

She pictured him pulling off his scuffed boots and dropping, fully clothed, onto his single bed. She concocted the single-bed detail. She'd never been to the Carters' ranch but knew Nathan had been sleeping in the house since the water pipes in the hired hand's trailer burst last winter. Would he adjust to bunkhouse living in Wyoming? Would he regret leaving employers who treated him like family? Would he regret leaving New Mexico and her behind?

****

Late Friday morning, Eleanor went to see Meryl Darwood about Charlotte Kline. Eleanor worried that Charlotte would skip the Darwoods' command-performance event. And if Charlotte gave the party a miss, the Darwoods might suspect her all the more of murder.

Eleanor waited in the tutor center for Meryl to finish an end-of-semester evaluation of a student tutor. Soon, a young man emerged from Meryl's office smiling in what looked like relief. He left the door ajar.

Eleanor peered into the office. "Have a minute?"

"For you, Eleanor, always," Meryl said. "Excellent timing. That student made my morning. He's one of our best tutors."

Today, Meryl looked a last-century vision in a full-skirted dress in a daisy print that emphasized her rounded figure. With her well-controlled hair and orange lipstick, she only lacked a pill-box hat to complete the church-lady look of fifty or sixty years ago.

They sat at a table stacked with paperbacks. With a "ta-da!" Meryl took one off the top. "*Season of Dreams*. With my compliments. A signed first edition." She said it with a touch of humor.

Eleanor flipped through the novel. "What an accomplishment! How do you find the time to write?"

"I do it in the evenings on my laptop. I sit with Gerald while he watches his golf shows. What's up, my friend?"

"I'm concerned about Charlotte. Have you talked with her lately?"

"Not much. I've seen her with the literacy tutors. She whips in, takes care of business, and leaves. Busy woman."

Eleanor felt as nervous as if she had come for an evaluation. How ridiculous! She had known Meryl for ages. Taking a steadying breath, she decided to be direct. "Gerald told Charlotte you suspect her of murder. She's deeply hurt you would think that."

Meryl's droopy eyelids widened like an alert owl's. "Gerald told her?"

"And me."

Meryl tsk-tsked. "He shouldn't have. We're shell-shocked about Paul's Kiefer's murder. We racked our brains and came up with the names of several people with motives, including me. Paul wanted this center to be turned into a place to experiment with all sorts of things, virtual instruction by simulated faculty for one. The silly man not only wanted to rid the world of college textbooks, I fear he imagined doing away with flesh-and-blood instructors. No more need for college faculty or the future teachers we train. Public school students would stare at screens all day. Such nonsense."

"Perhaps you exaggerate his intentions," Eleanor said.

"Oh no. His excitement about the prospects of artificial intelligence, in particular, scared me. But Gerald said Paul's ideas intrigued him. That the college could save hundreds of thousands of dollars a year by eliminating some faculty positions. Online classes are popular; some hardly need faculty. I got rather miffed at Gerald. Actually, I went on somewhat of a rant." Her grin softened her words.

"How did Gerald react?" Eleanor asked.

"He said perhaps I had rid the world of one flesh-and-blood faculty member. But he said it with a wink."

"Did he wink when talking about Charlotte?"

"Not at all. He said he wouldn't be shocked if she killed Paul to protect her sacred cows, the third graders' project and her adult literacy work. I might have nodded at that. Oh, why did he mention that suspicion to her?" Meryl shook her head without disturbing a single hair. *She must use industrial-strength spray.*

"You should talk to Charlotte," Eleanor said.

"I should speak to Charlotte," Meryl said at the same moment. "The next time Charlotte comes in, I'll apologize. Now, don't get upset, but let me tell you something Gerald apparently didn't mention."

"What's that?"

"When we spoke about motives, your name came up."

"I'm not surprised. The grapevine has it Paul wanted the department-head job. He felt I should clear the way for his younger leadership."

She considered mentioning that Wayne yearned to retire and that she hoped he wouldn't push her to do that too. She'd barely gotten her feet wet as department head. But this was not the time for confidences.

Under Meryl's alert-owl gaze, Eleanor added, "Paul must have shared his aspirations with some of the faculty. Vince Morrison. Kim Lamont. Faculty do talk. But I can handle what's said on the grapevine without murdering one of—"

"The grapes?" Meryl flashed her a smile.

Eleanor made herself smile in return. "I intended to say, 'my colleagues.' Meryl, did you not respect Paul? You're the only person I ever heard call him 'silly.' "

"I shouldn't have used that word or made fun of Paul's research. Gerald and I agreed that Paul reminded us of our Louis. Intelligent and ambitious. Did I tell you Louis may travel to China this summer?"

"On vacation?"

"Partly. He intends to see the Great Wall, but he also plans to look up some relatives and do more research on Chinese opera for his dissertation. All play and no work aren't possible for him, even during the summer."

For a pleasant few minutes, they discussed the Darwoods' adopted son. Then Eleanor suggested, "Why don't you call Charlotte? We three could have lunch."

"Eleanor, you're like a helicopter mom making sure I do my homework. Shall we keep it simple and meet in the Commons?"

Chapter 30

Deep into her work, Bethany ignored her buzzing phone until Zena began to leave a whispered message. "Pardon me for bothering you, Bethany, but there's something you should know. Can you get back—"

"Hi, Zena. I can hardly hear you. You must have a mob at the café."

"We're in the middle of a rush. Could you come over at closing time? I need to tell you something."

Mystified, Bethany said, "Okay, but what's it about?"

"The murder maybe. I'll explain when you get here."

****

The café's din hadn't diminished as Bethany paid upfront for a late lunch. She waited for a table behind a couple with a boy about two years old and a baby girl in a sling on the mother's chest.

Zena, her fiery hair barely contained by a bandanna, seated the family and brought them plates of spaghetti and salad. Catching Bethany's eye, she pointed to a free table and soon plopped down an identical meal. As two men in business suits thumbed their phones, she said, "I'll seat those guys and be back in a minute."

In more like ten, Zena brought a slice of white cake topped with strawberries. She dropped into a seat, angling it to keep an eye on the other patrons. "The berries are the frozen kind, but they're sweet."

"I love strawberries," Bethany said, digging in. "But I'm dying of suspense. What do you want to tell me?"

Zena pushed the bandanna off her eyebrows. "It's about a professor who came in today. He eats here fairly often and asks me to post flyers for one thing or another. He's big on the Heritage Festival."

Bethany's scalp tingled. "Do you know his name?"

"His first name. Vince. He's in your mother's department."

"Vince Morrison."

"I didn't know his last name. He flirts with me, but he's terrible at it. I feel for him. He's usually alone and has to sit with strangers when the place is crowded. But not today."

"It wasn't crowded? It sure is now."

"I mean, he wasn't alone. Well, at first, he was, but he paid for two lunches and said he'd wait to be seated until somebody meeting him arrived. Gosh, was he nervous! He jingled his pocket change and watched the door for about fifteen minutes until a woman showed up. I recognized her, but not by name. Normally, she's with a group who joke that they're the *starving artists*."

"Can you describe her?"

"Dark haired, slender. Honestly, too classy for a guy like Vince. She looked kind of like you, like a sister or at least a cousin."

"That had to be Laura Vansetti. Paul Kiefer's ex-wife."

"Really? Hell's bells."

"How did they act?"

"Not like lovers. The meeting didn't go well."

The tingling in Bethany's scalp intensified. "How

could you tell?"

"At first, I couldn't when I found them a table and served their lunches. But when I took them their desserts, I noticed they'd hardly touched the main course. Wow, was there an atmosphere between them! Like ice. They sat at a table for four, but nobody dared to join them."

Bethany nudged her half-finished cake to the side. "Did you hear their conversation?"

Zena sighed. "Not much. At first, I assumed they were talking about their relationship. But then I heard her say, 'Paul? Why would I? I'd need a motive, right?' "

"They were discussing—"

"Paul Kiefer's murder."

Bethany leaned toward Zena. "How did Vince respond to her questions?"

"He said something about Paul and colleges. 'Paul gave you his opinion of them. And then, he was murdered.' That got quite a reaction. She jumped up and fairly spat at him. 'I can't believe this! I'm out of here.' She left like an actor overdoing an exit in a bad play. Bethany, you're not eating your dessert."

"I'm too busy digesting your every word." Obediently, she took another bite. "Delicious." She dabbed her mouth with a thin cloth napkin. How much to tell Zena about Vince and Laura? She opted to confide in her friend. "I'm almost positive Vince didn't use the word *colleges*. I think you heard *collages*."

"Artwork! I should've realized. Dumb me." She blushed a deep pink under her freckles.

"No, no. I only know that because I talked to Laura Vansetti."

She told Zena about finding Paul's ex-wife, viewing her collages, and learning that Paul had belittled them.

"They divorced a few years ago, but it seems he still liked to hurt her." The café crowd dwindled as closing time approached. Bethany finished her dessert as Zena mused, "Kiefer must have been a nasty dude. What was Vince to him?"

"Paul's best friend in the C&I department, kind of a sidekick. They played tennis together."

"He thinks his buddy's ex-wife killed him. Could he be right?"

"Laura seems to have put her bad feelings for Paul into her collages. Besides, she's in a relationship with an art prof. I met him."

Zena's coppery eyebrows shot up. "A professor/student affair!"

"She's not underage. Supposedly, they became an item after she finished one of his classes."

"Too bad for Vince," Zena said. "You should've seen how he treated her. He pulled out her chair like a guy on a first date. After she walked off in a huff, he stared into space like some of my customers with nowhere to live. Folks who seem lost. You want to give them a hug."

Mischievously, Bethany asked, "Did you hug Vince Morrison?"

"No way, girlfriend!"

"Is it okay if I call and tell him what you overheard?"

"Go ahead. If my loose lips lose him as a customer, that's no biggie if it helps you find a killer. I'll get you a coffee."

Bethany took out her phone. *No message from Nathan.* She phoned Vince, and hearing his recorded voice, simply asked him to return her call. She didn't mention Zena or Laura.

Zena brought the promised coffee plus one for herself. Bethany preferred to get moving, but she settled into her chair as Zena asked, "What's shaking with that guy of yours? Nathan, right? You haven't brought him to lunch for a while."

Bethany told her about the job in Wyoming. She gestured with her phone. "I'm waiting to hear from him."

"Any chance you'd move up there too?"

"He suggested it, but it's too early to think about it."

"But I bet you do."

"All the time. While I'm trying to concentrate on my own job and my grad work."

From the kitchen came the sound of a guy singing in a jokey voice, "Help, I need somebody! And I don't mean just anybody…" A woman joined in, "Help, I need someone…"

Zena cocked an ear toward the singers. "What you need is to take care of yourself, lady. You seem exhausted."

"You noticed." Bethany drained her cup. "I get tired of the grad program, Zena. I might ditch it."

"Stick it out to the bitter end. An MBA can come in handy. It got me this high-paying gig."

Two teenage girls, skinny as broom straws, entered the café, hesitating by the cashier's stand. It was past closing time, but Zena hadn't locked up.

"Two more to feed," Zena said. "They can help with the dishes."

****

After lunch, Eleanor asked Jereen to hold her calls. Standing by her window, she gazed at the blue sky, going over in her mind what had transpired between Meryl and

Charlotte. She didn't know if their friendship had been patched up, even though, over sandwiches in the Commons, Meryl had apologized to Charlotte.

With a hand to her breast, Meryl had said, "I'm sorry Gerald upset you. He shouldn't have mentioned that we talked about you as a suspect. Everyone's name came up, mine included. Some could say Paul posed a threat to the tutor center, and I wouldn't have that. We even came up with a motive for Gerald—jealousy of a younger man who would be dean! Who refused Gerald's golf invitations and stuck with tennis, of which Gerald is no fan." Meryl had widened her eyes comically.

Eventually, Charlotte had told Meryl not to worry. Replaying the meeting, Eleanor realized that Meryl never said she believed Charlotte to be innocent. Instead, Meryl breezed through the plans for her party. A catered buffet and mariachis would keep people fed and entertained. May Zeller would oversee a group of student helpers.

Hiring students was Meryl's clever way to keep most of the faculty on their best behavior. Few professors would overdrink, tell rude jokes, or discuss the murder where students might hear them. Why, then, Eleanor wondered, did she dread having to attend?

****

At home, after a long afternoon at work, Bethany was pondering Vince and Laura's meeting when Eleanor phoned. She shared Zena's information with her mother.

"Vince isn't the most subtle person," Eleanor said. "If he accused Paul's ex-wife of murder, it's not surprising she'd be outraged."

"On the heels of my questioning," Bethany said. "She admitted Paul had said nasty things about her current artwork."

When Eleanor didn't respond, Bethany asked, "Mom, what are you thinking?"

"About another relationship. Charlotte and Meryl's." Eleanor described the lunch meeting she'd engineered. "Meryl apologized, but it will take time for Charlotte to get over the Darwoods' suspicions."

"The party might help."

"Possibly," Eleanor said, not sounding hopeful. "Come to dinner tonight. Your dad's grilling sausages, and I'm making that crusty zucchini we all love."

"Another time," Bethany said. "I'm tired, and Nathan will phone, I hope. By now, he must have given the Carters his notice."

"Will that be hard for him?"

"Sure. He bonded with that family, but he needs a change."

"Like you, dear?"

"Why do you say that, Mom?"

"Oh, I think you know. You may be tiring of Las Cuevas. Taking over the Foundation from your father would keep you here."

Hunger pangs told Bethany not to have an important conversation now. She put the phone on speaker and rummaged in her freezer for a meal to microwave. "Can we discuss that another time, Mom? I need to zap something to eat."

But Eleanor didn't let her go. "You're bringing Nathan to the Darwoods' party?"

"That's the plan."

"What do you intend to wear? If I may ask."

"A sundress, I suppose."

"Pantyhose?"

"Hmm. At least freshly shaved legs."

Eleanor's laugh filled Bethany's kitchen. "That mini bag I gave you last Christmas would work for the party."

Bethany hadn't yet used the embroidered Oaxacan bag. "Instead of my daypack. Yes, Mom. It'll be perfect."

"A woman sewed it with love at that co-op. Bethany…"

"What is it, Mom?"

"I dread this party with Paul's killer out there. You don't have any idea who that is?"

"If I did, I'd tell you. I'll watch people at the Darwoods' and listen for Paul's name to come up. But I suppose people will act as if his murder isn't at the front of their minds."

"We'll talk at the top of our lungs about our families and in hushed tones about campus politics," Eleanor said. "The golfers among us will take advantage of Wayne's putting green."

"Same as always."

"On the surface, yes. I have butterflies in my stomach about having to pretend we're celebrating the end of an ordinary academic year."

"My stomach has a growling bear in it. I'd better fire up the microwave."

To her mother's credit, Eleanor disconnected without another pitch to drive over for dinner. She knew when to accept a polite no. Bethany watched a meatloaf entrée rotate. She looked forward to an early night after—*please goddesses*—she heard from Nathan.

****

At ten-thirty, as Bethany finished watching the late news out of Albuquerque, which had nothing new on the murder, Nathan phoned.

"I told them," he said first thing. "I gave my notice."

"Well, hello to you too." Bethany heard the frustration in her voice.

"Sorry. I know it's kind of late to call. This is the first chance I've had."

Bethany let his apology hang in the air. "How did the Carters take the news?"

"Mrs. Carter pretty well but not the mister. In front of the boy, he said nobody, especially his worthless son, can fill my boots. He's not done being riled about Mickey's escapade."

"Understandably."

"I guess. But Mr. Carter shouldn't have said half of what he did. Mickey stormed off to his room, and after a while, we heard him drive away in my pickup."

"He took your truck? How did he get the key to it?"

"I left it in the ignition. Stupid, I know."

Bethany nodded, glad Nathan couldn't see her face. "Where is he now?"

"That's the thing. His papa and I went looking for him while the missus stayed at the ranch. We found my truck in a ditch and Mickey stumbling along in a daze. With a goose bump on his forehead from banging the steering wheel. The idiot hadn't put on a seatbelt."

"And you were relieved that nobody'd had an accident the last time we spoke. Is he okay?"

"We're at the hospital. He might have a concussion and a broken arm."

"For goodness' sake!"

"Yeah. He's a dumb cluck but a good boy. His papa's too hard on him. Makes me feel awful I'm quitting."

"Are you considering staying?"

"Thinking about it, but no way."

Bethany absorbed his answer with conflicting emotions. "How's your truck?"

"Might not be drivable. We left it where we found it. The boy's more important than my wheels."

Bethany wished Nathan could assure her that he would come to the Darwoods' party. But he only said, "I'll try to get the truck looked at, and then I'll call you again. The main thing now is for me to hunker down here. Mickey is getting an MRI to make sure there are no loose screws in his thick head."

"You're waiting with Mr. Carter?"

"And the missus too. She drove here not long after us."

"The Carters have two vehicles?"

"Yeah, their farm truck and Mrs. Carter's sedan. Why?"

Because you could borrow one of them tomorrow. "It's good she wasn't left stranded at the ranch."

"Bethany, about that shindig…"

Finally, he's thought of it. Shindig was one of his jokey terms, like loose screws. Was he about to warn her he might miss the party?

"You can count on me, darlin', even if I have to take a bus."

"Is there a bus?"

"Hell, I don't know. I'll get there somehow if my truck is out of commission. I won't miss your fancy affair."

"It's not mine. And I told you it won't be fancy."

"Still, you might get to see me in dress pants."

"Nice jeans or trousers, it won't matter. As long as

you show up."

"Okay. It's a date."

Her jaw pounded as she hung up. Did Nathan, who had no siblings, consider himself Mickey's surrogate big brother? Would he not quit his job with the Carters if the boy had a head injury? She chided herself for the thought. *Shame on me.* But who could blame her for wishing Nathan didn't plan to move two states north of New Mexico?

Chapter 31

Saturday afternoon, Nathan phoned to say his truck had been towed to a rural garage whose owner promised to get right on it—after he finished another job. As the hours ticked on and Nathan didn't call again, Bethany faced attending the party solo. She had received a special invitation this year as the scholarship presenter. Otherwise, Wayne could have done double duty as the Foundation's representative and a department head's husband.

From her closet, she selected a light green halter-top dress that skimmed the tops of her knees. As a concession to her mother, she wiggled into silk pantyhose before stepping into her dressy sandals with sensible two-inch heels. She applied an extra coat of mascara, smoky eye shadow, and crimson rose lipstick instead of lip gloss. With a twist, she pulled her hair up in the back and secured it with a wide clip, then finger-combed her bangs. Finally, she exchanged her everyday earrings, silver studs, for a dangly pair.

In her small bedroom, the backs of her legs touched her bed as she appraised her image from head to toe in the vanity's mirror. Meeting her gaze was a woman with heavy chestnut hair, dark eyes, thick eyebrows, and a nose that didn't seem the embarrassing honker of her girlhood. Her body satisfied her now, in her thirties. Under the dress's lined halter top, her breasts looked firm and in proportion to her waist, hips, and feet that no longer looked like clunkers.

Other women might have polished their fingernails and toenails, but in her case, that would have been going too far to impress people. Other women her age might have opted for higher-heeled shoes. But she had considered high heels dangerous footgear ever since she'd solved her first mystery: the death of a young woman who'd plunged down a staircase in stilettos.

Although Bethany hardly ever wore perfume, she owned several bottles of it, all gifts. She chose one at random, spritzed the air, and coughed at the vinegary smell. She'd forgo wearing scent but keep the pretty bottles.

As she reached automatically for her daypack, she remembered the Oaxacan bag Eleanor wanted her to use tonight. It had barely enough space for her keys, phone, driver's license, a credit card, and the lipstick. Her heart beating a fast tattoo, she had an urge to call Nathan. But no; she'd drive to this shindig, as he'd called it, on her own. She'd make an appearance to please her parents and the Darwoods, and to look for a murderer among the end-of-semester crowd.

****

SUVs, trucks, and a few sedans—none particularly new or flashy—lined the unpaved street in front of the Darwoods' hillside adobe residence. The couple lived near the top of the same neighborhood as Wayne and Eleanor. Bethany parked two blocks past the house and walked back. Beyond the arched entry, a smaller version of the three-tiered Mexican fountain on the campus quad splashed water noisily.

A student helper in a green education college T-shirt

266

manned the front door. Inside, a glut of guests chatted in the open-plan living space or circled a buffet on the dining-room table. Bethany accepted a glass of sparkling water from a young man bearing a drinks tray. She made her way past a fireplace, with enough space to roast an ox, to a patio where Lenny Ortiz and his fellow mariachis blasted the partiers. Catching her eye, Lenny gave her a showman's toothy smile.

Casting around for people she knew, Bethany spied Vince Morrison and Kim Lamont. Surprised to see them together, she watched Kim sip wine and Vince bend her ear. As two women squeezed past them, Vince snaked his arm around Kim's waist under her lacy shawl. In a clear rebuff, Kim stepped nimbly to the side. With her wineglass clutched to her chest, she left Vince by the patio railing. He ran a hand over his balding skull and gazed over the sloping lawn with a manufactured interest.

Bethany approached him. "Hello, Vince."

He reined in some powerful emotion—despair, Bethany guessed. His jaw muscles bunched like hers under stress.

"Ms. Jarviss." He drew out the "s" sounds.

"Just Bethany. I've been trying to reach you, Vince."

Raising his glass, he splashed red wine in the narrow space between them. He licked his wet hand. "Terribly sorry I didn't get back to you. I've been dealing with students. End-of-semester stuff." He stumbled and grabbed the railing.

The guy is drunk.

As if she had spoken, Vince scowled at her. "Yes, I started early. A whiskey at home. To give myself Dutch

267

courage, you see."

"For what? This party?"

He came so close that his nose nudged her ear. "I came with the lovely Kim," he whispered. "I called her and said no sense driving all the way up here in two cars. She said nice of me to think of it."

"She let you drive?"

He swayed on his feet. "No, actually. At her place, she took one look at me and insisted we come in her car. This red's potent stuff. It embold—emboldened—me. But my touch wasn't welcome, as you must have noticed. Shall we dance?"

Other people bopped self-consciously to the mariachis' rendition of a rock tune. Vince slugged down his wine and, with an unsteady hand, set the glass on the railing's edge. The glass plunged into the shrubbery.

"Whoops!" He swiveled his arms and hips in a 1960s twist. "Join me?" He wiggled toward her.

"No thanks." She held her sparkling water out of reach as he grabbed her free arm to steady himself.

"Well, Sherlock. If you won't dance, you must be here to sleuth." His leer rasped against her nerves.

"Like you've been doing, Vince." Her arm hurt, but she let him keep hold of it.

"What do you mean?" He said it like "Whuhduhyuhmean."

"I heard you contacted Paul's ex-wife," Bethany said. "You didn't mention that she goes by her maiden name, Vansetti."

He smirked. "You didn't ask."

"Vince!"

"I didn't remember that when you asked about her. I swear." He released her arm and raised his hand, palm out, and smirked again.

"You had lunch with Laura. At the Cuevas Café," Bethany said.

"How'd you know? Ah, the manager. A friend of yours?"

"How did you get Laura to see you?"

"I phoned to say I was sorry about Paul's death. She said no sorry needed and people should leave her alone. She said his department head's daughter had come snooping around with condolences as an excuse too. But when I told her Paul had been my best friend, she agreed to meet me to talk about who might've killed him."

Vince swayed as if the explanation had worn him out. But Bethany pressed on. "Zena said you seemed quite the gentleman. You pulled out Laura's chair like you were on a date and paid for her lunch."

"I like the same type of women as Paul did. Is that a crime?"

"No, but Zena said Laura got angry and walked out on you."

"Laura told me she saw Paul at the art building right before he died. He knocked her collages for a show she's in. I said, 'Wow, and then he was killed.' She took offense, like I'd accused her of murder. She ran out of the café like a calf from a chute." He giggled and belched.

Nathan would've appreciated the simile. But Bethany didn't react to it; people were staring.

"Vince, keep it down." She stared back to force the gawkers to look away. "I saw Laura's collages. She used a piece of a photo of Paul and herself, and not in a nice way. But I don't think she killed Paul. She seemed over him. She's about to get her MFA and is dating an art professor I met. Jason Dooley."

"Dooley. I know who he is. A puffed-up toad. She never mentioned him."

"Have you tried to contact her since your lunch?"

"Nope, but I called my friend in the campus police. Told him how she ran out of the café. Hinted she might be the murderer."

"Good goddess! What did he say?"

Vince slouched like a deflating balloon. "To stay out of it. She'd already been questioned."

"She mentioned it."

"Well, Bethany, you got more out of her than I did."

"I would've told you if you'd returned my call."

"Point taken. What are you drinking?" He peered into her glass. "Looks anemic."

"It's sparkling water. Let's get you a glass."

Grasping his elbow, she steered him into the living area to a corner chair. She hailed the server with the drinks tray and took a sparkling water for Vince.

He swallowed thirstily and belched again. "I'm not usually a disaster."

"Relax, okay?" She left him to sober up. *How would he get home? Would Kim drive him? Their problem.*

Across the room, in front of the unlit fireplace, the Darwoods held court. Bethany got in line and inched toward the hosts. The Darwoods had dressed in their party best. As she neared them, she spotted the college's crest on the dean's bolo tie and saw that Meryl wore copious turquoise jewelry with a dress of that color. When Bethany's turn came to say hello, the dean chided her. "You don't have a drink in your hand, young lady."

"I've had one already." She didn't mention that it had been water. The dean always encouraged his guests to loosen up with alcohol.

Meryl added a welcome. "Be sure to help yourself to the buffet. Where's your plus one?"

"He had truck trouble but might still make it."

The dean switched his attention to the people behind Bethany, but Meryl showed her concern. "I hope he does. You look lovely tonight, by the way."

Duty to her hosts done, Bethany noticed her parents greet a couple their age who headed to the buffet table.

Eleanor beckoned her. "Hi, dear."

"No guy in a white hat with you?" Wayne asked.

"Car trouble. He'll show up, I hope. But not in a white hat, Dad."

Eleanor shot him a cautionary glance. "Your father was about to fill a plate for us to share. Wayne, go on while I admire our daughter."

"Nice dress," he said. "Not too short."

"Nice bolo," she countered, patting the turquoise stone. The family had given him the tie for his fiftieth birthday. "The dean's wearing his college one tonight."

"Yes, I saw that." He turned toward the buffet. "Here I go, to forage for food."

"My hunter and gatherer," Eleanor quipped. "Bethany, your dad is on a social high tonight. Watch. He'll see somebody he knows and forget about the buffet."

"He thrives on chewing the fat at these affairs," Bethany joked. "He makes it look easy."

"You're adept at mingling."

"Not as good as Dad. He's like a politician pressing the flesh." Under her mother's scrutiny, she curtsied. "Okay, tell me. Do I pass?"

"More than pass. Hair, dress, purse…"

"Pantyhose."

"Well done. Do I pass too?"

Her mother wore one of her elegant sheaths—this one a pale apricot. "You look beautiful."

But Eleanor's attention had strayed to the growing crowd. Close up, Bethany saw that her mother's makeup barely concealed dark circles under her eyes. "What is it, Mom?"

"The atmosphere. Almost the entire college has turned out, all thinking about Paul Kiefer's murderer. We wonder if he's here. I overheard someone say the police may make an appearance. That the Darwoods might have invited Chief Marcos."

"She wasn't invited in the past?"

"No, why would she be? This is a college event, and I can't imagine the Darwoods asking Elisa Marcos to come this year. Putting the fox among the chickens, as the dean would say."

That would be for the good, Bethany thought, if the chief arrested the killer.

"See, your dad's not coming back," Eleanor said. "He's gabbing with that bunch from the phys ed department. I'd better mingle with my faculty."

"Vince Morrison is in that chair." Bethany pointed him out. "I took him a sparkling water. He's tipsy and feeling sorry for himself. Kim Lamont rebuffed him."

"I'll try to cheer him up." Eleanor edged her way through the crush, a petite, purposeful woman in pastel.

Bethany moved toward the buffet where May Zeller in a chef's apron, hands on sturdy hips, watched guests heap their plates. At May's elbow, Roxanne Vale, wearing a college T-shirt engulfing her thin frame, stood dead on her feet. She probably needed a rest as much as the money she'd earn as a server tonight.

May handed an empty platter to Roxanne. "Bring more shrimp and sauce, would you please?"

Roxanne cast Bethany a tiny smile and headed back to the kitchen as another server emerged with a plate of artfully arranged asparagus spears and a bowl of olives. Alma Gomez followed with pinwheel appetizers. Her college T-shirt hugged her breasts and fit neatly into her skinny black jeans.

Ignoring a stick-to-the-job look from May, Alma said to Bethany, "I wanted to serve wine, but I'm too young." She said it in a mock sad tone. "Ms. May only permits students twenty-one and older to serve drinks. I am kitchen help."

"A job that needs doing," Bethany said. "I see Roxanne's here. How did your meeting go with Dr. Kline?"

"Thank you for encouraging us to talk with her. She accepted our apologies and our essays. Women professors are kinder than the men. They do not look at us with big wolf's eyes." She noticed May approaching. "I must stay busy." Avoiding her boss, she moved to the far end of the table.

"Hi, May," Bethany said. "How's the student crew working out?"

May brushed a hand through her spiky hair. "Fine, but that one is a handful. I stopped her from flouncing around with a drinks tray like a flamenco dancer. She's too young to serve alcohol."

"She mentioned that," Bethany said. "But she must be twenty, so just wait 'til next year."

May came close to Bethany. "Did you notice we didn't set up a coffee urn like usual? Mrs. Darwood said to brew a pot in the kitchen and serve coffee to people who ask for it. Weird, huh? But the whole party feels weird. Something is in the air like a storm's about to break."

Bethany sensed it too. "Everyone is making a special effort to act like nothing is wrong."

"That's it, people are acting," May said. "Especially the killer if they're here." She inched closer so Bethany smelled May's minty-fresh breath. "Who do you think it is, Ms. Jarviss?"

"Bethany. Honestly, May, I'm at a total loss."

"Rumor has it so are the cops," May scoffed. "Hey, you're not eating."

"I'm waiting for my boyfriend."

Roxanne returned with two heaped platters. As she reached the buffet table and saw them watching, she stumbled. May, close by, grabbed the platters in a deft move.

"No harm done," May said. "I'll take care of these. Go on back to the kitchen."

As Roxanne scurried off, Bethany turned her attention to the mariachi music flowing into the house from the patio. Wishing Nathan were here to dance with, she noticed Gene Waverly, on the move like a sneak thief. She trailed him unobtrusively out to a deck overlooking a putting green the dean famously called his sanctuary. The sun had set, but yard lights shone over the practice area. Two men in shirtsleeves lobbed balls onto the artificial turf as Gene observed them.

He had donned khaki pants instead of his usual baggy jeans, a pale blue shirt, and—surprise, surprise— no suspenders. As Bethany drew near to him, she smelled the nutmeg and citrus notes of his aftershave.

Between his fingers, he rotated an unlit cigarette as if it were a miniature baton.

Seeing Bethany, he said, "No ashtrays. This used to be the smokers' area, but like a lot of things, that's a thing of the past."

"Like what things?"

"Trust, for instance. Everybody's looking at each other funny. This bash used to be okay, but tonight it's a big bust, and I don't mean a lady's bosom." It came off as a poor joke.

"You're right, Gene. The elephant in the room syndrome." Bethany spoke in a hushed voice. She didn't want to attract the attention of the men below on the putting green. "Did you speak to Chief Marcos?"

"In my office. She came with a campus cop who had peach fuzz on his cheeks."

"What did you tell her?"

"I came clean. Told 'em about that sweet interlude with Janet at the conference. That Paul knew about it. How I flushed Janet's pills at the house. The whole shebang. Then I held out my paws for the handcuffs."

"They didn't cuff you!"

He propped the unlit cigarette behind an ear. "No, but Chief Marcos made sure the boy cop wrote down my every word. She advised me to get representation, by which I took to mean a good lawyer. The one who handled my divorce gave me the name of a defense attorney in Santa Fe. Haven't called her yet. Hope I don't have to."

"Sorry this is hard for you, Gene. But it's good you talked to Chief Marcos."

"If I'm innocent, you mean. I said how-de-do to Kim Lamont tonight, and she turned red as a beet. I'm one

275

hundred percent sure she squawked to Eleanor about Janet and me and probably told other people. Everybody on the faculty is giving me the slit-eye."

"You're imaging it."

"Nope. They're looking slit-eyed at each other too. Suspicion is a terrible thing. I've heard some of the young faculty are thinking of jumping ship."

"What do you mean?"

"Going on the job market."

"There's always some of that. Faculty leaving."

"Well, I'm not," Gene declared. "I've decided not to retire. Going to stick it out a few more years. It's all I know how to do in this sorry life. Plus, I figure the school needs me."

"Have you told that to Mom?"

"Been working up to it. I'll promise to get off my soft butt and put in more effort. I might write a paper or two. Become a credit to the department."

A server came bearing drinks. Bethany shook her head as Gene said, "Don't mind if I do" and took a glass of red wine. The server melted into the house. "I need a smoke," Gene said. "Okay by you?"

When she didn't reply, he plucked the cigarette from behind his ear. "I'll take that for a yes." He flicked his silver lighter one-handed and lit up. As he puffed, he poured the wine over the deck's railing. "This'll do for an ashtray." He tapped ash into the wine glass and chuckled at his ingeniousness.

Bethany coughed as smoke wafted her way. Gene waved a hand at the noxious cloud. "I'll leave you to it," she said.

Watching the men below, he muttered, "Idiots' game." She didn't appreciate his smoking or his assessment of her brother's sport. She didn't expect Gene to turn into a model academician. Nevertheless, she liked the old codger.

Chapter 32

In the house, one of the phys ed faculty broke away from his friends to waylay Bethany. He'd seen her on her bicycle, he said, and asked if she was into mountain biking. His face registered disappointment when she replied that she mostly biked in the city. She realized he wasn't making a move on her but merely spreading the word about his bike club. When a fit-looking fellow joined the conversation, Bethany slipped away.

She saw Charlotte, alone, viewing the contents of a glass-fronted case. "Here by yourself, like me?" Charlotte asked.

"Nathan's truck needed a quick fix. I hope he shows up before too long. Jerry didn't come?"

"He's on chaperone duty at the high school. The spring formal's tonight."

Bethany checked out Charlotte's floor-length muumuu and peace-symbol earrings. "Are you going later?"

"Neither of us is hot on the other's affair. He has the perfect excuse to miss this one, and I'm avoiding chaperoning the umpteenth prom."

"What are you looking at in the display case?"

Charlotte stepped aside. The case contained Meryl's novels, displayed face out. At the top was the newly published *Season of Dreams*.

"A dozen novels," Charlotte said. "I didn't realize

she's written that many. For her last birthday, she told me Louis surprised her with a display case, but I'd never seen it until now. She's talented, I'll give her that."

Bethany took the grudging tone to mean Charlotte hadn't quite forgiven Meryl.

"I admire her novels," Bethany said. "She never writes down to her audience. She gave me *Season of Dreams*, but I haven't had a chance to read it."

"Me either. Eleanor must have shared that Meryl upset me." Charlotte sniffed. "I should get over it. My aura feels murky."

"Mom said Meryl apologized to you over lunch."

"Eleanor pressured her into it." Charlotte's earrings swung side to side. "How could she suspect me of murder? She pretended she and Gerald suspect everybody."

"That's probably true," Bethany said. "Maybe you ought to give her a break."

Charlotte hmphed. "We've been colleagues forever. Until this murder happened, we got along fine, seeing as we share the same dream."

"Keeping the tutor center open?"

"More than that. Functional literacy for every child and adult in New Mexico. We haven't achieved that even in Las Cuevas, but it'll happen."

A woman in a white pantsuit hailed Charlotte as Bethany's phone sounded. Nathan had texted that he was on his way. A rare texter, he probably didn't want to interrupt her at the party. She texted back —*Great! xoxo*— wishing he had estimated when to expect him.

The mariachis held forth with the familiar tune about a girl on a beach. Bethany longed to be someplace tranquil. Tired and famished, she saw no sense in waiting for Nathan before sampling the buffet. She put a few appetizers on a plate and found them delicious. Her attention went to the dean speaking to a cluster of younger men by the display of Meryl's books. Setting her empty plate on a side table, Bethany drew closer to the group.

"There's a dearth of books for adults learning to read," the dean said. "Meryl's stories fill that gap."

Nice of him to brag about her.

The youngest-looking man in the group asked, "Can works like these count toward tenure?"

"Not an issue for Meryl," the dean said. "My wife isn't tenure track. Directing the tutor center is a staff position. Meryl writes these little books because it's her passion."

"But theoretically," the man persisted, "if I wrote a popular novel, could I put it on my publication list?"

"Why, are you a closet novelist?" The men smiled as the dean stroked his chin. "No, I don't think that would be acceptable. Popular writing is not at the level of research-based academic papers. Even if you were in the English department, you'd have to produce a literary work for it to count. What have you written?"

The fellow probably was a first- or second-year assistant professor. Short and pale, with wispy blond hair, he looked shy. "I'm trying to write children's books. For children in preschool and kindergarten."

"Nice to do in your spare time," Gerald said. "But for your career, you'll need a solid record of journal publications."

He turned his back on the display case. Nearby, Eleanor and Meryl listened intently. Meryl laser-beamed a glare at Gerald. If he noticed, he didn't let on. "Peer-reviewed, national journals are best," he said. "And it helps to know the reviewers." He winked and sipped wine.

The men, unaware of the women behind them, laughed compliantly. Meryl put a hand to her mouth and, with a swish of turquoise skirt, left them. Bethany filled the gap next to her mother.

"Pompous ass," Eleanor said, clearly referring to the dean. "Let's see if Meryl's okay."

Down a wide hall, one door stood ajar—to the dean's book-lined study, Bethany knew from previous visits. They found Meryl leaning over his desk, her hands pressing on the polished oak surface. On it were standard office items: desk lamp, landline phone, stacking tray, and an NMU mug holding pens and pencils.

"Meryl, dear," Eleanor said, keeping her distance. "What's the matter?"

Straightening up, Meryl brushed tears off her cheeks with her fingers. Without a word, she crossed the room to a bookshelf, reached high up, and took down a thick, black-bound volume.

"What's that?" Eleanor asked warily. "Something important?"

Meryl read the title aloud: "*The Case for Specialized Training of Undergraduate Student Tutors in College of Education Programs.*"

Eleanor went to Meryl's side and read, "*By Gerald Davis Darwood*. His dissertation?"

Not answering, Meryl dropped the bound book on the desk, returned to the bookcase, and reached for the closest in a row of thick binders. She opened the binder, to a random page, it seemed to Bethany.

"Manuscripts," Eleanor said with a side glance at

Bethany. "Also Gerald's?"

"Articles for peer-reviewed journals. He keeps the journals in his campus office," Meryl said, her voice bitter. "Evidence of a successful academic life. Gerald always called us a team, the Darwoods. Doing what was needed to advance his career. My support was a given."

Meryl closed the binder and set it atop the dissertation. From the bookshelf, she selected another binder, carried it to the desk, and placed it on the other works. Eleanor stepped out of the way as Meryl repeated the action with two binders at once. The growing stack reminded Bethany of something, but what? *Got it! The pile of publications I knocked over in Paul Kiefer's home office.* A pile that included Meryl's books.

"When I started writing my novels, I spaced them between Gerald's publications," Meryl said matter-of-factly. "His took a great deal of my time."

"Did you discuss his ideas with him? Proofread his manuscripts?" Eleanor asked cautiously. "It's natural for wives with strong English skills to assist their husbands in those ways."

Meryl yanked a lacy white handkerchief from a dress pocket. She dabbed at her turquoise-lidded eyes and let the hanky fall to the floor. Neither her mascara nor her lipstick showed the slightest sign of wear. Her face to the world remained intact.

"Help?" She took down another binder and set it on the pile. "You underestimate me, Eleanor. But people do underestimate faculty wives."

"You're more than a wife," Eleanor said. "You write novels. You direct the tutor center. You're a wonderful mother."

"Adoptive mother. Yes, my Louis appreciates me.

He gave me that beautiful display case for my novels as a birthday gift last year."

"Yes, you told me," Eleanor said as Meryl scooped up half of the binders and rested her chin on them.

"Perhaps you ladies would help me take the rest to put in the case," Meryl said.

With a puzzled frown, Eleanor asked, "Why these?"

Bethany stepped forward. "I can answer that, Mom. Because she wrote all of this. Isn't that true, Meryl? Starting with the dean's dissertation."

Meryl appeared affronted. "Oh no. I started with his college papers when I was his girlfriend. What a slapdash effort he made! Mostly handwritten notes without proper sources. I did the research too and cited the sources correctly. Gerald showed his gratitude by not dating other girls. When he started graduate school, he married me."

Bethany felt appalled as Eleanor asked, "His dissertation? You wrote it? And his journal publications?" They stared at the stack Meryl struggled to hold.

"Every one of them. I would start with vague ideas of Gerald's, but he was too occupied with teaching and committee work to develop them. I built quite a publication record for him over the years. Then, when he became dean, he didn't need to publish as much. I had more time for writing in my own name."

Eleanor's face blanched. "Why don't you put those back? Wait until the party ends to add them to the display case?" She spoke as if to someone threatening to jump from a high ledge.

Meryl didn't budge. "Gerald is right," she said. "Without academic publications, one's career goes nowhere. I've been such a fool."

"You have a fine career," Eleanor insisted.

"As only a staff member, as Gerald pointed out to those junior faculty. I hold a master's, not a doctorate. I never had the time to acquire a terminal degree. At first, when I was young, it didn't seem important. And I had a number of miscarriages and often didn't feel up to par. The years simply passed. Now, I see the difference between people's respect for Gerald and how I'm viewed—as less educated than him because I'm not as intelligent. People assume he created a cushy job for his wife, you know. And they're not exactly wrong about that."

"You're a vital member of the college," Eleanor insisted. "Now, let me have those. Raise your chin, dear." Eleanor took the stack, faltering under its weight. Bethany rushed to help as her mother plopped the burden on the desk, knocking the phone and its base off the edge. Meryl stared, stony-eyed, while Eleanor bent to retrieve them.

"Paul Kiefer learned that you wrote the dean's publications, didn't he?" Bethany asked Meryl.

Eleanor's head shot up. "What?"

Meryl took down another binder from the bookshelf.

"Paul figured it out," Bethany said. "He must have realized Meryl sandwiched her early books in between writing papers that were supposedly Gerald's."

Meryl tossed the binder like a spinning disk. It knocked off the NMU coffee mug and sent writing implements skittering across the floor.

"Stop it, Meryl. Please!" Eleanor cried. She moved between her friend and the bookcase. "Don't tell me what Bethany says is true. Plagiarism is a serious academic offense!"

Meryl shook her head in vigorous disagreement. "Plagiarism is stealing someone else's academic work and passing it off as one's own. I didn't plagiarize."

"Well, then Gerald did," Eleanor said.

"Not true. He didn't steal anything."

"But what you two did is wrong. You could both be discredited. Terminated by the university."

Bethany edged toward Meryl. "Did Paul threaten to ruin your lives—yours and the dean's?"

Meryl's head whipped around. "I don't know what you're talking about. Paul never said anything to me." She gaped at the doorway as the dean's imposing figure filled it.

Chapter 33

Gerald Darwood shut the door and assessed the disarray in his study. "What's going on, ladies?"

"Gerald…" Eleanor put her arm around her friend. "Meryl has told us about her writing, all of it. The dissertation. The journal articles. All hers. A lifetime of scholarly effort to advance your career."

"She apparently didn't know Paul found out," Bethany said. "He heard Meryl speak at the education conference. He must have recognized her competency. I think she spoke so authoritatively that Paul wondered why she didn't write for academic journals. Then, he came back and looked at the timing of the articles and her books. He recognized the pace of a single author. Meryl, not you."

"I've read what I thought was your work, Gerald," Eleanor said. "Article after article. I respected you for writing them."

"I did write them. Meryl helped, that's all. The work is mine. Tell them, old girl."

At the "old girl," Meryl whipped a binder off the desk. She ran at her husband and smacked the binder against his chest. "Liar!" The binder dropped from Meryl's hands as Eleanor pulled her back.

"You're a murderer, too, Dean Darwood," Bethany said.

"Oh, really?" He crossed his arms and planted his

feet, his back against the closed door.

Not intimidated by his stance, Bethany said, "Paul posed a threat to your career and reputation. He wanted early promotion, tenure, and more. Probably release time from teaching to set up his new lab."

Meryl struggled free of Eleanor. "Gerald, is what she says true? You killed the poor man?"

"Poor man? Ha! A smug, presumptuous young bastard. He didn't want to pay his dues but expected to leapfrog to the top. He demanded that the tutor center be closed and the literacy program terminated. Eleanor, he wanted me to persuade you to retire so he could be named department head. He would have orchestrated the management of the college behind the scenes."

Bethany spoke up again. "And you feared that sooner or later he would push you out and take over as dean. So you drugged him with Roxanne Vale's misplaced pills in coffee you served him in your office. What did you do, walk him back to his office and when he was practically comatose, bind his head in packing tape? Without leaving fingerprints because you wore disposable gloves you stole from May Zeller's housekeeping closet?"

"No, I took the gloves from our kitchen."

"You planned Paul Kiefer's death?" Eleanor asked.

"Very thoughtfully."

Meryl continued to tremble, and an involuntary moan came from deep within her throat. Eleanor wrapped her arms around the larger woman and patted her stiff hairdo. "Now, now. Take it easy, dear. It'll be all right."

The dean stared scornfully at his wife. "Stop making a scene, Meryl. Our guests will hear you." He flung open the door and marched out of the room.

"I'm calling 911," Bethany said, reaching in the Oaxacan bag for her phone.

"No." Eleanor said. "I'll call Chief Marcos and ask her to come without fanfare." She guided Meryl into the dean's chair, then picked up the delicate hanky and handed it to the distraught woman.

"I'll see where Dean Darwood's headed," Bethany said.

"Be careful," Eleanor said. "He might be dangerous."

A danger to others or himself? Bethany wondered. A quick check of the master suite, three more bedrooms, and their associated bathrooms turned up no one. In the main part of the house, the party continued full force. Bethany scanned the crowd. *No dean.* She followed the sounds of music and laughter to the now-packed patio where people line danced. Charlotte was in the front row, kicking up her long dress. Not finding Gerald Darwood, Bethany backtracked and went out to the deck where she'd spoken with Gene.

The dean could have taken the stairs down to his four-car garage and made his escape. But there he lingered, chatting with the guys on the putting green. One handed him a putter and a ball. The dean dropped the ball and lined up for a short shot. Bethany texted Eleanor and stood still, trying not to attract the men's attention. Did the dean expect life to go on as usual? Seeing the sturdy putter in his hands, she realized it could be a weapon. Gerald might grab one of the faculty members, hold the club to his throat, and shout to the police, "Keep your distance, or I'll hurt him!"

But that wild imagining faded when the dean's ball

rolled into the cup to polite applause, and other men took their turns. Bethany stayed riveted to her vantage point—for ages, it seemed—until Elisa Marcos, in street clothes, arrived with a uniformed campus officer.

The chief's calm authority halted the play in an instant. "Hello, Dean Darwood. Will you come with us, please?"

The dean handed his putter to the nearest man and went quietly. Bethany slipped down the stairs and, at a distance, trailed the police officers, with the dean between them, around the garage to the front of the property. Behind a double-parked NMU squad car, a city police unit sat, lights flashing. An officer handcuffed the dean and guided him into the back of the SUV without incident. Only then did Bethany notice the putting-green group and other party guests viewing the astonishing sight. She rubbed her throbbing jaw. It sickened her to contemplate that murder had resulted from a married couple cheating the system to which they'd devoted their lives.

A solemn Chief Marcos approached her. "Your mother said in her call that you got Dr. Darwood to confess to murder."

"In some detail."

"He's not talking now," Chief Marcos said. "Are you absolutely sure he's responsible for the death of Paul Kiefer?"

"Definitely. Ask Mom what he said. Ask Meryl Darwood, for that matter."

"We will. And all of you will need to give statements at the city station while the details are fresh in your minds."

Too fresh. Bethany shivered.

****

She gave her statement, then waited with her father while her mother gave hers. Eleanor had called Charlotte, told her that the dean would likely be charged with murder, and asked her and May to shoo the shocked crowd out of the Darwoods' house.

Meryl also gave a statement and rode home with a female officer. Unseen by his wife, Gerald Darwood waited for his attorney. Eventually, Bethany and her parents were free to go.

In the police station parking lot, news crews buzzed around with notebooks and cameras, asking questions Bethany and her parents ignored. Among the crush, Nathan, in a dress shirt and trousers, waited by his truck's banged-up front end. Bethany wanted to run to him and jump into his embrace like in a TV romance, but she merely gave him a faint nod as she got into her SUV. He followed her home, and in her living room, tightly embraced her as she related the bare bones of the Darwood drama.

He nuzzled the top of her head with his chin. "Sorry I missed the party."

She drew back to look into his eyes. "They were doing a line dance you would have enjoyed. I can't get over the fact that the dean killed a faculty member. Poor Meryl, but she cheated on Gerald's behalf for years."

On the sofa, Nathan wrapped her in a Navajo blanket and held her close. "The dean was a lazy fraud and his wife a big fool," he concluded.

"That sums it up," Bethany said. "It breaks my heart. The Darwoods are my folks' friends. I never suspected that Gerald killed Paul Kiefer or that Meryl wrote everything the dean put his name on."

"Until you figured it out."

"At the last minute."

He laughed. "'Course it was the last minute, darlin'. Like when you find a thing you lost at the last place you look for it."

****

In the morning, Bethany gave Nathan the Cuevas Café T-shirt. He kissed her and said as a thanks, he would cook them a powerful breakfast.

Over eggs and bacon, he ventured, "You know, it's not abnormal for a fella to get a girl to do his homework. I had a girlfriend in high school who did that for me a time or two. Sure you won't help me out that way if I enroll at the big U in Laramie?"

She rolled her eyes—comically, she hoped. "Ha! No way will I do your work. But I'll help you study for tests."

He buttered a piece of toast. "You could come with me. Live on the ranch."

She noticed he wasn't proposing marriage. "I'm sorry, Nathan. I can't."

"Why not?"

"My parents need my support, and I have a job to do. And an MBA to finish. I'm sick of school, but it's important I see it through."

"You'll visit me in Wyo?"

"Wild horses couldn't... You know."

****

Nathan wouldn't stay for lunch. He was eager to check on Mickey. He planned to remain with the Carters until the hospital discharged the boy, but he vowed not to let their problems prevent him from going to Wyoming. He would cause no fuss about Mickey taking and crashing the truck. The insurance companies could deal with the accident. "I remember being young and dumb," he said. "Thank the Lord the boy's not dead."

Bethany loved him all the more for his generous attitude as they kissed passionately. She ruffled his sandy hair and let him get on the road. Waving goodbye, she felt her spirits slump.

She phoned Don and Joni to tell them about the dean's arrest, learned Wayne had beaten her to it, and encouraged them to phone Eleanor. "Mom's more shaken up than you might think." *I am too.* She took a long bike ride and a longer nap, awakening in the late afternoon to Eleanor calling with a dinner invitation. Discovering she felt famished, Bethany readily accepted.

****

Gerald Darwood continued to be held in police custody, although he would probably make bail soon, Eleanor said as she and Bethany made salads while Wayne attended to the grill. "I went to see Meryl this morning."

"Any reporters around?" Bethany asked.

"No, but May was there, cleaning up. Meryl insisted on helping, and I did too. We packed the leftovers for May to take to the city shelter. Meryl wrote her a check and ones to pass on to the student helpers, although that could have waited. Meryl seemed so calm that I'm worried. I'll keep an eye on her. I didn't invite her to dinner, though. I wanted it to be just the three of us tonight."

Over the meal on the deck, Eleanor brought up a new point about the murder. "I never told anyone, but I saw Gerald meeting with Paul in Paul's office a few times."

"Was that unusual?" Bethany asked.

"It wasn't abnormal for Gerald to stop in our doorways to say hello, but he never went into our offices. We always met in his. In the back of my mind, I thought, *Paul's the newest member of the old boys' club*. I tried not to resent it. Now, I believe Gerald wanted a reason for his DNA to be found at the murder scene."

"You must be right, Mom. He wore gloves, but he knew he'd leave his DNA in Paul's office. He admitted he planned the killing."

"He didn't count on you investigating it," Eleanor said. "I'm grateful you did. Elisa Marcos must be too. She called this morning and said as much, but you can't expect her to say it in public. She let me know the police investigation didn't turn up Paul's hold over the Darwoods."

Wayne, who had stayed mostly silent, said, "I assumed Gerald was an honest man. He had us all fooled."

"So did Meryl," Eleanor said. "We underestimated her capabilities as a researcher and writer. It's sad she will never work at a university again."

It hurt Bethany to watch her parents grapple with their friends' downfall. "At least Meryl wasn't in on the murder," she said. "That should be some consolation to poor Louis."

"If I were him, I'd take his mother along on that trip to China," Wayne said. "I mean it. They should leave Gerald to twist in the wind."

"She wouldn't go," Eleanor said. "She's a stand-by-your-man type."

"To the extreme," Bethany agreed.

"Like you two ladies," Wayne said in an obvious

Rita A. Popp

effort to joke. "But you two have better men to stand by."

"What, now you think Nathan is good enough for me?" Bethany heard the pique in her voice. "A mere cowboy?"

"Don't get your feathers ruffled," Wayne said. "I like the young man, I really do. I've been thinking I could fly you up to Laramie any time you like. I haven't had my plane off the ground in a while."

Bethany accepted the peace offering. "Sure thing, Dad. Eventually, you can do that. But I'll drive up the first time I go."

He didn't argue but said briskly, "Now, who's for a second burger?"

****

On Monday, Bethany went to the office determined to focus entirely on her job. But thoughts of Nathan and of Mickey Carter's broken arm distracted her. Nathan hadn't needed to mention his damaged hand for her to see that he empathized with the boy. Nathan would stay in touch with Mickey and encourage him to put on a brave face as he recovered. Her cowboy was truly one of the good guys.

From time to time, Bethany thought with concern about her mother. She would also need a brave face to lead a department rocked by murder. But the tiny, mighty Professor Jarviss would be up to the challenge.

****

Eleanor wasn't surprised when she was called to the president's office to learn that the Darwoods had resigned from their respective university jobs. A senior male faculty member in the College of Arts and Sciences had been appointed acting dean of the education college. Charlotte Kline would direct the tutor center. Eleanor

294

was authorized to fill Paul Kline's position with adjunct instructors.

Dr. Ramirez, all business in a dark suit and tie, didn't mention the word murder. But Eleanor expected he could hardly avoid it with the head of University Communications, who waited in the outer office.

"You won't let my department hire a full-time, tenure-track replacement for Paul?" Eleanor asked, trying not to sound strident.

"Budget constraints," Dr. Ramirez said. "I trust you will find adjuncts with quite adequate technology skills to teach Kiefer's classes."

"But I thought his skills were special. He had a reputation as such a promising young academician."

"Yes, but everyone's replaceable, Dr. Jarviss."

Eleanor took that nugget of wisdom as her exit cue.

A word about the author…

Rita A. Popp writes light and twisty mysteries and other entertaining fiction. She is the author of the previous Bethany Jarviss Mystery, *The First Fiancée*, and a novelette, *Passing on the Farm*, published by The Wild Rose Press. Her mystery short stories have appeared in online magazines and two Sisters in Crime Guppy anthologies. She and her husband divide their time between their home in Colorado and cabin in the New Mexico mountains. Find links to Rita's fiction at https://ritapopp.com.

****

If you enjoyed this mystery novel, please consider leaving a comment at your favorite book retailer or reader website.

Thank you!

Thank you for purchasing
this publication of The Wild Rose Press, Inc.

For questions or more information
contact us at
info@thewildrosepress.com.

The Wild Rose Press, Inc.
www.thewildrosepress.com